DELHI NOIR

DELHI NOIR

EDITED BY HIRSH SAWHNEY

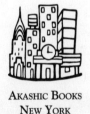

AKASHIC BOOKS
NEW YORK

This collection is comprised of works of fiction. All names, characters, places, and incidents are the product of the authors' imaginations. Any resemblance to real events or persons, living or dead, is entirely coincidental.

Published by Akashic Books
© 2009 Akashic Books

Series concept by Tim McLoughlin and Johnny Temple
Delhi map by Sohrab Habibion

ISBN-13: 978-1-933354-78-1
Library of Congress Control Number: 2008937355

First printing

Akashic Books
PO Box 1456
New York, NY 10009
info@akashicbooks.com
www.akashicbooks.com

ALSO IN THE AKASHIC NOIR SERIES:

FORTHCOMING:

In memory of Shiv Lal Sawhney
1933–2009

TABLE OF CONTENTS

PART III: WALLED CITY, WORLD CITY

INTRODUCTION
Everyday Anguish

Delhi, a city that's been reborn in various locations and forms throughout its thousands of years of history, was in the midst of yet another colossal transition when I arrived here four years ago. This latest metamorphosis was being fueled by legislation that opened up India to private and foreign investors. International brands like the *Wall Street Journal* and Chanel were setting up shop. The city's cruddy public transportation system was being revolutionized by an ultramodern metro. My mother's massive Punjabi family—Partition refugees who'd happily lived in a one-bedroom Connaught Place flat during the 1950s—were driving Hondas and Hyundais and comparing plasma television prices.

For the first time in decades, members of the educated elite were experiencing a gleeful surge of nationalism, and they wanted to savor it. They bragged about the new malls and cinemas going up in Gurgaon, a quasi-American suburb in which civic planning plays second fiddle to corporate whims. They reveled in the number of billionaires who called their city home, as well as the rising values of the houses their parents had built. But things weren't—and aren't—as good as everyone wanted to believe.

Every morning, papers abound with alarming stories: accounts of the unmitigated corruption and contract killing that make this city of more than fifteen million tick; indications of increasing divisions between rich and poor that lead servants to murder masters and foment Maoist movements in the country's hinterland; synopses of so many rapes and sexual assaults that readers become numb to them. Yet the everyday depravity and anguish of Delhi life remains confined to news copy. Despite notable exceptions like Namita Gokhale and Arvind Adiga, authors of literature—particularly those who write in English—usually choose to ignore the capital's stains.

Other Indian metropolises have had writers who've chronicled the perils of urban existence, and some of these individuals have done so by employing the devices of crime and detective fiction. Mumbai, India's film capital, lays claim over Vikram Chandra, who published the mammoth noir tomb *Sacred Games,* and Altaf Tyrewala, who wrote an impressive slim book called *No God in Sight.* Looking futher back, the iconic Urdu author Saadat Hasan Manto called Bombay home, even though his macabre stories were set in different locations. The legendary Bengali filmmaker Satyajit Ray also wrote detective stories, as did Bengali Sharadindu Bandyopadhyay, whose enigmatic Sherlock Holmes-esque Byomkesh Bakshi mysteries are set in Calcutta.

What then explains the lack of noir literature—and fiction in general—set in Delhi? The answer may be simple. Good crime fiction, however seductive and pleasurable, forces readers to reckon with the inequity and cruelty inherent to modern societies. It's only natural that Delhi's book-buying-and-publishing citizens would avoid such writing. Any insight into their hometown's ugly entrails would threaten their guilt-free gilded existence and the bubble of nationalistic euphoria in which their lives are contained. They are too dependent on the power structures and social systems intrinsic to the city—embassies, government offices, and corporations; rural poverty and illegal immigration—to risk looking critically at these things.

Thankfully, there are writers who are willing to see Delhi as it is, and this anthology contains stories by fourteen of them. *Delhi Noir*'s contributors are diverse: They are Christians, Hindus, Muslims, Sikhs; Punjabis, Biharis, Bengalis, and Keralites; men and women; gay and straight. Many reside in the capital, but others have addresses in Uttarakhand or the U.S. Some have published critically acclaimed books, and a few are still working on their first manuscripts. What they have in common is the inclination to write delectable literature that doesn't shy away from the city's uncomfortable underside. Their fiction isn't politically correct and refuses to pander to popular perceptions about India or its capital, perceptions that conform with the agendas of governments, glossy magazines, and multinational corporations.

I've borrowed three popular slogans that are tattooed across the city to divide these fourteen stories into sections. The title of the first section—*With You, for You, Always*—is the well-known motto of the Delhi Police. These stories range from humorous to perverted, but all scrutinize the presence (or lack thereof) of the cops who man the front lines of the capital's law-and-order system. Newcomer Omair Ahmad's detective story forces readers to come to terms with the fact that the Congress-led government was complicit with the massacre of innocent Sikhs in the wake of Prime Minister Indira Gandhi's assassination. Irwin Allan Sealy's tale about a vigilante autorickshaw driver who avenges sexual assault on the Ridge is defined by the wry, rhythmic prose that garnered him a place on the Booker Prize shortlist in 1998. Author and civil servant Nalinaksha Bhattacharya invites us into the life of a police officer who extorts sex from the wives of low-level central government employees. His is a sardonic, hard-hitting parody of the Indian television serials that are voraciously consumed by all rungs of society—those who live in brothels, mountain villages, and the extravagant farmhouses of Delhi.

The second section's title—*Youngistan* (land of the youth)—is a spoof of a Pepsi advertising campaign that attempts to appeal to India's 200,000,000 young people aged between fifteen and twenty-four. Unlike the folks in the ad, however, lives in these stories don't get easier by drinking a cola or encountering megastar Shah Rukh Khan. In Delhi-raised New York resident Mohan Sikka's "Railway Aunty," an orphaned college student stumbles into a prostitution ring that lurks beneath Paharganj's veneer of civil servants and backpackers. Bihar-born Delhi resident Siddharth Chowdhury bewitches readers with his raunchy, violent musing on life in a university dormitory. His prose alters the DNA of the English language, and is the literary version of good jazz.

Walled City, World City, the slogan heading the final section, stems from a *Times of India* campaign that encourages Delhi citizens to forget the city's painful past, its riots and pogroms. This bullish advertisement makes a simple comparison between Delhi's history—Mughal rule, colonialism—and its current aspirations—superpowerdom, cosmopolitanism. But Tabish Khair, author, academic, and a former *Times of India* reporter, reminds us that border crossings aren't just comfortable flights on 747s. They also define the lives of countless young farmers and laborers who've abandoned rural India for the capital to cook, clean, and shine shoes. Veteran Uday Prakash scrutinizes the promise of social mobility in the "new India" and exhibits the vitality and universality of Hindi-language writing. Closing out this volume, the always provocative playwright, author, and illustrator Manjula Padmanabhan transports readers to a nightmarish futuristic vision of Delhi as a "world city."

These fourteen stories span the length and breadth of Delhi, from familiar spots like Jantar Mantar and Lodhi Gardens to more off-the-beaten-path neighborhoods like Gyan Kunj and Rohini. Together they give you an alternative map to the city, one that doesn't shy away from its strident flaws and yet also sheds light on beauty in overlooked corners and conversations.

Delhi readers will be well acquainted with this volume's Blue Line buses and Mughal tombs, and also with most of its contributors. But this is the first time they will see original works of fiction by such a varied, talented group of authors in a single book. Non-Indian readers will be unfamiliar with many of the names in this book, which will hopefully offer them a rare taste of a different type of Indian writing: literature that fascinates simply beacuse it's well written—not exotic. For these readers, we have provided a glossary of the Hindi, Urdu, and Punjabi words used in *Delhi Noir*. It will hopefully make the richness of Indian language and culture accessible to an international audience without compromising the quality and flow of these stories.

Hirsh Sawhney
Delhi, India
May 2009

PART I

With You, for You, Always

YESTERDAY MAN

BY OMAIR AHMAD

Ashram

The call, when it came, was unexpected, but then most calls in her life had been. She'd been looking up a number in her cell phone when it suddenly started blinking and vibrating. Her thumb punched the answer button before she had time to process things, and the thin, tinny voice said, "Suhasini? Suhasini?"

The little screen showed Sunny's name, but she didn't really feel like raising the phone to her ear. Even in the afternoon it was too early in the day for Sunny. Irritated, more at herself than anything else, she punched the speakerphone button and cut the caller's desperate "Hello?" with her own voice. "Tell me, Sunny, you need money?"

For a moment there was no answer, and she thought he'd hung up on her. Sunny had never hesitated to say anything but a hurried "Yes" when asked if he needed money. It was what made him such a good snitch.

But his voice came through again, hesitant now. "Suhasini?"

"Yes, baba, Suhasini," she said, speaking to him as if he were a small child. "Damnit, you're calling me, you should know who you've dialed. Or are you stoned again?" He might have been one of her more reliable informants, but this didn't mean she liked him.

"Listen, Suhasini, Triloki gave me something for you."

"So?" She thought it was odd that Triloki would give

Sunny anything for her. Triloki knew where her office was if he needed to send anything. He'd been her senior partner, after all, until she'd found him blackmailing one of their clients.

They hadn't been in touch for the last two years despite the fact that the private investigator community in Delhi was such a small one. Her annoyance with Sunny became one pitch higher. Sunny had always been a resource for Suhasini. She was the one who had found him stealing the drugs from the hospital and decided that he was better use as an informant than in jail. It was bad form to tap somebody else's snitch. It made the informants uncomfortable and more nervous than they already were. But Triloki had always taken liberties; she liked to think it was his way of flirting with her. Maybe she had been eager for that, for him to cross boundaries, to be more than just business partners, which was why the betrayal had hurt so badly.

"He said to get it to you quick. Gave it to me yesterday. Said it had to do with Arjun Singh."

"The politician?"

"No, no, the collector—you know, old things, what do you call them, un-teek things . . ."

Un-teek? she thought, until the sounds rearranged themselves. *Antique*. Arjun Singh, the antique collector. She'd heard of him.

"The one who lives near Nizamuddin?" she asked.

"Closer to Ashram, in a haveli near Hotel Rajdoot."

"Yeah, yeah, near the railway station, not the dargah. Why don't you bring it over and stop pissing yourself?"

She'd been pushing him since the mention of Triloki's name, but even she knew when she'd gone too far. This wasn't her usual style. Detective work, like all good intelligence, re-

lied on confidence building. You didn't build much with rude-
ness and insults.

"Busy, I'm busy. You want it, you come yourself." His
voice was brusque, the whine gone from it in his attempt at
manliness.

"Right, right," she tried to be soft, but it was too late now,
and after some useless information that was a waste of her
time, he hung up. She would catch him for lunch, and maybe
he would speak after being fed. It was only much later that she
realized that he hadn't asked for money for the information,
or even hinted at it.

Had she realized this immediately, it might have saved her
from something, but then again, maybe not.

Arjun Singh rang right afterwards, almost as if they'd co-
ordinated it.

"Hello?"

"May I speak with Ms. Das?" the voice on the other side
said. The language was impeccable, intonation precise. She
could hear money, great amounts of it, in that voice. Old
money. This was a voice nurtured by wealth and generations
of connections.

"Speaking," she said, trying to clear the crudeness that
had come from speaking with Sunny from her own voice.

"Ms. Das, I hear you are the best detective in Delhi," the
voice said.

"The agencies are always the best," she found herself saying. "They have the resources. And Jaidev Triloki has a good
reputation." The last bit surprised her as it came out, and she
wondered why she was still defending the man's reputation.

There was an intake of a breath, almost a sigh. "I am old-
fashioned, madam, and I prefer to employ people rather than
agencies." There was a pause, another intake, another sigh.

"And I'm afraid Mr. Triloki can no longer help me. He's the one who suggested I contact you."

What the fuck? she thought, but the words that came out were professional. "Could you tell me who you are, sir, and why you need a private detective?"

"My name is Arjun Singh, Ms. Das. I am a collector of time."

"I'm sorry, Mr. Singh," she replied sarcastically, "I can't help you find time."

There was a moment of silence, and she cursed herself inwardly. She couldn't afford to speak to a client, and a potentially rich one at that, like this. Most of the old clients had gone with Triloki, and new ones had been hard to find.

When Arjun Singh broke the silence she could hear the edge to his voice. It wasn't anger as much as strain. Something was riding him hard. "Only God can give us time, and He is hard to find these days," he sighed. "But I believe you can help me."

She bit down on the next sarcastic reply that came rushing to her lips, and only said, "How, exactly, can I help you, Mr. Singh?"

"I need help finding someone. I would like to speak to you about it in person, if that's all right with you."

"Of course," Suhasini said. "My office is in CR Park—"

"Could you meet me at my house this evening?" he interrupted. And as she hesitated, a note of pleading entered his voice. "Please, it's terribly important."

And somehow she couldn't say no. She jotted down *Purani Kothi, behind Hotel Rajdoot,* although she didn't need to, not after Sunny's call.

The address confirmed he was rich, to own a whole building like that, but also that he wasn't one with a taste for the flashy. The area was old, and built-in, with such tangled alleyways that she had always referred to it as Jalebi Central. It was twisted up, like the orange-colored sweets they sold there.

The only case she'd ever investigated in that area was for the government, or at least that was what she had assumed. Triloki had been with the Intelligence Bureau before, and they had received a number of cases through that route. Though he'd never explicitly told her that was who it was for, and payment came in tax-free bundles of cash. He'd always been the one introducing her to these things, and she'd walked right along, Mary's fucking little lamb.

They'd been hired to take pictures of a Kashmiri politician. A meeting had been arranged for him with a young woman. A classic honey trap, it was assumed that the politico would have one night of fun, and the government would have enough embarrassing photographs to make sure that he didn't have any more fun afterwards. Except that he just wasn't up to it. The government had a habit of overkill, and this politician had been worked over so many times in custody that, although he invited the nubile young thing to his room, he only wanted to talk. It was all rather pathetic, and Suhasini, in the next room with the video lead showing her the pointlessness of it all, had been overcome with a strange feeling. It was the only time she'd ever felt any sympathy for the militants.

"I'll see you at 7 in the evening, Mr. Singh," she said, and hung up. But after she put the phone down, the remark about Triloki came back to her. She located his number on her cell phone and was about to dial when a sense of caution stopped her and she set the phone down, again. Then she pulled out her second cell phone, the one that didn't reveal her number on the receiving end, and called Triloki.

There were only two rings before someone picked up. "Hello?" said a rough voice that wasn't Triloki's.

"May I speak with Jaidev Triloki?" she asked.

"One minute," said the voice, and then there was the sound of muffled voices in the background.

"Hello, this is Jaidev," said another voice, smooth, full of authority, and so confident that she almost answered despite knowing that it wasn't him.

"Hello?" the voice said again.

"Mr. Triloki?" she finally asked.

"Yes, this is Jaidev Triloki," the voice lied, smooth as an oiled snake.

She was so baffled that she did what she had always done as a child when caught by surprise: She lied. "This is Aparna, Mr. Triloki, from the Academy of Investigators in Vasant Vihar."

"Yes?"

"We wanted to invite you to be one of the keynote speakers at our inauguration ceremony on February 17. The home minister has agreed to be the guest of honor."

"I'm sorry, I'll be out of the country at that time," the man who wasn't Triloki said. "But thank you for calling."

Suhasini just stared at her cell phone for a while, trying to make sense of things.

At that moment her first phone started vibrating. The screen glowed, telling her it was Triloki calling.

She didn't know what to do and watched the phone vibrate slowly across the table. Then she grabbed it, stabbing the cancel button. A moment later it started vibrating again, again from Triloki's number. She canceled the call a second time and quickly text messaged him, *In meeting. Problem?*

There was no reply for a few minutes, and she told herself

to relax. Maybe Triloki was in some sort of trouble and had asked a friend to answer his phone while he dropped from sight. Maybe he was just calling up to tell her that, and also to notify her about the package with Sunny. He'd served with India's premiere investigating agency, after all. He knew what he was doing.

The message that came back from his phone shattered the idea: *Are you attending inauguration of Academy of Investigators?*

What's that? she messaged, and there was no reply. She waited, watching the phone suspiciously, but even after a good quarter of an hour there was no reply. Whatever Triloki was involved with, he was in big trouble.

Picking up the phone, she called Sunny and received a suspicious "Yes?" for her pains.

"Where are you?" She was in no mood for his tantrums, and just wanted to get to the point. The brusqueness must have had its effect, and he replied tamely enough, "Nizamuddin."

"I'll be at the railway station in half an hour, at 5 o'clock. Meet me there. Bring the package." She sensed him about to protest and added, "Sunny, it's not a good time."

It took her five minutes to lock up. The guard at the gate nodded to her and she asked, on impulse, "See anybody strange, Altaf?"

He shook his head, "No, madam. Nobody strange."

"Keep an eye out, all right?"

He nodded back at her. Altaf and his brother, Abdul, had been hired by Triloki six years ago, when the agency had first opened. They knew what kind of people could come looking for private detectives.

There was very little traffic on the roads, and she was happy that it was a Sunday. It took her barely fifteen minutes to get to the Nizamuddin Railway Station but another five minutes to find a decent place to park. It was a long walk to the station, and the damned road smelled of piss. But at least the walk allowed her to make sure nobody was following her.

Sunny was already there, looking anxious and shooting suspicious glances at the policemen around him. She rarely met him like this. He was guaranteed to attract the wrong sort of attention. The policemen gave Sunny the once-over, and then her too.

"What is it?" she asked, and he thrust a grubby envelope toward her. "Just this?" and he nodded energetically. "Okay then," she said. She wanted to tell him to fuck off but restrained herself from being stupid with anger again. "You'll find the packet in the usual place," she added, letting him know he'd be paid.

He nodded, scuttled off, and was lost among the crowd in moments. She thought about going inside the station to read Triloki's letter and have a cup of tea. There was a certain anonymity to the crowds there. But Sunny's antics meant that she could be assured of the policemen paying close attention to her.

Instead she strode back to her car, and then over the bridge. On a whim, she decided to walk into the alleyways of Jalebi Central, midway between Nizamuddin and Ashram. It wasn't the sort of place you found women on their own, certainly not ones dressed like her in a shirt and jeans. Had it been later in the day, after the sun had gone down, she might have driven elsewhere, but she just needed to walk.

This had been a prosperous part of town at some point in time; you could tell from the bits and pieces of old buildings, the edges of bungalows now gone. It had become a refugee zone after Partition, and the construction had the hallmark of the era's ugly structures. These places were to be lived in and nothing more, small boxy buildings with unfinished brick surfaces everywhere. Now it was full of pushy Punjabi families; large, loud, and boisterous. Usually she couldn't handle it, but right now the shouting, the four-story buildings with barely any space between them, and all the hefty women somehow made her feel better.

Yet after a few moments the claustrophobia got to her, and she was relieved to finally make it through to a tea shop near Mathura Road, with Hotel Rajdoot looming nearby and the flyover to the Ashram crossroads just beyond it. It wasn't that big of a building, but here, in the tropical jungle of alleyways and bylanes, it looked much larger than normal. Nevertheless, it still maintained a grubby air, as if the paint just couldn't hold, or maybe the combined sweaty existence of everybody living in Jalebi Central somehow tarnished all the buildings in its vicinity.

Right next to the hotel was a bungalow which you couldn't really see from the road. Purani Haveli, where Arjun Singh lived.

She ordered a cup of tea and tore the envelope open. The tea stall owner gave her a look—she wasn't the usual sort of customer—but she ignored it.

There was only a single sheet of paper, with Triloki's spiky handwriting.

Suhasini,

There's no real point in saying sorries at this time, but I wish the thing with Suparna had never happened. I don't know what came over me, she had so much money and here I was poor after so many years of work. Anyway, that doesn't matter now, but maybe this case I'm working on is a penance of sorts. I know I'm not doing it for money.

And that fucker, Arjun Singh, doesn't even understand how things work. He won't even give me the diary. If you take this case, get the diary. That's your only chance, your only safety. I've got nothing, but I'm going to confront that fucking politician. My work with the IB will help. I've got to prove that there is some good in me. If you get the diary, though, I've told Ramdev, the police inspector stationed at Nizamuddin police station, about the case. His number is 98--------. Don't trust anybody but him. I'm sorry about everything. Remember me kindly.

She folded the letter and put it in her packet. Taking a sip of her tea, she thought coldly that whoever Triloki had gone to confront hadn't been very impressed by his IB background. She recalled the voice over the cell phone this morning and figured that if it was the same man, Triloki hadn't stood a chance.

Suddenly, unexpected tears came to her eyes. *Such a waste. The poor fuck. What was the point of doing penance now? So he had blackmailed Suparna for a few lakhs—big shit. Her husband was a property developer; God only knew how much of their money was stained with blood and deceit.*

In a burst of sudden anger she punched Arjun Singh's number into her cell phone. He picked up on the second ring.

"Hello? Mr. Singh, this is Suhasini Das. I am already here. Can we meet now?"

He didn't ask why, just told her to come. There was some satisfaction in that, in getting on with work rather than having to wait. She reached the gate of his house in five minutes. The guard had been forewarned of her arrival, and he escorted her down the long driveway to the house.

Something was subtly wrong here. She could just sense it,

like something glimpsed out of the corner of her eye. There was a long car parked in front of the house, a canary-yellow Chevrolet, beautifully maintained and at least a couple of decades old. And the house too seemed somehow old and yet new, like something from a classic film. It was a beautiful bungalow out of place here and maintained in a way that had gone out of style twenty years ago.

The guard let her into the house and asked her to sit in the drawing room. As soon as he was gone, she got up to look around. Things felt even stranger here. The calendar hanging on the wall was out of date—in fact it showed the months of 1984. But it was brand-new, as if somebody had just unpacked it. There was a large poster for the Hindi film *Naam* that she remembered from her college days, but again the thing looked almost untouched, un-aged.

"Thank you for coming here, Ms. Das."

When she turned to face the person entering from a side door, her voice caught in her throat. He could have been an actor in some period film. The hairstyle and the cut of clothes were perfect for the early '80s. What was even more disconcerting was that she knew Arjun Singh was in his late forties, yet the man standing before her looked like a twenty-year-old. It was only when she stepped up closer to shake hands that she noticed the small wrinkles, the skin at the edge of his neck, the very subtle signs of age almost perfectly hidden.

"I'm sorry for the rush, Ms. Das, but I have very little time. Mr. Triloki has been working on a case for me for five months. There is a man who I have been looking for . . . for a very long time, someone who took something very precious from me."

Suhasini nodded. It sounded a not-too-unusual story.

"Mr. Triloki located that person," Arjun Singh said, "and

was supposed to set up a meeting in two days. Except then Triloki disappeared."

"Who was he searching for?" she asked.

"Rajan Pandey," Arjun Singh said, and seeing the blank look on her face, explained, "He isn't a high-profile person, just a party worker, a fixer."

Surprising herself, she nodded. "I've heard his name." She couldn't remember when, but the reference seemed familiar. She'd always been good with names and numbers, just not very good at linking them together. Triloki had called it her best asset and biggest flaw.

Arjun Singh looked at her oddly. "It took Mr. Triloki four months to even find where he was."

"He's in Delhi, lives in a big place in Greater Kailash II," she found herself replying, unsure where the information came from, just that her brain had secreted it away at some point from some investigation. "In K-block. Lots of money and manpower."

Arjun Singh's eyebrows rose. "Yes, yes," he said. "Maybe I should have come to you first."

"What do you want him for?" she asked.

"It's difficult to explain," he replied.

"Try, Mr. Singh, try."

He sighed, and then suddenly realizing they were still standing, said, "Why don't we sit down, Ms. Das?"

She did but remained at the edge of her chair. Arjun Singh took off his watch and gave it to her. "Do you notice anything about this?" he asked.

It took her only a glance. The second hand was moving backwards, and as it completed a full sweep, she saw the minute hand move back. Looking up, she said, "What is this?"

"Do you know what today is?" he asked, and at the shake

of her head, answered his own question. "It is the twenty-fourth anniversary of the day that Indira Gandhi, the prime minister of India, was gunned down by her Sikh bodyguards because she had ordered an assault on the Golden Temple, the holiest of Sikh shrines. This was also the day that her son, Rajiv Gandhi, assumed the leadership of the Congress Party, and during the days that followed hundreds, thousands, of innocent Sikhs were killed by mobs while his administration did nothing."

Suhasini nodded her head. She was still in Calcutta at that time, but she remembered when the news of the assassination had come through. There had been mob violence in Calcutta, but nothing like what happened in Delhi.

"You may not realize, Ms. Das, but I too am a Sikh. I started shaving and cutting my hair after my involvement with left-wing student politics in college. I became an atheist and rejected all of that. But I was still a Sikh in some ways at that time, something I understood when, that day in Delhi, they started killing people of the religion I no longer believed in.

"For two days I waited, safe in my apartment two blocks from here, where people only knew my name and had never seen me as a Sikh. But then I decided I'd hidden for too long and that the world posed no threat to a rational man. My faith in rationality took me out for a walk.

"Nevertheless, despite my rationality, I was fearful. I may have been clean-shaven, but other Sikhs had also tried to save themselves by shaving. Often this act had not been enough though. They had been recognized and attacked, sometimes by their very own neighbors. So just to hide that small fear from others, from the mobs that were hungry for blood, I did one more thing. I walked out with a lit cigarette in hand, explicitly breaking the Sikh taboo against tobacco. To hide my identity, to identify myself as only a man and nothing more.

"But they were burning Sikhs that day, and the smell of burning hair is deep, cutting. The weak stink of tobacco cannot compare. The smell of charred flesh is enormous, and swamps your senses. And the screams, they are of a different register than the fizz and spark of a match lit for a cigarette.

"The first five minutes revealed nothing. And the cigarette died. Emboldened, I lit another, walking farther out of the inner alleyways of this place. And then another, as I walked farther still.

"It was at my fourth cigarette that I faltered. The wind was strong and snuffed out the match. I moved a little way to try and find shelter, but none was to be had. I could hear screaming now, and was beginning to get scared again. I needed a cigarette. It was my only shield.

"So when I saw an alleyway in Nizamuddin, just before Humayun's Tomb, I turned into it, cigarette on my lips, matches in hand.

"They were gathered there. All five of them. Four killers, and one sacrifice. Quiet and isolated from the world. The man kneeling on the ground had been beaten and kicked. His clothes were torn and blood oozed from the wounds on his face. There was blood on the steel rods that the other men held, and over it all was the smell of kerosene. It had been poured on the pleading, weeping man huddled in the corner, into the used car tire draped around his neck so that it sloshed around as he tried to move. But in the endless animal stupidity of the mob, the murderers had forgotten to bring the matches. Or maybe one of them had remembered and lost them, and they had been caught with their bloodlust high, like rapists rendered suddenly impotent.

"And then I arrived in the alleyway, and even before my eyes had registered what was there, I lit the match and brought it to my cigarette, to the profanity that was to save me that day.

"Maybe it saved me from something, maybe it didn't.

"The cigarette fell from my open mouth, but the match-box was still in my hand. The leader of the gang held out one commanding palm."

Arjun Singh paused and summoned the will to continue. Despite the care he had taken at maintaining the youthful façade, he looked old, very old. She could now see the signs of the artificial stiffness caused by botox injections.

In a soft voice Arjun Singh continued: "It has been almost twenty-four years now, but I saw God that day, in the eyes of the man I betrayed. I heard him plead, 'Bhagwaan ke naam mein . . .' ('In the name of God . . .')

"But I was carrying profanity that day, hiding behind it, us-ing it to keep myself safe. And when that one hand stretched out to demand the matches, I gave them."

Arjun Singh stopped again, taking a long, shuddering breath.

"Twelve years went by until I could find the courage to make my way back to that alleyway. It was blackened and sorrowful still, and something spoke to me. And for another twelve years I retraced my steps, day by day, week by week, year by year. I've made myself back into the man I was at that time. I have even watched all the films backwards from then to the present.

"Look," he pointed at a large framed photograph on a wall. "Isn't that me?" And Suhasini had to agree. From a distance, Arjun Singh had walked backwards in time and looked like the man he had been twenty-four years ago. In a soft voice, he concluded, "Only two days are left, and I need to walk back that way. I need to go back there and say 'No' to the man who had asked me for the matches that day, to Rajan Pandey."

For a few long minutes Suhasini just sat there. As the story had unfolded she had found herself leaning back in the chair, leaving way for the tragedy to spill out. She could find no words to respond. It was all mad, fucking mad. She had heard her own mother talking about being forced to flee the area of British India that had become East Pakistan. This part of the world was full of tragedies and full of mad people. Arjun Singh's insanity was just of a different flavor. Triloki must have thought it was manageable and worth it if he had taken on the job. Nevertheless, she couldn't figure out how to react. It was Arjun Singh who broke the long silence.

"I thought I was going to have my chance to face him. Triloki found him, identified him. But now Triloki has disappeared."

It was then that she asked, "What about the diary?"

And suddenly she saw the shrewdness flash in his eyes. The man might be insane, but he hadn't earned this money or his reputation as an antique collector by being stupid.

"What do you know about the diary?" he asked suspiciously.

"Triloki left me a note," she offered, and it only made him more suspicious.

"You're all in this together!" he suddenly shouted. "Get out! Get the fuck out! I told him I wouldn't give up the diary. I told him. Get out!"

She rose slowly. There was no idea what he was going to do. "All right, Mr. Singh, I'm leaving. But *you* called me, not I, you."

Arjun Singh just glared at her. "I knew I shouldn't have trusted Triloki," he muttered.

And that was just one step too far. "You trusted him? I don't know what the diary is, but one thing I know for sure is that you didn't trust him with it." Furious, she pulled out Triloki's letter from her back pocket and threw it at him. "Read it, you mad bastard. Triloki thought he was doing something for nothing. He risked his life for you, and he lost. I've been calling him on his cell phone, and some person pretending to be him picks up the phone. In all likelihood he's dead. All for you and your fucking weird crusade. Keep your motherfucking diary, and rot!"

She turned and stormed out of the house, too angry to think. As she made it out of the gate, she felt a thrust of regret. She shouldn't have thrown the letter at Arjun Singh. It was probably the last thing Triloki wrote, and now that crazy antique collector, that Sikh-in-denial, would have it.

Jumping into her car, she revved the engine and left the streets of the area, of Jalebi Central, in a burst of exhaust smoke.

It was late evening and she was back at her office when Arjun Singh called. She didn't pick up. He tried three more times until she finally answered. "Mr. Singh," she said, "I'm not interested in working for you. Get somebody else."

"Ms. Das, please." There was terrible strain in his voice. "I apologize. I have worked all my life toward this day. I'm sorry I overreacted."

"Mr. Singh, you are a rich man, no doubt you can hire many private detectives. Please do so, and stop bothering me."

"You don't understand," he said. "You don't understand about the diary. It's the private diary of one of Rajiv Gandhi's personal secretaries. It's a record of everything that happened during those riots, seen from the prime minister's office. After I rescued myself, after I confronted Rajan Pandey, I planned on helping all of those who died in those days to find some measure of justice, and this is my only tool."

And now it all became clear to Suhasini. "And it would be the perfect bait for a person like Pandey," she said.

"But I can't sacrifice the justice of thousands for my own deliverance." She could hear the anguish in his voice, but her mind was already running ahead of her. She could see how Triloki must have planned things, how he had failed without the diary.

"You don't have to sacrifice anything," she said. "You can offer to sell it to him, and he'll come to you. He has to. The diary is political dynamite, and all he knows about you is that you are an antique collector, somebody who can be paid off with money. Triloki set things up with an inspector at Nizamuddin. I'll make sure he's there. You can lure Pandey with the promise of selling him the diary and then confront him. We get Pandey, and you don't lose the diary."

When Arjun Singh didn't answer right away, she said, "Mr. Singh, this is the only way," and was surprised at the pleading in her own voice. It seemed very important to her now to complete this thing, to make sure that Triloki's last assignment was finished properly, his penance completed.

Maybe it seemed that way to Arjun Singh as well, because he said, "I should have trusted Triloki. I'll trust you instead."

"Thank you, Mr. Singh."

"Please," he replied, "please, just make this work," and hung up.

She looked at her phone and didn't know what to do next. The name Rajan Pandey niggled at her, and she realized that she didn't know how to contact him. If he was the fixer he was supposed to be, then there would be no real way to access him, not for somebody like her. On an impulse she dialed Triloki's number on her second cell phone.

This time it was the smooth voice that picked up. "Hello?"

"Rajan Pandey?" she asked.

If she hadn't been concentrating she would have missed the hesitation, and the slight rise in the pitch of his voice, as he replied, "Sorry, you have the wrong number."

"No, I don't, Mr. Pandey," she said. "It's you that has the wrong number. In fact, you have the wrong phone, Triloki's."

"Suhasini Das," the voice said.

"Very good, Mr. Pandey," she answered.

"You aren't inviting me to an inauguration again, are you?"

The voice was so cool, so controlled, it made her ears burn. "No, Pandey." And now she spoke in anger: "I'm inviting you to look at a diary."

"You have it?" Now he was dead serious, no jokes at all.

"You haven't even asked which diary," she said.

Laughter erupted from him, hard, cold, bitter laughter. "I know which diary," he said. "Triloki was most . . . cooperative."

Bastard, she thought, *I'll enjoy taking you down.* "Day after tomorrow. Morning, at 10 o'clock, near Hotel Rajdoot. You know where that is?"

"Yes, I know where that is," he said. "Where exactly?"

"I'll let you know," she said, and hung up. And then she called Arjun Singh. He was both elated and panicky, but she managed to draw from him the address where he wanted to confront Pandey and the promise that he wouldn't step out of his house until she arrived.

She made one final call.

"Hello, Inspector Ramdev?"

"Who is it?"

"This is Suhasini Das, Jaidev Triloki told me to call you."

"Yes, yes, he said you'd call." Ramdev sounded far too hearty. "What's the matter?"

"I need your help. There's a meeting where there will be a person turning up. He's well connected, Triloki probably told you about him," she said.

"You want security?"

"Yes," she answered, and gave him the details. He reassured her that he would be there, and he sounded happy. Ramdev probably had no idea of how badly things had turned out for his friend Triloki, and this was no time for her to tell him.

She spent the next day with Arjun Singh, walking the streets of Jalebi Central. She checked the place where the killing had happened so many years ago, and all the approaches to it. She wanted to make sure that there was nowhere that Pandey could run, and no direction from which he could catch them unawares. She met Ramdev, who, despite the hint of delight on his face, seemed like a reliable man in a tight spot, competent and tough.

She spent the night at Arjun Singh's house, traveling backwards in time at every moment, full of oldness and oddity, and could hear the man pacing upstairs as she slipped into sleep.

She woke up in the middle of the night, groggy and ill at ease, to the sound of something smashing. She rose from the bed and quietly made her way to the door. Opening it softly, she looked around until she spotted Arjun Singh. He was walking purposefully with hammer in his hand, and she saw him stop before a clock and take a mighty swing. Then smash it again. He was done with time marching backwards.

She crept back to bed, but her sleep was filled with bad dreams, and she rose in the morning feeling more tired than when she went to bed. When Arjun Singh appeared he was wearing clothes that were precisely twenty-four years old and had a small brown diary in hand. They walked to the alleyway, and from there she called Pandey.

"I'll be right over," was all he said.

As they waited, she saw the policemen slowly arrive, filtering in one by one as if they were there by chance. Ramdev parked his jeep ten feet away and gave her a grin, tipping her anxiety to fear. There were too many of them, and they were far too close. Pandey would see them and escape. She was getting ready to signal them away when the sleek Mercedes arrived, precisely at 10. She recognized the numbers on the license plate, and suddenly she remembered where she had seen Rajan Pandey's name before. It had been on a file on Triloki's desk, a case he had been investigating.

And then the car door opened and a man stepped out. She recognized him from the photographs in that file on Triloki's desk. Rajan Pandey, the man that Suparna, the builder's wife, was having an affair with. Rajan Pandey, whose pictures had been used by Triloki to blackmail Suparna. Rajan Pandey, the seed that had destroyed Suhasini and Triloki's partnership.

Pandey looked past her and waved to Ramdev, and Suhasini knew she had been tricked, badly beaten. She turned to Arjun Singh, wanting to warn him, but he was already rushing ahead toward the culmination of his long dream. "See!" he shouted, waving the diary. "See! This is the truth, the truth that you can't burn. I won't give you any matches today!"

And then the driver also stepped out of the Mercedes. It was Triloki. "You can always find matches," he said, "if you know where to look." And he tipped his hat at Suhasini.

HOW I LOST MY CLOTHES

BY RADHIKA JHA

Lodhi Gardens

Until I lost my clothes I was a regular sort of guy: lots of clothes, lots of problems, a little luck—mainly with women. I had a family that was insisting I get married again, a dog with a chronic skin disorder, a flat with a mortgage, and a growing infatuation with heroin, better known as brown sugar or "sister" on the streets. On the plus side, I was the educated, intelligent CEO and sole employee of a global consultancy company. My three ex-bosses back from when I was still a salary slave were all women who believed in me and continued to give me enough work to keep me dancing with sister all night long.

The night before I lost my clothes was a night like any other. I had a report to finish, a feasibility study of a new iron ore extraction process the Koreans wanted to sell to an Indian company. The report had been due the previous week. I'd done all the work and only had the conclusion left to write, so I'd gone to the bar at the Habitat Center at 7:00 to celebrate. By 11:45 p.m. I was home, well lubricated, a little horny, and ready to earn my next few hits of sister.

I opened the computer and went to *My Documents*. But the file wasn't there! Believe me, I looked for the file everywhere—in every single directory, folder, and subfolder, even the hidden ones. I searched for it by keyword, by date, by name, by subject. But it was nowhere to be found. I stared at the computer and suddenly felt certain that my ex-wife, the custodian of our only child, had somehow gotten to it and erased it. So certain was I that I sent e-mails to my lawyers and hers, to her parents and to mine, to her bosses and to mine, to the police, the supreme and high courts, the prime minister, and a few friends of the family who happened to be ministers at the time. Then I sat back and waited for news of her arrest to arrive.

My mobile phone rang after fifteen minutes.

It was one of the she-bosses, Sheena, the one for whom I was doing the feasibility study.

"I don't believe this," she said. "Do you know what time it is?"

"I'm telling you, it's true," I insisted, raising my voice. "I was going to print it out and mail it to you tomorrow, but the bitch got to it first. She must be spying on me."

"And how is she doing that?" Sheena asked sweetly.

"I don't know." I looked suspiciously at the walls. "Maybe she bribed the maid again."

Silence on the line. I could see Sheena shaking her head, her shoulder-length iron-gray hair brushing her cheeks.

"Do you know what time it is?" she asked for the second time.

I looked at my watch. 1:29. "Time? What has time got to do with anything? This is an emergency, we need to find her and put her in prison," I said impatiently.

"It's 1:30 a.m." she continued in the same deadpan voice. "I have to work tomorrow morning, you know. I can't sleep till 11 like you do."

I sensed a lecture coming and groaned. "But you've got plenty of time to sleep. Stop talking and go to sleep now. I'll find her and the file and get them to you tomorrow. Promise."

The moment the word was out of my mouth, I knew I'd made a mistake.

"You won't," she sighed. "You won't because you haven't done it. You've just been boozing and womanizing instead. How can you be so irresponsible? Think of Akshay, for God's sake." She went on for another five minutes, telling me how I had mucked up my life, finishing with, "Do you have a death wish? If so, just tell us and we'll leave you alone. But remember, you have a son to think about."

"I know, I know," I said when she'd finished. "Just go to sleep. I'll find the report and get it to you tomorrow. Promise."

The phone went dead. I got up and threw it off the balcony. Then it struck me that if the police called I wouldn't know, and if they couldn't find me they would let her go. So I decided to go to the police station myself. I left the house and began walking. I had no choice. My car was gone, not stolen or sold as normally happens in this city, but simply misplaced. It would turn up eventually. It always did—for the car was so filthy no one wanted it in front of their house.

I walked along National Highway 3 toward Delhi, past the NOIDA golf course, the shopping malls, and the beehive colonies with their peeling façades. People in cars honked as they drove by. Truckers flashed their lights and motorcyclists cursed. But I hardly noticed. I was a man on a mission, filled with a superhuman strength. I walked over the sewage drain that was the Yamuna by way of the Japanese Bridge. As I entered the city, Humayun's onion-shaped dome glowing palely in the moonlight, my objectives changed and I headed up Mathura Road to the roundabout with the little Lodhi tomb and then turned left toward the Oberoi flyover. I was going to score some sister.

* * *

There was a party going on under the flyover. Four men had just scored some sister and were huddled over a small scrap of paper. One man, his hands trembling like a fish out of water, was trying to light a match, cursing fluently in a mixture of English, Bengali, and Assamese.

"Hey, even your language smells like fish," I told the guy trying to light the fire. "You can't light a fire like that. Let a real man from the north do it for you." I grabbed the match-box from him. *Oberoi Hotel*, it read. I looked at him again. How had he gotten his hands on it? His clothes were in tat-ters and his hair was matted. I couldn't tell when he had last bathed, but it must have been some time ago. He smelled pretty bad. But he still had his shoes. Surprising, for someone in his condition.

The matches were damp and smelled of urine, which is why they wouldn't light. So I threw them away and took out my lighter instead. I also took out my stash and added to the stuff on the foil. The others looked at me jealously, or, to be more accurate, they would have been jealous if there had been space for that in their minds. But in the world of sister, once the flame gets going everyone goes really quiet. All shivers, shakes, and itches stop. All feeling melts away. We become the flames, making love jointly to our sister. The world is for-gotten along with the itches.

Soon she was warm and ready and we prepared our nee-dles. The fish-eater leaned sideways and pulled out a needle from his shoe. I shuddered, wondering what diseases he had living inside him. He was going down really fast, it was obvi-ous. I wondered if he still had links with his family, or whether he was even educated. As if he'd read my mind, he looked straight at me and asked, "Didn't you go to Doon School?"

A burst of sunshine warmed the night. Doon School was

the place I had loved most in the world. All my nicest memories were associated with it. When I was full of sister I invariably went back to those cedar-paneled rooms where twenty boys slept together, the sweet scent of our slumbering bodies filling the air. I gulped, nodded. "Yes, yes, I did. I am a Dosco," I said proudly, my eyes becoming misty.

"Which house?"

"Hyderabad," I replied.

"Kashmir," he said.

A brother.

Okay, you guessed it. It was the brother who stole my clothes.

When I woke up, I couldn't recognize the roof over my head. It seemed all broken in places and there were two ugly brown lampshades hanging from it that were closed from the bottom like socks and gave no light. What light there was came from above them. I just couldn't figure it out. So of course I panicked. Waking up after a night with sister is a serious matter in any circumstance, but when one doesn't recognize the roof over one's head, the panic button gets pushed down hard and stays down.

I couldn't move or breathe. It was as if rigor mortis had already set in. Only my brain refused to stop. If anything, it worked with lightning speed: If my house had miraculously grown mold, it calculated, then it meant that the Yamuna, toxic and polluted, had flooded, and the mold on my ceiling was toxic and polluted and the dappled light above it was actually a phosphorescence even more toxic and polluting. In short, I had to get out. But my legs refused to obey me. I looked down at them—and a stranger's legs stared back at me.

Then it all fell into place.

He'd taken my clothes and he'd taken my legs too,

so I couldn't go after him. That was my first really clear thought.

But what made me really mad was that he had taken my underwear as well. He should have left it for me, it wasn't even clean. Yet I couldn't hate him. For that's what brothers do, don't they, wear each others' dirty underwear?

It took me a little while longer to realize that I wasn't in my house either and that what I had taken for a roof was a canopy of leaves, and the strange moldy things were in fact beehives. The brother must have woken up before me and seen me lying there in my nice clothes and decided to swap. Dragging me into the junkies' park next to the Oberoi Hotel, he had stripped me of my clothes and abandoned me.

I lay back on the grass, stared up at the sky, and wiggled my bare toes. Indeed, they were mine. Then I wiggled my shoulders, and the cold tickle of grass told me that I wasn't dreaming. I looked down, and that's when I felt the full impact of my nakedness.

For till that moment I had never really looked at my body. I knew what I could do with it and I knew what I couldn't do with it. But as an object in itself, it was a stranger to me. Women hadn't seemed to mind it too much and they'd certainly liked what it did to them. But as I looked at my body in the full light of day, I knew that it was really nothing to be proud of. My dick, curving a little to the left, seemed lost, a steam engine trying to hide in a scantily clad hillside.

I got up and looked around for the brother's clothes. But they were nowhere to be found. Beneath my feet, condoms, bits of old newspaper, plastic wrappings, rags of all sorts, and needle cases crunched and scattered, just the usual garbage. I dropped onto my hands and knees and pretended to search. I knew I wouldn't find anything though. A junkie sold his underwear long before he sold his outerwear. It was less necessary.

Ten minutes later I gave up. As I suspected, I had found nothing. The brother had either sold his old stuff to someone else or he'd left it under my head and someone even more desperate than him, possibly one of the silent guys he had been with, had taken it. I took a deep breath and the scent of urine and other waste filled my nostrils. The park was empty, most of the junkies having abandoned it for less smelly pastures. I wasn't a junkie, I thought angrily. I was a victim. I should go and report the theft of my clothes at the police station. So I climbed over the low iron rail separating the park from the road and stood on the pavement.

It was still early and cold. I had goosebumps. I thought about going to the flyover where several hundred people lived, ate, had sex, and slept in tightly wrapped bundles. Someone there was bound to have some extra clothes. Yet I hesitated. What could a naked man offer a poor man in exchange? So I stood on the pavement and stuck my hand out for a lift instead.

No one stopped. That didn't surprise me. What did, though, was that many didn't even notice I was naked. I persisted, sticking my hand out and waving it ferociously. How dare they ignore me like that? I was no domesticated chicken, I was a man. I had my pride.

Suddenly, as if God had heard my silent complaint, all the cars froze like they were waiting for me to choose which one I would get into. Then I realized that the traffic light had changed. The drivers had their faces turned forward like robots. Lost in their own private worlds, they never even saw me, not even when the light changed.

I was getting a little desperate when a brand-new Lexus

pulled up right beside me and inside it I noticed one of my ex-she-bosses, the nicest one. "Sharmilaa, Sharmeelaa," I called happily, feeling my luck kick in.

She was listening to Indian classical music, the window rolled down. Her famous Bengali lips were pursed as if she were about to kiss someone. She was frowning slightly, the way she always did when she was worried. Probably her husband, I thought. The man was a serious handicap and I'd told her to ditch him many a time.

"Sharmila," I called again, approaching the window.

She heard me before she saw me and her head began to turn. I can never forget that moment. Me, rushing to the passenger side of the car full of hope, her face as she got a glimpse of me. She leaned over and quickly locked the door. I grabbed the handle and tried to open it.

"Sharmila, it's me," I said urgently, tapping on the window a little harder than I'd meant to, "don't be scared. I have been robbed. You must take me home."

She wouldn't answer, struggling with her window instead. I rushed around the front of the car to her side and bent down so she could see my face. "Sharmila, don't be a fool. Someone robbed me of my clothes. It's me. You know me."

She refused to look at me.

"Sharmila, don't be stupid now. I don't have time. You have to take me home. I have a report to hand in," I said impatiently.

She didn't budge. Just stared angrily at the car in front of her.

"I don't know you," she said at last through tightly pinched lips, "why are you embarrassing me like this? If . . . if you don't get away from my car I'll call the police." Her face took on the stubborn expression I knew well.

"Sharmila," I cried, stepping away from the car, "don't do this, you'll regret it later. Where's your heart?"

She looked me full in the face then. And the truth struck me like a bolt of lightning. For that's when I realized that in fact we were no longer people but animated passport photographs. If our bodies were allowed to assert themselves at all, they could only do so under the cover of night—and their needs were quickly dispensed with. But now that my body had been unveiled in broad daylight, my head had become invisible. I had ceased to be me. I was just a body, not a person with rights or brains.

I saw this clearly then, as I stepped back onto the pavement and watched Sharmila drive away. Strangely, what upset me the most is that she hadn't been in the least curious about my body. After all, we'd worked together for years. I'd fantasized about making love to her any number of times—even though she had a distinctly pear-shaped behind. And she must have done the same. And yet, when I was there in front of her, she didn't even sneak a peek. I sat down on the pavement, my knees clamped together. I must be really ugly, I thought sadly.

My pride in tatters and along with it my self-confidence, I wondered what to do. Who could I go to next? I had friends, or at least acquaintances, right there in Nizamuddin, two hundred yards away. At this time they would all be rushing their kids to school or getting ready for work, drinking that last cup of badly made masala tea, shouting at their wives to release a little of their pre-work tension. I bet if I just waited where I was, at least a half-dozen familiar faces would show up. But after Sharmila, this thought made me shudder.

I sat down on the edge of the pavement, making myself as small as I could, and watched the cars go by. It was rush hour. No place for a human on the road, especially a naked one. A traffic cop had arrived, creating more confusion than there had been before. But unlike the drivers of the cars who simply ignored me, he must have felt proprietorial about the crossroads and shouted, "Hey, what are you doing? You can't sit like that. You're troubling the traffic."

Troubling the traffic? How could I have been troubling the traffic? He was the one troubling the traffic. Since his arrival the traffic jam had quadrupled in length. I'd have explained that to him if he'd given me half a chance. Instead he called the other cops, the ones who wore khaki uniforms and sat around in white Maruti Gypsies that had the words *With You, for You, Always* painted in red on them.

There were three of them inside, all in khaki, two in front including the driver and one in the back.

"So you are the one troubling the traffic?" the policeman on the passenger side shouted out of the window.

I smiled at him. "No, officer. I am just sitting here thinking about what to do." I smiled again. It wasn't worth antagonizing an enforcer of the law—especially when you were naked and had needle pricks dotting your arms.

"He's thinking of what he's going to do," the policeman on the passenger seat said, turning to the others. "What do you think he should do?"

There was a short silence.

The man in the back, who was writing something down in his book, said, "He should come with us."

The policeman in the passenger seat leaned out of the car and said, "Hey, you're a lucky guy. My boss likes you. You can come with us. We'll help you think."

I didn't like the look in the man's eyes. "No. I have to go home," I said. "I have important things to do, a report to hand in. Thank you for your offer though," I added.

The policeman didn't smile. "And how are you planning to get home? Is it nearby?"

"No," I answered fatally, "I live in NOIDA."

Suddenly the man in the back who wasn't wearing a uniform leaned forward. "Get him in," he ordered.

The passenger door opened and the khaki uniform got out. Did they have extra uniforms in the police station? I wondered.

I was forced to sit between the silent driver and the one in the passenger seat, my knee jammed against the gearshift.

"I have a car too," I said as the jeep started. "Why don't you let me go home and I'll come back to visit you in it? I really have to hand in my report or I'll lose a lot of money."

The fat one who seemed to do all the talking shook his head gravely. "We can't let you do that," he said. "You'll catch a cold. And you'll be a traffic problem. There could be accidents. Let rush hour pass and we'll take you home."

I looked out of the front of the jeep. It was nice being so high above the ground. The early November mist still hadn't cleared. "That's okay. I'm quite used to the cold, in fact I like it. I went to boarding school in the mountains; in the mornings we exercised in shorts. God, it was cold, but I liked it."

No one said anything. Behind me, the man was writing away, his pen making a *scratch scratch* sound. The driver changed gears noisily, jamming the gear shift into my knee even harder.

"You'll like the station too. We'll give you food and clothes and take you home later," the policeman said, laughing. "Isn't that right, sir?"

The man in the back didn't reply, but his pen went on scratching.

Food and clothes sounded good to me, so I gave in. We

drove to the police station and came to a jerky halt under the porch. There was bougainvillea growing up the side of it and over the top, a riot of purple and white like a fancy lady's hat. I studied the building critically while the fat guy went around the back and opened the door for his superior. It was a nice piece of colonial architecture. Two women in khaki saris came outside and, seeing me, covered their eyes, giggled, and ran back in. Suddenly I longed for a really stiff drink.

The driver came out with a filthy old blanket which he threw to me. "Cover yourself," he said roughly.

"I thought you couldn't speak," I said, grabbing it. Then I added, "Hey, this is filthy, give me something else. I could get leprosy or something from this."

"Shut your filthy mouth," he replied.

I was taken into a reception area where a rather bored policeman fingerprinted me.

"Why are you fingerprinting me? I'm not a criminal. The criminal is out there somewhere, wearing my clothes. I'm a victim," I protested.

"We fingerprint everyone," the man across the desk replied laconically.

The fat policeman who'd brought me in said, "He's dangerous, this one. Got a big mouth. The boss wants him kept carefully. He's probably a Muslim terrorist."

I was led down a corridor, my hands handcuffed behind my back, then down some stairs into another dark, featureless corridor that smelled of toilet. We came to a cell and the policeman fished out his keys and threw me in. The blanket slipped off my shoulders and I was naked again. There was no one else in the cell—I was alone.

I don't how time passed. When someone eventually came, I had lost all track of it. Time and clothes. The two were closely related in this case. The brother who had stolen my clothes had stolen my watch as well, the bastard. It was a Seiko. A final gift from my wife.

The interrogation began. I was tied to a rope, which was tied to a loop in the ceiling that must have once held a fan. They beat me with their belts.

"Who are you?" they asked.

"I already told you! It's in your register!" I shouted.

"Are you a terrorist?"

"You crazy? I'm a businessman, a CEO. You're making a big mistake. I came willingly, I'm a victim. You'll pay for this." Already I felt less certain. No clothes, no watch, no wallet. Even I didn't believe myself.

The beating went on for a while. I stopped speaking. They quit when they grew tired. Beating someone is an exhausting job, like manual labor, I guess. And none of them were in good shape.

One peed into a bucket of filthy water and the other threw it over me. They left.

I shivered in the dark and began to sneeze.

Much later I was fed some stale chapattis and a bowl of watery daal. Then I was given a pail and a filthy rag and told to clean the cell. After the cell, they made me clean the toilets. I'd never cleaned a toilet in my life, and I didn't do a very good job of it. But they didn't care. The idea that they'd made me, a Brahman, clean their toilet was what really pleased them. No one really cared if their toilets were dirty, they just wanted to see me, a "sahib," cleaning them. It proved what I had always believed, that India is a country of ideas, not actions.

As I was working on the last one, there was a commotion outside—sirens, lights, agitated footsteps. "Sonia Gandhi, Sonia Gandhi," someone called. The place emptied. The man who was supposed to be guarding me ran too. I followed him, not wanting to be alone with the rats, and arrived at the front door just in time to see a convoy of Maruti jeeps racing away from the station. I simply walked out after them. No one stopped me. It wasn't even dark.

On the street, the cars were still packed like sardines. I dodged between them, not giving them a second glance, until I came to the red light under the flyover where the policemen had picked me up that morning. I saw a bus in front of me and leapt inside.

At first no one reacted. The people in the last seats in back looked at me in surprise when I got in, then quickly turned away, confirming my belief that naked, I was not impressive. But there were too many of them to be scared. I was simply not their problem, I was the ticket collector or conductor's problem. They stared stonily in front of them just like the drivers of the cars had.

The bus was fairly crowded. Not packed like the Delhi Transport Corporation buses, but profitably full, like the privately owned bus lines always managed to be. The aisles held a decent number of standing passengers, the conductor somewhere in the middle. The moment he saw me he came charging toward me with all the aggression of a raging bull.

"Get out of the bus," he said without preamble.

I ignored him, staring longingly at his jacket, a cheap Chinese windbreaker with *London Fogg* written in red.

"I said I want you off the bus," he repeated, puzzlement creeping into his eyes.

"Why? Can't you at least let me stand on the step? I've been robbed, my clothes have been stolen. I need to get home.

I'll get off soon." My voice came out all thin and whiny. Not at all like my usual confident foghorn.

"I don't care. You just get off the bus or I'll throw you off," the conductor said loudly. Other passengers turned around to look.

"You should be ashamed of yourself. Letting innocent ladies see you like this," an older man, a government clerk–type, told me.

"I am, I am. Give me your clothes then, I'm sure you have more," I replied.

A murmur of disapproval passed through the crowd.

"Hey, hey. Just joking. I'm getting off at the next stop, promise," I said placatingly.

Hearing this, the conductor leaned out a window and banged hard on the side of the bus. But the driver didn't react. He'd just built up a head of speed which he wasn't going to lose till the next scheduled stop.

Now it was my turn to smile and the bus conductor's to feel stupid.

"Have you no shame? Get off this bus now," he ordered.

"But how can I? The bus is moving. Have you no pity?"

"Pity-shitty chodo, that's not my problem. You cannot be in this bus without a ticket, that is all."

We'd just passed the Lodhi Road Crematorium at this point, and I was hanging onto the railing on the top step when the bus came to a crashing halt, squealing brakes and all. We peered out of the windows to see what had happened, expecting to see a dead man.

And that is exactly what we saw—but not quite as freshly dead as we expected.

A dead man was crossing the street along with an enormous cortege of the living, that's why the driver had been forced to stop. Inside the bus, everyone's lips began to move in prayer and fingers clutched at lucky charms hidden under shirts and sari blouses.

I had an idea. The dead were generous people. They didn't need their clothes.

The bus began to move slowly. I didn't wait. I leapt off it and joined the marchers. They pretended not to notice me, or perhaps they were so lost in their grief that they really didn't care about the naked man in their midst. Or perhaps death made them look at such things in a more tolerant, philosophical light.

As soon as I was through the gates, I was quite literally pushed aside by an even larger mass of mourners who had obviously been waiting for the deceased. Must have been an important man, I thought. But he was dead now. Luckily for me, he wasn't getting an electric cremation, for then I would have lost the clothes. Instead he was being given the full treatment, with priests and incense and oil and wood. I climbed a nearby tree and watched.

Beneath me, the cremation ground was a sea of white. The man's family, who'd been standing at the entrance greeting everyone, arrived—two sons in their forties, and a sister or wife who took one look at the body on its bed of wood and fainted.

The sea of white parted as the woman was carried away. The pundits began to mumble and the sons, their flabby bodies pale in the smoggy light, began to throw ghee on the pyre. The smell made me hungry and sick at the same time and I wished they'd hurry up. I watched the cloth anxiously. If my calculations were right, while the top cloth would be a goner, the sheet on which the body lay would be all right.

The flames rose high. It struck me suddenly that the dead man and I were similar. We had both been robbed of our clothes while we were defenseless and dreaming. I wondered what would happen if the man came alive after the crowds had left and found his body half-burnt and naked. Would he lie back down and ask for more wood and oil, or would he demand some clothes? I knew what I would do. I would demand clothes and go a.s.a.p. to find my son.

But the man didn't move a muscle. The smoke thickened and grew bitter and people began to drift away. The pundits finished their work and the family moved to the entrance to say goodbye to the guests. Soon there was only an attendant left, a grizzled old man with coal-black skin who was no doubt paid by the family to make sure the body burnt till the end. Bones, I vaguely remembered, took a long time and a lot of oil and wood. The body would take four or five hours, and then the family would return for a box of ashes that they'd carry to the polluted Yamuna, where they would pay more money for more prayers.

Up in the tree, I shifted uncomfortably, the bark rough against my skin, the mango leaves filled with dust and diesel exhaust, praying that the old watchman would leave to take a pee or have a smoke. But to my surprise, he didn't. He remained where he was, morosely watching the pyre, the white hairs on his beard and head getting picked out by the flames.

The fire burnt well. The ghee, it seemed, had not been adulterated. I heard the bones crack and a new, truly awful smell filled the air. I began to cough and the old man looked up in surprise. But the leaves of the tree must have been dense and plentiful or his eyes were weak, because he didn't spot me. I decided to abandon my post and rescue my sheet straight away. What if there were secret caches of oil in the wood that were even now destroying it?

I got down on the ground and armed myself with a piece of wood from the pyre. Then I crept around the old man and hit him on the back of his head. He turned just as I swung, perhaps his hearing was especially sharp or else it was pure coincidence, and the branch smashed into his face, breaking his nose. He let out a cry and then fell slowly, like in a movie. I dropped the branch and dashed around to the other side of the pyre, scrambling up the unburnt logs even though the heat was something terrible.

Through the smoke and my tears I saw the edge of a sheet gleaming whitely just above my left hand. One more foothold, and I had the sheet grasped firmly and pulled.

I hadn't thought it out at all though. I could have saved myself the trouble by simply stealing the clothes of the unconscious guard. Instead I burnt my hands and feet and almost got myself killed. When I used a burning branch to free the sheet, the body came along with it. We both tumbled to the ground, the body's half-burnt face on top of me. I don't know how but his eyes were open and staring into mine expressionlessly.

I threw the body off me—it was unbelievably heavy—and grabbed the sheet on which it had lain. The sheet still smelled sweet like rose water, and I wrapped it around my waist like a lungi, taking care to conceal the burnt bits. Then I ran, I ran as fast as I could out of that place of death.

I made it to the Lodhi Hotel compound on the other side of the road. Of course, there was no Lodhi Hotel left. It had been bought and torn down, Russian kitsch to be replaced by modern kitsch. Back in the old days the hotel had belonged to the government and was filled with pretty Russian hookers. I had liked it then—the idea of a government building filled with hookers always managed to stir my desire. Now it was a construction site.

At first no one bothered me. I wandered amongst the screens and piles of rubble, drinking in the sweet music of many chisels hitting stone. Then I heard a voice behind me. "Hey, what do you want? This is private property," it barked. I ignored the bark. That's what you do, ignore dogs that bark. I had a lot of experience with dogs.

The music of the chisels stopped. Everyone was looking at me.

"This is no dharamshala, this is a hotel. You will get no money or food here. Get going!" the guard shouted, banging his stick. I noticed that his uniform was black and red and he looked out of place in that world of sandstone and cool white marble.

"*You* get going," I said calmly, "*you* don't belong here."

The man raised his stick and would have struck me but I was saved by the appearance of a pretty blond creature in a kurta and hippie skirt. "Stop, stop!" she called.

The guard immediately became deferential.

"What does this man want?" the woman asked.

"I don't know, madam," he replied dubiously. "But don't worry, I'll chase him away. He's probably a thief."

"I am no thief." I said scornfully, "I was just looking."

She turned to me, and to my surprise she actually looked at my body and my face. And I felt them respond to her.

"Work, I want work," I said in English.

She seemed taken aback. Her eyes narrowed in suspicion. She was no fool. She had seen the junkies in the park by the Nizamuddin Bridge underpass. She looked at my lungi. "But you have no clothes," she muttered.

"They were stolen," I replied.

She peered at me sharply, suspicion hardening into con-viction. "Then go get some," she said coldly, "and we'll con-sider you." The wall that all white women had inside them had gone up. It felt harder than stone.

The guard wasn't following any of this, but he understood, like all good guard dogs did, her change of tone. Grabbing me by the shoulder, he hustled me out. At the gate, maybe because he had a sense of humor or else because he was genuinely sorry for me, he picked up a sheet of pink plastic and handed it to me. "Here, you can make this into a shirt," he said.

I clutched the plastic to my chest, tears blurring my vi-sion. Once outside, I found I was right by ground zero, the place it had all begun. But this time I decided not to go back into the park. Instead I walked along Lodhi Road, past the church, past HUDCO where Sharmila sat each day on the twelfth floor, giving misguided middle-class couples extremely expensive housing loans, past the gas pump that sold Norwe-gian smoked salmon and pork chops, past the Islamic cul-tural center and the Ramakrishna Mission, past Tibet House and the Habitat Center—all the landmarks of Delhi's cul-tural life.

I came at last to Lodhi Gardens. The sun was almost gone but inside the gardens the privileged continued their lei-surely parade—ayahs with children, bored overweight moth-ers, joggers, sedate couples, bureaucrats, cell phone–wielding politicians, upwardly mobile businessmen. No one gave me a second glance as I slipped into the garden. They were all too interested in watching each other. The ministers and bu-reaucrats pretended not to see anyone. The others watched the ministers and bureaucrats. I walked amongst them till I came to a hexagonal tomb encircled by palm trees and slipped inside. There I would wait for darkness to fall, thinking about my old life and what a sad mess I'd made of it. Footsteps interrupted my thoughts. Voices, giggles.

I looked around desperately for somewhere to hide.

The only place I could see was between the two tombstones in the middle of the room. I had barely squeezed myself in there when the lovers arrived. She had a terrible shrill sort of giggle which was nasal and unmusical. His voice was okay.

"Ao na," he was saying.

Giggle, giggle. "Na, na."

"Ao na."

"Na, na."

"What are you scared of? Do you think your mother will jump out from behind a pillar?"

Giggle, giggle again. "Na, na darling. I was just—" She stopped.

"Just what?"

"Thinking."

"Let me do the thinking for both of us, okay?"

"Okay, darling."

Naturally, thinking is the last thing a man does when he is with a woman he desires. Women are different. They can think anytime because nothing rears up between their legs to block the forward march of their brains.

Footsteps. Giggle, giggle, silence. I raised my head carefully. Long hair, plastic heels, socks with sandals. A silly pink woolen hat with bunny rabbits and a pom-pom dangling from the top. *Take it off,* I begged the man silently, *she'll be much prettier without it.* And sure enough, as I watched, the man lifted his hand and swept the hat off. But that was only the beginning. Before my astonished eyes, the coat came off too, and the shoes. And then the rest. When they were down to their underwear, the clothes in a heap beneath them, the woman made a feeble protest which was just as soon disregarded. Then I was watching the man's naked butt go up and down, up and down, between her naked knees, and I swear to you they both seemed far more naked with their underwear around their ankles than I had seemed with nothing on.

Afterwards, she cried a little and he held her in his arms looking bored. Then, while she finished dressing, he went outside to smoke a cigarette.

Night fell and the tomb went silent. Just as I was about to get up and go look for food, another couple arrived. They were quicker than the first, more experienced. They didn't even bother to take off their clothes. After they left another pair entered. This time they were both men. I didn't look. When they were finished, I dashed to one of the open arches and leapt out. All that copulation was beginning to stress me out.

Now, a different Lodhi Gardens met my eyes. Gone were the self-important bureaucrats, the children, the ayahs, the sedate lovers, the exercise freaks, and the tourists. In their place, under each halogen lamp, there stood a couple in a perfect Khajuraho pose.

Soon I began to feel really cold and a little uneasy. There were only men left, many of them alone, and they seemed to know I was wearing nothing underneath. One approached, expensively dressed.

I had an idea and let him follow me into the Mughal sentry tower beside the rose garden. When he arrived, I told him abruptly to take off his clothes. "How much?" he asked first.

"Free if you take off all your clothes first," I replied.

"You want to see my jewels then?" he asked.

I didn't know what he meant, so I nodded.

He began to take off his clothes.

I didn't move a muscle until they were in a pile on the floor and he was naked before me. Then I took off my dead man's sheet, threw it over his head, kicked him in the groin a few times, and stole his clothes.

Decently clothed once more, I said goodbye to my days of consulting and ventured into the hospitality industry. Lodhi Gardens' lovers paid me to ensure an uninterrupted session in a tomb. I provided a bed, water, and talcum powder for after, and I even charged those who were waiting to watch. After all, they were one big family of lovers, weren't they? And watching others gave them ideas. So everyone was happy.

As for me, I invested in the stock market, stopped taking drugs, and grew rich. My son and wife eventually moved back in with me and we all lived happily ever after in a brand-new flat on the right side of the Yamuna.

And every once in a while, when I find myself on the Japanese Bridge to NOIDA, I think about the man whose clothes I stole. And I wonder whether he ever realized the gift I'd given him or whether he simply wrapped the dead man's sheet around him, crawled back into his car, and drove home to his empty life.

LAST IN, FIRST OUT

BY Irwin Allan Sealy

Delhi Ridge

A wise man would have gone home when he heard the tube light smash, but my wife calls me an unwise man and I must be, since I smoke as well as drive an autorickshaw on Delhi roads, and I butted in.

For that matter, a wise man would have finished his BCom and gone into marketing, but I thought: No office for me, no boss for Baba Ganoush. And this looked like the life back then, not that I'm saying it isn't still, some days, maybe even many days. But autorickshawry has its own traps and it's always tempting to get that last fare, just one more, and that's the one that takes you out of your way—when it doesn't land you in trouble.

God knows there's trouble enough by day on Delhi roads. And three wheels aren't the steadiest undercarriage when the going gets rough. Better than two is all you can say, and probably not all the time either. You see some sights on the road that you'd like to forget, and when it comes to the crunch, the guy with the least steel is the loser. I've seen some two-wheeler accidents where the helmet didn't help much more than the severed head. Bastard Blue Line buses! people screech, me too, but might is right in the jungle.

Keep well in, I tell my passengers, and they do. (As if it would make a whole lot of difference when the bus rams you.) But a wraparound shield is better than nothing—even if the dents are starting to join up on my Bhavra. The Bee is what I named her in the good old black-and-yellow days before this greenie shift.

You could say I own the buzzer. I've paid back most of the deposit on her to the Punjab National Bank, and I can usually go home by 9, maybe 10. Mornings I start early with schoolkids, twelve monsters packed in with a little removable wooden bench, schoolbags outside. And I don't always work late. I've saved a bit of money in term deposits at the PNB. If I overdraw on the current account, they automatically take it out of the next deposit: last in, first out.

Most days I wear a clean white polyester safari to work. Impractical, I know, and the wife never fails to remind me, though secretly she likes me in it. No pen in my pocket, no comb either. Good Agra sandals, size eleven, and I don't tuck one foot under me as I drive. It's hard enough having to double over just to get into the driver's seat. No holy pictures along the top of the windscreen, just the Shah Rukh poster at the back on the one side and Deepika on the other. I have noticed men sit right up against my life-size Deepika, the shot in the black negligee that got everyone going. Women cozy up to the King.

Anyway, this night I was cruising along the busy Mall Road in Civil Lines looking for a last fare when something about the peace of University Road pulled me in toward the Ridge. I left the rat race behind and sailed along past those sedate college gates in top gear, engine purring. All the walls have gotten higher since I was a student—maybe that's saying something, if only that I haven't gotten any shorter. I switched off the stereo. I was one of the first to install a system back in the twentieth century when the vehicle was new. There was always a Sufi fat-boy tape rolling to drown out the noise of the day. Nights nowadays you want to listen to the silence, when you can.

Directly opposite the main gate of Delhi University, where the road goes straight up to Flagstaff House, the hill stretch has been closed to traffic and an autorickshaw stand has sprung up at the barrier. A handful of peanut vendors and ice-cream carts congregate there during the day. At night, of course, it's deserted, and so it was this night, but sometimes you can pick up a late fare. I did a U-turn and drew up beside the gate. Ten or fifteen minutes under the entrance lights might be well spent, I thought. People don't like to walk along the Ridge.

The Delhi Ridge is a wilderness of rocks and thorn trees, nature's last stand in this gray city, the nearest thing we have to a forest. A hundred years ago they planted this barren upland with a Mexican tree that ran amok. Up along the crest are paved paths the municipality has laid in an attempt to tame the manmade jungle. Monkeys use the watershed as a safe base for raids down either side; peacocks honk at first light and then retire, leaving the field to a treepie with a harsh call—half heckle, half jeer. Morning walkers do their laughter therapy up there, and power joggers go by in pairs, tugging at the elastic bands of their tracksuit cuffs to consult expensive watches. But a careless jogger could ruin a pair of Nikes on the broken glass of last night's rumfest, if he's lucky. If he's unlucky, say he was working late, there's a higher price he could pay among the syringes and condoms and gutka sachets that lie strewn in the red-brick dust. Even by day you'd jump if someone came up behind you on those paths. You don't go there after dark unless you have a minder. Or unless you are the minder.

Of course, lovers go there because there's nowhere else to go. Students mostly, from the DU campus. There are park benches where they can sit and make out by day. I used to go up the

Ridge during my spell as a student, before the old man real-ized I was getting ideas and married me off. In the early days the wife and I took the boys there for a joyride once or twice, before they grew embarrassed about an outing on the work-horse. We'd sit and watch the monkeys by Flagstaff House. In winter they sun themselves and pick one another's fleas. A big male will turn up and simply roll over in front of a lesser creature, and the chosen one will leave whatever it was he was doing. I tend to believe in the chosen.

The newest tribe are the gardeners who arrived when Nehru Park was created. But joggers and gardeners and ca-noodlers and watchers tend to move on once the sun sets. Everyone does except for the diehards, or those who blithely believe a special dispensation hangs over them like a royal parasol. And who knows, maybe they're mostly right.

They can be wrong. Every once in a while you read in the paper about a rape on the Ridge. I used to pay special atten-tion to these snippets, partly because of my old association with the university.

That evening, I was parked outside the gates and starting to look at my watch when I heard the tube light smash. Few night sounds are more chilling, none more deliberate. After all, a tube light is something we carry with special care when we must, upright beside us. As if it were the body's ideal twin, smooth and colorless and fragile. It breaks in a shivering white cascade with the sound of heaven collapsing. If spirit had sub-stance it would shatter like this, something between a gasp and a cry. And that's how it sounded, scary but somehow, how to put it, binding.

I sat up in my seat and looked at the Ridge, studying the darkness. Curiosity, of course, but partly the witching of that weird sound. In a minute I thought I heard a sort of cry, an earthly pain. I didn't stop to think. I started up the auto and zipped across the road, made an S around the double barrier, and headed uphill in the direction of the noise.

Next thing I heard was running feet, the *stamp-stamp-stamp* of cheap shoe leather. I pulled over and keyed off and waited. It was a young man and he ran straight into me. It wasn't that my dim headlight was switched off, just that he was running downhill and used the machine as a brake. He slammed into the windshield and stood there bent over and winded. Even by the faint light of my beam I could see he was bleeding. His face was cut up and he looked frightened. So frightened he'd lost his voice and could only point back up the road the way he'd come.

In the background I could see Flagstaff House like a stage set, a black cutout of a tower against the gray of the November sky.

"Get in," I called, and shoved him into the passenger seat, "and hang on!"

I turned the auto around on a five-rupee coin and was about to get the hell out of there, but he grabbed me by the shoulder and found his voice.

"She's still there!"

So he wasn't alone. I armlocked the handlebar till we were facing uphill again and began the slow climb in the old machine. Come on, Bee! Even to me, the journey seemed to last forever.

At the top of the rise the boy jumped from the auto and ran a short way toward the tower calling the girl's name, but his wild turns of the head said she was not where he'd left her. I looped the tower in the machine, leaning on the horn and shouting words of support and threat into the dark. It must have been the purest gibberish, and a greater silence was the only reply.

"Get back in!" I called, and the boy obeyed but hung out of the auto scanning the side of the road. I've made a career of watching people's faces in the rearview mirror and his was intent, as if unaware of the volume of blood trickling down his forehead. The pain wouldn't have hit him yet. He seemed to be reading the night, willing it to disclose his harmed lover.

And then she appeared, or a figure appeared that the boy recognized, because he hopped out again and ran toward the brush. She was walking very slowly, smoothing down her kameez over and over again. The dupatta, if she wore one, was gone. The boy took her hand and led her tenderly toward the auto.

I took them straight downhill, jinked back around the traffic barrier, and turned left onto University Road. It was a clear run to the next corner where the road climbs back over the hill to the Hindu Rao Hospital. But a 212 bus coming the opposite way strayed across the white line and broke our momentum. "Blue Line bastards!" I shouted, but we'd lost it and had to toil the rest of the way up to the crest. Then we raced down the other side of the Ridge and into the hospital gates.

Well, that's it, I thought as I headed home; you don't see people twice in the big city. But of course you do, maybe just the ones you think you won't. I told you I read people's faces in the mirror and it's true you can tell straight off the talkers, the tippers, the nasties, the hunted, the doomed. I had watched the girl in the mirror whenever a car came the other way and I guessed she wouldn't report the crime. She still had her silver chain, a necklace of eyelets each with its little silver tear. The pain had finally struck the boy, and last I saw them she was leading.

The next day and the next day and the next I looked in the papers, but there was no report. Ah well, I thought, you lose some, you lose some.

Then there was a story: a savage rape on the Ridge. But the description didn't match and the date given was for the day before, a whole week after my little adventure. Over the next fortnight there were two more incidents; in both cases the girl's dupatta was taken and the boy's face messed up. The police issued descriptions of the assailants, two men in their late thirties. People were warned off the Ridge at night. An officer criticized trends in women's garments with words I remembered from twenty years before. And the general suggestion was that these things wouldn't happen but for the foolishness of the couples. Well, I thought, clipping out the stories, maybe all that hot young blood buzzing in the brain does make you a little careless.

Next morning I was tooling along University Road when I saw the boy. He didn't return my look—maybe after a month he really didn't recognize me—and ducked in at the main gate. On an impulse I parked the Bee and gave chase. It was him all right and he remembered me, but he didn't want to be reminded of that night.

"Well," I said, "you might want to forget it happened, but whoever did it hasn't stopped."

He looked genuinely surprised, like he hadn't read the newspapers. I invited him for a coffee. In my day I used to wonder—a tea man myself—what drew people to the university coffeehouse, although the place had an undeniable glamour. I still don't know. As we sipped the filthy stuff I took out the news clippings from my pocket and laid them on the table between us. He glanced over them with a troubled expression. The scars were healing nicely on his face; with a bit of luck they would melt into worry lines.

"Look," he said, when he had read enough, "what's it to you?"

My heart contracted. I hadn't imagined he needed winning over. I'd steered clear of asking after the girl, figuring she'd slipped out of his life.

"Just tell me if you could recognize the guy again."

"You mean the guys," he said, stressing the plural in a defensive way.

"The guys. Have you ever seen them again?"

He searched my eyes as if looking for a handhold, then gave up. "They hang around the metro station in the mornings. The main guy is built like a bouncer. He wears the same safari suit every day."

"What color?"

"Sort of a darkish color."

"Black?"

"Not quite black."

"You mean like gray?"

"No, no, darker than that."

"Sort of a blackish gray?"

"More like a grayish black. But darker."

"Blackish black?"

"Ya. Almost."

I saw I was getting nowhere fast. I made a last bid. "Listen, I'll be at the metro station in the morning. Just point him out and I'll take it from there."

"Take it where?" he asked despairingly, and I let the question dangle.

I didn't really expect him to be there the next day but he turned up.

"The safari wala's not here," he said, "but the other guy is. By the sweet potato vendor, pink shirt."

He pointed toward the granite steps where the metro terrace descends to street level. A small sleek mongoose of a man in a red cotton overshirt was stabbing at a leaf plate with a toothpick while sweeping the concourse with his eyes. I dropped my gaze as the little pointed head swiveled toward us. When I looked up it had darted away. His bottle-brown hair was topped by a blue-and-white baseball cap worn the right way so the brim hooded his eyes. Fake Diesel pants with faded chaps were standard, I assumed, but the bulge in the back pocket could have been either a cell phone or a knife. I had never seen a man wear three shirts before, four if you counted the tee. True, it was winter and the outermost, a florist's dream of canna lilies, was zippered.

I was already moving toward him through the horde of students. I must confess I didn't stop to thank the boy, nor did he seem keen to stick around. I'm not a big sweet-potato fan myself but the other item on the menu was a salad of yellow star fruit, sour to frizzling insanity, and I stood six inches from the sidey and ate it without turning a hair. Right then a Mallika bombshell went by and I groaned and staggered theatrically and caught Sidey's eye. He winked at me and grinned and I left it at that.

It wasn't till the next day that I saw the bouncer. I arrived there early and had to wait. I'd dropped off the schoolies and gotten rid of the little bench so I sat in the back of the Bee in the Deepika corner and smoked. Tobacco first, then a sweet cigarette. Back in the '90s I'd taken to sucking on them whenever I felt tempted and now I had two habits (three if you count stopping by the flat to trouble the wife when a fare brought me within stroking distance). Same red-and-white Phantom pack from childhood, little smooth white sugar sticks with a red dot on the end. Some days if you suck hard enough the red dot actually glows.

A cobra—that was my first thought when the villain appeared. I swear I expected all the cool university chicks to go into a frenzy of squawking the way forest birds do when a snake appears. But they stalked on by in their hiphug Pepe jeans with their video cell phones gripped tighter than their textbooks, and the cobra watched them pass with a bland insouciance only Sidey, stationed at the sweet potato stand, could rightly read.

He wasn't in a safari suit (I felt a little vindicated in mine) but in white drill pants pressed to a knife's edge, elastic boots, and a black balloon jacket that gave him a slightly unmoored look. Or maybe that was his natural walk, weaving a little, like a wrestler, not a drunk. Sidey fell into step beside him and the two of them walked up University Road without bothering to take in the scenery. I had expected to watch them ogling, but instead I found myself tailing them in the Bee, hanging a good way back. What surprised me more than their disinterest in the girls was Sidey's face. You expect a planet to light up when the sun appears, but Sidey's face fell into a total eclipse. His eyes took a haunted half-shadow and even the cap looked crestfallen.

I parked the Bee at the Flagstaff Road barrier, told the ice-cream wala the wife needed a branch of babul leaves, and trailed them uphill. At the top they took Magazine Road and I waited at Flagstaff House pretending to watch the monkeys. The road, once simply a path, follows the crest of the Ridge through the man-made jungle, low dusty thorn trees with twisted gray trunks and a canopy like mustard gas. On either side, beyond the park benches and half hidden by the brush, are power substations and water tanks and gardeners' tool-sheds like bunkers. Also ruins from Muslim times, tombs and such. Built with a prospect on what would have been a barren ridge, they now huddle blindly in the jungle, peculiarly functionless unless to conceal a walker caught short by nature. Turds and worse await the unwary foot.

Cobra and Mongoose sat down on a bench and looked about them. A gardener had set a hose with a ratchet spring to green the grass by the caged bougainvillea and was standing back to inspect the spray as it ticked around in a wide circle. Satisfied, he drifted off to join his fellow workers for a smoke by the garden gate at the far end of the park. Cobra and Mongoose watched him go, then idly observed the itinerant spray. Idly I imagined the eye of the hose coming around to fix them with a stare. Stray walkers came and went along the long park road; a couple sitting on a nearby bench rose and made for the far gate where the 212 goes by.

When the coast was clear Cobra got up and vanished into the forest, Mongoose trailing after. I stayed put. I knew there was no way out of the park except at the far end or back in my direction. They were gone ten, maybe fifteen minutes. I was getting restless when they reappeared and took the road to the far gate, strolling side by side as before.

I went to their bench and sat a moment to see what they saw. Rising out of the bushes opposite was one of those curly-wurly ocher buildings from Mughal days, a hunting lodge maybe. I sauntered into the forest and entered the ruin from behind to find two rooms; the roof of one had fallen in and the floor was grassed over. In the inner room hung a musky odor that told its own tale. A stair led up from the outer room but the way up was barred by an iron door; a heavy padlock hung from the hasp. I picked up the biggest stone I could find, lifted it with both hands, and brought it crashing down on the lock. The lock gave and hung there broken jawed; I unhooked it and threw it into the bushes downhill. (Any crook can remove a government padlock and replace it with his own, a nice rusty old job, and people will walk on by thinking: official.) Upstairs I found an empty chamber with a pillared balcony: nothing but fallen birds' nests on the floor. On the way back down I noticed a loose slab at the landing and lifted it. Underneath lay a yellow cement sack neatly folded in half. I took it back into the chamber and looked inside. There were four lengths of fabric in there, three colored and one white. They were not new but clean, some printed, one embroidered; together they seemed a strange valueless hoard. It was only when I unfolded one that I realized what it was: a woman's dupatta.

I went straight back down to the Bee.

"Wife's going to be angry," the ice-cream wala forecast.

"What?" As I drove off I realized he meant I'd forgotten the babul leaves.

I headed over the hill past the Hindu Rao Hospital along the 212 route, cursing the Blue Liners as I flew; sharing the same prey, buses and autos are natural enemies. I hung a left at the chaiwala by the cell phone tower, then hard left again, and cut the engine, rolling to a halt right where the silk cotton tree that overhangs our whole neighborhood is anchored. Just short of home.

I hadn't come to trouble the wife. I was there to call on a man dead five hundred years.

He stood nine feet tall, my ancestor, going by the grave. Called the Grave of the Nine-Foot Saint, always freshly painted green, it sticks out two feet into the main road, the remaining seven closing off the sidewalk. Huge blood-orange flowers flop down on it in summer, followed by a delicate rain of cotton that whitens the precinct like snow. It's an island of peace for a military man.

He was a military baba, my ancestor, the man whose name I bear. Baba Ganoush. Baba G., my wife calls me for short, or just Baba, though I don't really qualify. Babas were either plain holy or soldierly holy, and I'm neither. My military baba had no secret weapon: *He* was the weapon. He moved the army. He had a retinue of 786. Baskets of purple eggplants and potted marigolds moved before him in the field; caged songbirds and urns of rose water came behind. The night before a pitched battle, his linked light-boys dressed up as houris and oiled their bodies and did calisthenics for the host. Before the phalanx of warriors he drew a box in the dust with his ring finger and danced a victory dance that spun every watching soldier into heaven.

I stood by the grave and felt my shirttail begin to lift and billow. His spirit clad me, sliding over my skin like a lover's hand. The air grew red and I was racked with pain and filled with heretical notions. Blood is our element, I remember thinking, not water. We swim in it from one life to the next, passing like a wet flame from wick to wick. So little to the body, I was thinking the other day while I bathed, the soaping is so quickly done, so little to do.

Go! I heard my Baba say. Fight, with love in your heart.

I went to a hardware store and bought a quarter-inch brush, a small tin of enamel blue, a cheap screwdriver, and a key ring with a red disc; on the sidewalk I bought a second-hand padlock. Then I went home and parked the Bee and kissed my wife. Not now, I said, detaching myself when she sent the boys out to play. I opened the paint can and outlined eggplants and marigolds on the nose of the Bee and rose water urns and caged bulbuls on her tail. The paint was still wet as I rode over the hill again and padlocked the iron door in the curly-wurly ruin.

Next day I tailed the pair again. They did a repeat of the hill walk and parted at the gate on the 212 route, Sidey looking more depressed than ever. I tailed him home to a Maurice Nagar flat and made some inquiries with neighbors.

The morning after I was at the DU metro station early. This time I braved the sweet potato but asked for an extra squeeze of lime.

Mongoose turned up in his floral jacket and ordered the same. We exchanged a wink when a Bips lookalike passed by on gel-pen refill heels. I chucked my leaf plate and ordered another.

"And one for my friend here!" I said.

"No, no," he protested, but only formally. He was already chucking his leaf.

"Something else, these babes, no?" I said, strolling him gently away. He was walking before he knew it.

We drifted up University Road toward the gates. He seemed happy to get away from the metro, but kept looking back all the same.

"So, Mr. Raju," I began.

Mongoose stopped dead in his tracks. "How do you know me?"

"Oh," I brushed away an airy cobweb, "we have our ways."

At the *we* I drew myself up to my full height, laid a long finger on my shoulder, and tapped twice where some silver might adorn my epaulettes. He remained standing so I prodded him along with little shocks of home address and house history, even a little detail about a tiny nephew who might need a polio shot. (I picked that up from two door-to-door health workers.)

"And how is the, um," I gestured up the Ridge, "shikar these days? Happy hunting?"

His eyes bulged. Sideys break down more or less right away so I was at pains to let him know I knew he was just the accessory.

"And your friend, the big gun?"

He was dumb and dry-mouthed. I walked him up the slope past the tower to the curly-wurly lodge in the forest.

"We've had to change the lock on your door, I'm afraid." I produced the key ring that my older boy had painted in police blue-and-red; he had added off his own bat the sinister Delhi Police motto: *With you, for You, Always.* "Go on, open it."

He undid the padlock but lacked the strength to climb the stair.

"Don't you want to go and see?"

"I believe you."

"All right. What can you tell us about your friend?"

Right then the cell phone rang in his cargo pants. Mongoose jumped where he stood. It was Cobra, I could tell. The timing shook me too; the sidey simply came unhinged.

"If it's our friend," I said, "tell him you'll meet him tomorrow."

He obeyed. But Cobra had other plans and after hearing him out, Mongoose hung up in an ecstasy of fear.

"What's up?"

He looked unseeingly at me, his finger and thumb worrying a burr on the cotton jacket.

"Hey." I frowned and slapped him.

He began to whimper, edging away from me and then back as if pushed from the other side by an unnamed force. The phone slid into his pocket and he gripped the barred door like a prisoner who doesn't realize he's on the outside. "He's crazy," he wailed. "He's mad!"

"What's this drama-shama?" I growled.

He slid down the door like a bad actor and squatted there with his forehead lodged between two bars.

"Hoy!" I booted him in the bum to no effect. I was aiming a harder kick when he began to speak.

"He's going to kill somebody. And he wants me to help."

"Kill who?"

"Somebody. Anybody. He says no more fooling around. He says next time we use the knife. He says finish off the bastards. He says they need to be taught a lesson. They keep coming here and polluting the morals of the nation. But then he himself . . ."

"He himself what?"

He hung his head.

"He himself what?"

"Brings me here."

"When are you seeing him?"

"He says we'll have a drink this evening. He says we'll want a bit of warming up. He wants me to bring a bottle of Walker. Where am I supposed to get the money?"

I thought for a bit. "Okay, you get a bottle of Patiala whiskey and go to the rebottlers behind Kashmiri Gate. They don't charge much. Your job is to get him drunk, okay? You don't drink in here? . . . Good. Get him drunk and then walk him to Flagstaff House. I'll be waiting there at 10 o'clock. In an autorickshaw. We'll take him for a ride. Just get him drunk. And keep yourself sober. Do you think you can manage that?"

He seemed to come to life and we parted at the 212 bus stop.

"Ten o'clock!" I called as he climbed on his bus.

At half past 9 I was parked and waiting. I moved a couple of lovers on in a gruff policemanly voice and, as I watched them go, wondered where the knife would have gone in. Then there was nobody. I sat in the Bee and twiddled my thumbs and watched the night. The tower looked bleak and aloof, the Ridge close and unfriendly. Another feather of gray would have tipped the night sky into blackness. Brooding on my ancestor I realized that at this hour before the battle he would be drawing his mystic box in the dust and beginning his slow dance of death and transference. I simply sat and nibbled at a sugar stick. Before I knew it I had emptied the box.

At 10:10 I heard voices. They were singing but they were not houris. It was my quarry, drunk, both of them. Cobra was spitting threats at the world in between lines from an old song.

There's a boy across the river
With a bottom like a peach

"Get in, you idiot!" I whispered to Sidey, who was busy playing the Lucknow game of After You. He obeyed and snuggled up to King Khan.

But alas I cannot swim!

Cobra needed help and I brought myself to touch him. His balloon jacket felt dry and scaly, so I pinned him by the neck, bent him in two, and simply sprung him in. He turned to Deepika and began to slobber all over that sheer black negligee. I got in at once, started up, and took off, veering clockwise around the tower. My passengers were thrown left in a crazy centrifuge, Cobra leaning precariously out of the Bee.

"Hang on!" I yelled, and we plunged downhill, racing the way the boy had run the night of the tube light. Down below I jinked around the traffic barrier and left onto University Road. It was a repeat of the hospital ride, only this time I had the villains.

The Bee buzzed like the beauty she once was. I felt I was playing an instrument whose dark sweet drone underlaid the pair's drunken bawling. In days past I could tell the engine's semitones up and down the scale. I swooned to certain piston tremolos and awoke in time to pump a sweet glissando on the brake. Bee and I were partners in a dance whose music was in our blood. We moved in unison: I could trust her with any step, and she responded with an enabling precision; I could jiggle the schoolkids into giggling hysteria, sway a pouting beauty, or hit a bump at speed and bounce a snark straight up into the iron beam.

What to do? I was thinking as I sped through the dark. I had no plan. I watched the two men in my rearview mirror, but really I was looking a lot further back. Rape is a tricky business to judge. Unless you've felt the hot blunt thorn of it in your own flesh, your opinion isn't worth a lot. For a moment the mirror showed me just one face in the backseat, then as the bastard split in two I knew what I would do.

At the corner where the road goes over the hill, a north-bound 212 was about to take the curve onto University Road. There's no median strip there and downhill buses always cut that corner. There's a moment when their headlights are shining clear up the Hindu College Road when in fact the bus is heading down toward the university gates. I switched off my light and spun the Bee around in a tight U-turn. Cobra flew out into the bus's path. Last in, first out.

I watched him go in the mirror and thought he flew a little further than I intended. Well, that's destiny, I thought: He's meant to lose a little less. I turned the U into an O and sped off into the night, but not before I saw the bus drive over his feet.

Enough to put him out of action, up on the Ridge anyway. Then I dropped the Mongoose home. As in *dropped*.

Well, that's that, I thought. You don't see folks again in the big city. It's getting bigger all the time. That's progress: fluorescent lamps replacing tube lights, four-wheelers replacing three.

But maybe a month later I did see Sidey again. I had a passenger so I couldn't stop, but he was looking fresh and expansive on the sidewalk and he gave me a long cool wink as I went by.

It wasn't till I arrived home that I got to thinking about it. The wife had made baba ganoush after scorching the eggplant skin on a naked flame in her painstaking way. It's the family favorite, picked up from an aunt in the Gulf, and it usually goes down in a great hurry, no chewing, but I was about to swallow when I saw that wink again and then all I remember is the wife and boys looking strangely at me because I just kept chewing on that mouthful.

I haven't seen Mongoose lately but I often see that shrewd little pair of eyes fixed on me. Then one of them closes in the blackest wink, and I'm left wondering: Which of us was the sidey?

PARKING

BY RUCHIR JOSHI

Nizamuddin West

The cop van, slowing down on the street below, he doesn't like, even though he doesn't really notice at first. He's not planning to spend long on his terrace, just enough to catch one more shot of her walking away with that young ass of hers, maybe exchange a wave as she gets into daddycar and drives off. There's music playing behind him, on his comp, and the just-opened bottle of vodka waiting. It's what you do after a good love session, except she's young and doesn't drink what he does, doesn't listen to what he does, and on top of that, the Aunty is waiting at home, dinner ready, while the owner of daddycar is away, businessing out-of-country.

There's all kinds in this neighborhood, the semi-rich retired, the Government Service Detritus, the bourgeois Mosey refugees who've been forced out from other parts of Saarey Jahan ka Kachha, the old '47 rehvaasis refusing to die, the solid slum-class that's accrued around the Dargah, the Sufis and qawwalis who've dittoed, and now the new hippies, do-gooding goras with their blond and barefoot children kicking up dust as they trail along behind their crazy rent-paying momdads.

This afternoon they've decided this is also where Osama's hiding—totally best place for him, actually—and they've been fucking for him, doing it for O Bloody Laden, hoping he can hear them in his lonely hole, maybe even see them from one of the high mosque turrets near the tomb. It's been good, great even, and funny too, especially when she's shouted, "Oh, Sam, let's do it for Osama!" and then when they've collapsed in a postcoital heap of sweat, laughter, and sheets. He hasn't wanted it to end just yet, but she's pulled the plug, both on the Most Wanted Man on Earth, and on him, suddenly the Least Wanted Man.

"Babe!" He hates that "babe," coming from her, which is not the same as coming from the Yankietta who had a right to use it—same as we, us, have a right to use "bhenchod" and goras, like, don't.

"Babe, you know, na, if I make it back in time for dinner then we peacefully get another whole day before Dad returns, right?"

"Right . . . didn't know you were still in Class Ten, but yeah, okay, go."

"Fuck you, uncle, I might as well be in Class Eight, okay? For you I'll always be in Class Eight, a horny Class Eight thirteen-year-old, okay?"

"Okay."

"You'll take what you get, na?"

"Yeah. Now go."

"And dude, I've been here from 1:30 to now, 7:30, which is six hours, so you're not seriously complaining about what you get and take, ya?"

"No. Now go." He hates the "dude" even more than the "babe."

"I'm not complaining about this either, na? So, like no complaints and see you day after?"

"Ya, ya, ya, now GO!"

She places a goodbye tongue in his mouth, like she's depositing cash at a government bank—rightful, superior, slightly disdainful of the clerk on the other side of the counter—and goes. Bolt door behind, turn around, and, like, beautiful choice: Go to kitchen, pour second drink vs. Go to computer and carry on hitting the downloads and get the rest of the Joy Div stuff before the broadband does its late-night slowdown.

He goes out to the terrace to get one last visual taste of her, catches her as she walks into sight under the lamppost, fixing her spaghettis, pulling uselessly on her low-low salwar bottoms, sees her turn right into the little gali across the way where he's told her to avoid parking, and then he sees a bloody thana Qualis, blue-light mundu spinning as it casually, absentmindedly crawls up and blocks the gali where she's parked. The blue light goes off but neither of the two thullas sitting inside makes any move to get out.

It's not that she can't drive, problem is she tries to drive like she's Schumacher's little sister, bloody Ferrari sitting in an Indica. That's also fine, it's just that her slow-driving is pretty bad: the parking, the backing, the maneuvering in narrow situations—it's the opposite of watching her on a dance floor, where she mongooses through a maze of groping hands with nothing really managing to touch her. Here she's liable to touch everything, including the cops' Qualis. If she had any sense she would drive the way her car's pointing, straight into the service lane on the other side of the gali, and nose her way out from there, but she's a headbanger and he knows she'll reverse toward the main street and hit her horn.

Unbolt door and pull open, he's already halfway down the stairs, tucking the hanging drawstrings back inside his shorts, when his mobile starts to sing.

"Sam? Babe, can you please come down here fast?"

"Yah, coming, what's up?"

"Cops hassling me."

"On my way. Be polite."

And that's how the scene will always play in his head: Cops sitting fat in van, him on stairs, and-but-then by the time he reaches daddycar they are on the road, in the lane, ugly eyes reaching deep into the crack of Tia's ass as she bends into the open front passenger door, attacking the glove compartment for papers. Then one guy, the tall, tough-looking one, is standing right behind her, his eyes still searching down while the fat one flicks his glance between the papers and Tia's deep cleavage. In his head, a shout—why are the damn things so big anyway? He's not a tit man, he didn't ask for them to be so big, a size or two smaller would have been just fine, caused a whole lot less trouble on these tit-obsessed streets.

Samiran will always remember this as himself being hog-tied, witnessing a visual gang rape. The fat cop doesn't even take his eyes off Tia's stack when addressing Sam.

"Tu kaun hai? Who're you? Where do you live?" The "tu" would be insulting if the cop had done it with some thought, but Samiran is suddenly sharply aware that for this thulla he is a default "tu," nowhere near worthy of the effort of an "aap." Samiran is now very conscious of his dirty T-shirt and frayed shorts, his unshaven jaw, his Tia-smelling face. There's no point trying to tell them he does ad research for the net component of a big national weekly mag, but he tries anyway, with the succinct version. "I am from Press, mai Press ka hun."

The words come out flat and weak, and he will remember the cop's eyes cranking up to his face, the briefest of curiosities and the quickest of dismissals. Nizamuddin is full of high-powered media, both this side and that side of Mathura Road, and both the thullas have dealt with a few. Sam can tell they are thinking, *This dirty chut is no big threat.*

"Press card hai?" There's a fat mole on the left side of the fat cop's nose which is shining slightly with sweat as the lamppost catches it. Sam feels like that mole is the central black hole for all the malevolence coming out of the bastard. No, he doesn't have a press card, he's not a journalist, and now he is very aware that he doesn't have a magic number he can call, any contact who can disable these bastards. With fury he realizes exactly where he stands in the Delhi pecking order.

Tia, to her credit, isn't trying to cover up one inch of her skin. She's standing there, erect, tits jutting at one cop, butt showing the finger to the other. Before the cop realizes it, she's taken the papers back from him and gone into attack. She uses her English, not bothering with Hindi and not bothering to modulate her fake American twang. "What's the problem? I don'nderrstand what the prawblem is!"

The fat cop points at the problem. The problem is the guy Sam knows as "K-5," and he's standing there, just outside his gate, the front gate of K-5, in track pants and a long kurta, grinning like a monkey with gonorrhea, the words *Got You!* almost blazing in neon across his forehead, just under his backpointing baseball cap.

"Parking," says the fat nose-mole cop, "Suspicious car parking. We have a complaint."

"Who's complained?" Samiran feels the blood hit his head.

"*We* complained!" says K-5, dripping self-righteousness. "We didn't know who this car was. Never seen it before. Times are bad, could have been a terrorist car, how do we know!?!"

Samiran gets it like a thwack in the face. Tia always parks her car in this lane, right in front of K-5's side entrance where there's usually shade. They always tell her not to park there because that's where they park their third car. And she always tells them they don't own the lane outside their door. Once she actually told this guy to fuck off. Today is clearly revenge day, with a little help from friends in the local thana. K-5 has obviously called the cops to come and have a look, and everybody's lucky because this is exactly when the girl's decided to come down to her car.

Sam turns to Tia. "Listen, why don't you move the car out to the main road? We'll just sort this out."

As Tia gets in and starts backing up, Sam turns to the cop. "Okay, bhaisahab? Now you know who the car belongs to and where people were visiting. Theek hai?"

"Terey kehne sey okay nahi ho jatta hai!" ("It's not okay because *you* say it's okay!") Tall Cop is now right behind Sam, using the same "tu."

Sam rearranges the movement on his face, trying to stuff down the anger. He wants Tia out of here and he wants to gun these scum down. On their knees, begging before his .357 Magnum, one close facial, the fat one first, so the tall guy can see what's coming, Fat One's brain and face splattering onto the road and into the gutter—no, actually, mostly on the tall guy's boots, *Gazpacho soup kabhi chakhaa hai, bhenchod?* (*Ever tasted gazpacho, sisterfucker?*), and then, as the Champion Rapist of Haryana starts to shake, as he covers his head, babbling "Nahi bhaisahab, nahi huzur . . ." a bullet straight in the cock, and then as the hands jerk to crotch, then and only then, one slug straight between the eyes. Then, next, a long shot to bring down the cockroach-pimp K-5 as he tries to run, just enough to bring him down but not fully kill. Then, a big smile into the fucker's face before blowing him away. Two dead cops, one squashed cockroach, somehow nobody else around for miles, and he goes up, carries on with his downloads, finishes half the bottle of vodka around a long shower with proper water pressure . . . and he wants Tia out of here.

Now, backed out on the main road, Tia has the same idea. Her Indica is finally pointing in the right direction. As he and the cops walk out of the gali, Sam realizes the chick's bravado has run dry. Her face is now saying, *Shit. Daddy. Daddycar. Aunt. Trouble. Big shit.*

As they get close, he waves at her. "Achha, now you go!" He calls out, "I'll take care of it."

Him saying this overlaps exactly with her saying, "Dude! I gotta go!" and she takes off, smoothly enough, like her normal fast takeoff, no extra engine-gunning in panic, but no quarter given to the speed-breaker that sits a few yards down, and none to the two stray dogs dawdling in the middle of the road who yelp away right and left as she zips straight through them.

Telling Ajit three days later, Samiran still feels a throb of fear. "That's when the cops got heavy. She zips off and the fat one says, 'Who said she could go?' Tall One says, 'Why did you tell her to go? That's very suspisuss!' Fatso says, 'You know we can take you into custody right now?' Tough Guy says, 'Shall we take you to the thana? Shall we check your house? Which one is your house?' . . . And I could see the fat bugger was, like, looking at me as a Revenue Area, but the tall one was acting like I was going to be a Recreational Area. Then, suddenly, this K-5 bastard pipes up and points up here and says, 'That one! That's his barsaati!' and that was it, man. I just lost it."

"Lost it, how? You didn't abuse, I hope?" Ajit looks slightly worried.

"Nothing like that, I just got tough myself. Told them to stop calling me 'tu' and try 'aap.' Told them they could come and check me out anytime, said to them, police harassment big in the news so they should be careful not to be used by some malicious neighbors. Finally said you can never tell who is who in this town, and tried to look like I fucking meant it."

"So they took your number?"

"Yeah."

"Called what time this morning?"

"About 9:30."

"Fat One or Tall One?"

"Fat One, I think."

"So he's going to drop in around 1 o'clock?"

"That's what he said."

"So," Ajit looks at his watch and smiles, "lunchtime may mean he's looking for some lunch money. Revenue Area. You said you are Press, but his SHO's phone is still intact, two days, no call from anybody high, so he's going to try his luck again."

"So what do I say when he comes?"

"Nothing. You relax and enjoy."

Chandran looks up from Sam's computer. "Yes, man, you just relax. Let Ajit convey some pnownage."

"Huh?" Sam is slightly confused.

"Ignore him," Ajit says. "These bloody Southies speak in another language."

"Some nice stuff you have here." Chandran is completely engrossed in Sam's iTunes library. "Can I rip this sometime?"

"Sure, take what you want."

"Great, thanks. In fact, I have my drive with me so I'll do it right now." Chandran gets up and stretches. "Which was the complaint guy's house again?"

Sam points at K-5 through the thin curtains. "The corner one. That's the main gate, on the main road, and that's the lane, with the side entrance, which they think they own."

"And this . . . You got their right name, anh? The family's name?"

"Yeah, think so, it's what it says in the colony directory. Siddiqui."

"Right, right . . . And next to them is who? In this one, just across the gali?"

"Flats, three different families." Sam leafs through the directory. "Ghufran, Abbas, Khan."

"And then this one, to our right?" Chandran is now pointing at a wall of Sam's front room, gesturing beyond the view provided by the window.

"Kashmiris. Renting, so name not in this owners' directory. Some big carpet business."

"You're in this corner house, so everyone has a nice view of your barsaati, huh?" Ajit is grinning again. "Nice, clear view of all your activities too!"

"Well," Chandran stays serious, "nice view works both ways sometimes. Sam has a nice view of these guys too. In fact, we are higher here than most of them."

"A bit," agrees Sam, "but there's nothing to see, usually."

"Whereas you, my boy, are a one-man, live-action, neighborhood porn channel!"

"I wish. Anyway, I close my curtains."

"But isn't this Tia the one who makes a lot of noise? What will curtains do? That little neighbor of yours can probably hear her all the way across the road. Every time she moans he probably sizzles. You need sound padding, like they have in those posh fuckotels abroad."

Samiran doesn't say anything. Ajit is a friend but Chandran he's meeting for the first time. Ajit sees this and fields.

"It's okay, these Southies are sexless. They get their kicks from world domination."

World domination or not, Chandran stays focused on his immediate plan. He pulls out a small external drive and plugs it into Samiran's computer. Then he puts on the headphones. By the time the doorbell rings, he's got all of Sam's jazz, most of his early punk, and nearly all of his Velvet Underground bootleg tracks. As Sam goes to open the door, he can hear Chandran singing in a low voice, *"Now you know you shouldn't DO that, don't you know you'll stain the CARPET . . ."*

Fat Cop and the mole on his nose are even uglier in daylight; it's as if two malevolent creatures have come visiting, one attached to the other. The thulla doesn't wait for Samiran to move aside, he shoulders past him as if it's his own house and Samiran is some kind of minion who just happens to be there. Once inside, the cop looks around with interest, taking his time, checking out the narrow corridor that leads from the door to the main living area, peering at the Che Guevara poster and the small framed stills from the Apu trilogy. In the small no-man's-land that joins the rooms, the kitchen, and the door to the terrace, the man discovers Janis Joplin, with her hands crossed over her privates but otherwise naked. The cop tries to decipher the flower-power calligraphy announcing the ancient concert but goes back to staring at Janis's smallish tits. And then interrogating her crossed hands, trying to get her to part them.

"Mishter Chakkarvarty, you are very fond of naked women, hain?"

Samiran stays silent, wondering where Ajit's gone. Chandran's singing has stopped too. For all the cop can tell, the two of them are alone.

"Mishter Chakkarvarty, you have a servant-woman who comes to work for you, no? What she is thinking of this picture?"

Good point. Sam remembers the momentary awkwardness when Farida and Janis first met, the day after he put up the poster. And then Farida's curtain of dour indifference dropping back in place; the complete absence of any emotion as she dusted over JJ's naked hippy-waif body, the silent adding of the poster to the other bad things Farida encountered when she came in every morning, the other things she ignored, the booze bottles, the unmade bed, the girls who would sometimes be filling the bed or wandering around the barsaati, clothed, mostly, but their very presence conveying the opposite.

The thulla lets go of Janis and pushes open the terrace door with the very tips of his fingers, like not wanting to tamper too much with the scene of a crime; but his ownership air is fully in place as he walks out onto the terrace— *Chakkarvarty, you have come as summoned. Now let's talk.*

"So where is that madam who was driving the car that night?" The cop's voice is hard without any warning, even the word "madam" is like a slap. "We can either talk to her or we can talk to her father . . ." The cop looks down at a piece of paper in his hand. "We can talk to Mr. . . . Avinash Prabhu, C-343 Defence Colony."

Samiran folds his arms, mouth still shut, wondering what Ajit is playing at. Samiran's silence seems to send the cop into greater fury. He drops the "aap" he's been using so far and reverts to the "tu." "What makes you think you people can turn a decent family neighborhood into a whorehouse muhalla? Hunh?"

Samiran clenches his fists under his armpits, fighting to keep his face impassive. A pigeon comes and settles on the parapet behind the fat cop. After examining the situation, it starts a slow sentry march up and down the parapet, pecking every now and then at live goodies in the lime paint, being a total sidekick to the cop.

The policeman pulls up a cane chair and sits himself down. He takes out a little notebook and a battered rollerball from his tunic pocket. "What is the girl's mobile number?" His voice is quiet, final, pronouncing death. "We need to talk to her."

Samiran opens his mouth, wondering what to put through it. Ajit's voice is suddenly very audible, speaking in oozingly respectful, clear, official Hindi.

"No sir, no, no, no need for that, not yet. No sir, please, Saikia sahab is usually very tough in these cases, sir, overtough sometimes, so why disturb him? Why bother DCP Corruption, sir, for such a small thing? It would become a policeman's whole career at stake, sir, because of a small mistake. No, no sir, no, no, there is no demand for a bribe, just a case of . . . how to say it, overzealous imposition of a certain morality . . . and, you know, malicious neighbors with nothing better . . . Exactly, ji, exactly!"

Ajit has walked out onto the terrace as if there's no one else around, his phone trapped between ear and shoulder. He ignores Samiran and the cop and goes to the parapet, making the pigeon flap away. "DCP Saikia, you know, will immediately suspect the other motive . . . Sir, yes sir . . . His new anticorruption campaign, yes sir . . . Well, he has just been posted from the northeast, no, sir? I don't know if they harass girls there for wearing small-small clothes, no . . . Oh yes! Hahahaha! Yes, yes sir, army-paramilitary may rape women, but local police will not arrest a boy-girl for kissing! Hahaha, quite right, sir!"

Samiran sees that Ajit is using his hands to carry two glasses and a bottle of beer, all of which he gingerly manages onto the parapet. He listens intently to the other party as he pours the beer, making sure the head of foam is just right in both glasses.

"Ji, sir, Nizamuddin thana, I think . . . Yes sir, Wahi sahab, the officer is right here. Should I just ask him and call you back? . . . No? . . . Okay, okay, I'll just ask him right now."

Ajit hands a glass to Samiran and turns to the cop. His tone is politely conversational, equally for the cop and the benefit of his phonee. "Sir-ji, please, can you tell me your name?" Before the cop can answer, Ajit bends to take a look at the name tag on the cop's left tit. He speaks into the phone: "Subinspector U.P. Singh, sir . . . Yes, I will just ask." He turns back to the cop and smiles kindly. "Sir, thoda, please, aapka full name? DCP South wants to know your name."

The fat cop is sliced into two zig-zagging parts, two halves that fit perfectly but which are barely able to cling to each other. One part of him clearly wants to snatch the phone from this new stranger and slap him unconscious; the other part seems to want to vault over the terrace wall and parachute away. Samiran imagines he can see thin seepings of blood where the blade has cleaved the man. When the voice comes out, it's barely audible, so squeezed is it by the juice-press of rage.

Ajit straightens up and announces into the phone: "Sir, he says his name is Ujjwal Prakash Singh. Nizamuddin thana, na?" The thulla jerks out the smallest of nods. Ajit listens a beat longer, allowing the bloodlines to well up further, and then, "Okay, sir, yes sir, I will tell him." He snaps his mobile shut and takes a deep pull on his beer.

"Nice, no? This one is much better than the usual bird-piss we get, no? Genuine German wheat beer. Deepti says her friend will be importing it now regularly." Samiran forces himself to gulp from his own glass. Ajit turns to the cop. "Sir-ji, your mobile is on and working?"

"Yes."

"The thana will have your number I take it?"

"It is naat so eejhhi to threaten me, my friend." Fat Cop is now pushing out his English, trying to jump start it. "You and your friend will get into the deeper trouble."

"*Threaten*, sir-ji? Threaten who? Who is threatening anybody? What are you talking about? I am just trying to bring about a friendly solution to the little problem we seem to be having." Ajit sticks to his smoothly purring government Hindi. "Oh, sorry, we haven't met. Ajit Karlekar, Delhi Government." He puts his card down on the low table between them.

Fat-fuck's phone has a ring-tone that Sam can't quite place. His voice is cautious as he answers it; Sam can see that the guy's hoping the whole thing's a crazy bluff, in which case he'll be able to tear into Ajit and him, but he can also see that the guy has a sinking feeling about the whole situation; after the first few moments on the phone, Sam can see anxiety cloud the small eyes; he can almost feel the mobile phone winch the man up from his chair, almost hear the voice that makes the man spin around and move away from them. Even from behind, Samiran is sure he can see the sweat spots enlarge, turning the khaki a darker brown under the man's armpits; and if, maybe, he's imagining that, he's certainly not imagining Fat Cop's smell, which is now sharp and impossible to escape.

Sam can't take his eyes off the thulla but Ajit is engrossed with his mobile, sipping beer and text messaging intently. All Sam can hear from around the cop's back and spreading ass is a binary progression of *Sir-sir-sir-ji-ji-sir-ji-ji-huzoor-huzoor-ji-sir-huz* . . . a word or syllable getting chopped off here and there as the other side cuts in. At one point, Fat Cop says a name which Sam assumes is that name of the Haryanvi rap-ist Tall Cop: "Sir, ASI Neb Chand, sir, yes, Neb Chand, he a good—" and then Neb Chand's goodness is also abruptly cut off. Sam notices the sidekick pigeon is back, waddling and cooing sympathetically as the man nods into his Nokia.

The phone conversation twists Fat Cop around again, and he's back to facing Sam and Ajit. Still listening and nodding, the man starts to give in to the September heat. His non-phone hand goes first to middle of stomach, through his shirt, right into the belly button, one scratch, two, three, then to the side of his paunch, as if drawing a median around the earth, the fingers fiddling between the liver area and the right kidney, and then, as someone on the other side ups the ante, the hand goes down to the crotch. But there Fat-fuck stops, suddenly aware that he's being watched.

The next time Samiran sees Fat Cop, however, the man com-pletes the gesture. He begins by fiddling with his balls and then giving them a good, full-turbo mauling. It's late after-noon a month later and Samiran is looking down from his bedroom window, watching Fat Cop standing outside his en-trance, three floors below. Fat Cop is standing there because he has been summoned by Samiran to counter a new police-man, Third Cop, who has entered the frame from outside, entered all the way from Mandawali thana across the river.

Third Cop has also come into Samiran's life courtesy K-5. Though the pimp-rat hasn't connected Sam to the sharp misfortunes that have befallen him and his family over the last four weeks, he has figured out that the local cops from Niza-muddin are no longer able to help; somehow or other they've been disabled, turned even, so that any complaint seems to almost backfire. K-pimp has therefore called upon the thulla talent from around his factory, obviously bribed them, and sent them, sent this Third Cop, after Sam. Chandran, in the meantime, has picked this up on his magical radar and given Sam an early warning, advising him to call Subinspector Singh, which Sam has promptly done.

"Sir, you know I don't have a problem with any police, but it would be good if your colleague didn't waste his time or mine."

Sam has kept his voice sweet and full of request, since he now knows that this is how menace is best communicated to all but the extremely dumb. Sam has learned a lot since he and Ajit saw U.P. Singh out of his flat over a month ago. "You don't kick a man when he's down," Ajit had explained after shutting the door. "You put a leash around his neck and tell him which way to crawl."

After the phone call on the terrace, Fat Cop, Fat-fuck, SI U.P. Singh, the Tia-hassling, tit-staring thulla, had looked like he'd been sitting on a large, slow-growing cactus bush for many years. Ajit, on the other hand, had been ready with a smile and a cold Pepsi poured into a tall glass. Every time the SI tried to raise the subject, to apologize, Ajit stood at the net and volleyed it, turning the subject away to some other topic of general interest. The message was a) *Sir, we are now all here in this friendly, postproblem atmosphere, why bring up what is already past?* and b) *You motherfucking bug on the asshole of a cockroach, you may think your humiliation is complete, but actually it's just starting.*

In the final sum total there had been both spectacular stick and some small carrot. As Delhi Deputy Commissioner of Police (South) Shri Satish Wahi sahab's secretary instructed Singh on the phone, Neb Chand, the wannabe-rapist, was to be transferred to some punishment post. But it was Singh who was to secretly sing out the damning report about Tall Cop's harassment of innocent young women. It was also going to be part of Singh's general duties to make sure Mr. Samiran Chakkarvarty, ace web analyst and highly connected press-person, was not hassled by anyone or anything, including nasty neighbors. In return, apropos a discussion on mobile phones, Ajit had gone into Sam's bedroom, rummaged, and came out with a large manila envelope for Singh. He'd handed this to the cop who was stuttering out his goodbyes. "There are some phones in this magazine, sir, so please take a look. The descriptions are in Russian but model numbers are in Normal, take a look and let me know what you like. I will see what I can do when my cousin returns from Russia—phones are cheaper there than even Singapore or Hong Kong." With which Subinspector Singh left, carrying a six-month-old Russian *Playboy* containing three pages of obsolete mobile phones and seven pages of evergreen Playmates of the Year.

Sam had made a small mistake as the cop was about to exit. "Zaroorat padi to mai tum ko phone karunga, thik hai?" ("I'll call you if and when I need you, all right?"), he had said, but using the familiar "you" with relish. Fat Cop's eyes had flared. At the same time, Sam received a small kick in the back of the shin from Ajit. It was explained to him later that the "tum" was an off-note in the complex and beautiful symphony of Ajit's subjugation of U.P. Singh. As Chandran had then underlined, "These kinds of sodomizings are a *verre delegate business*, machaa! Best to leave it to the experts, you understand?"

HISSING COBRAS

BY NALINAKSHA BHATTACHARYA

R.K. Puram

On a drizzly November morning, around 11:00, Inspector Raghav Bakshi parked his Gypsy under a neem tree and looked at the shit-yellow two-story government quarters surrounding a bald patch of land that was meant to be developed as a park. On Sunday mornings one could see the neighborhood kids playing cricket or badminton here, but the park was now deserted except for a couple of stringy goats grazing in a corner where there were still a few clumps of grass leftover from the previous monsoon. R.K. Puram Sector 7 was a colony for the babus who slogged from 9 to 5 in government offices, the Bhawans stretching from India Gate to Rashtrapati Bhawan in Lutyens' Delhi. The wives of these babus, having bundled off their kids to school and their husbands to office along with their lunch boxes, were now enjoying a couple hours of break from the drudgery of running their households on shoestring budgets. Later, after having their frugal lunch of roti, sabzi, and achaar, they would switch on their TVs to enjoy their favorite soaps on Star Plus, Sony, or Zee, mushy serials that glorified the virtues of joint families shepherded by benign and supportive elders.

The inspector was here, in fact, to inquire about the accidental death of one such matriarch, a sixty-five-year-old woman named Kamla Agarwal who'd presided over the measly quarters of her son and daughter-in-law. Five days ago, the old lady was "brought dead" to the emergency room of Safdarjung Hospital with multiple skull fractures. The police-man on duty had registered the case as a "death caused by a fall from the top of Malai Mandir," an imposing south Indian temple situated on a hillock that overlooks plebeian Sector 7 on one side and swanky Vasant Vihar on the other. The very next day, after the postmortem, a no-objection certificate was issued for the cremation and the paperwork was passed on to the R.K. Puram police station. Inspector Bakshi would have treated the case as a routine one, but then came an anony-mous call from a woman alleging foul play. Bakshi decided to give the Agarwals a good sniff, just in case.

The inspector rang the doorbell outside quarter no. 761 and a swarthy woman in a green-and-yellow synthetic sari opened the door. She had a gray shawl draped around her shoulders. As he announced the purpose of his visit, Bakshi noted that the buxom woman, who could have been in her late twenties, adjusted her shawl to cover her bosom. Ushered into a ten-by-ten room painted a dull shade of yellow, Bakshi took a quick inventory of its furnishings: a twenty-inch Onida TV mounted on an aluminum cabinet; a fancy wall clock em-bellished with a Radha-Krishna icon; a drab government cal-endar with too many holidays marked in red; a faded print of a nondescript landscape showing sunrise or sunset. This was a babu's no-frills basic dwelling, he thought, and the message that it conveyed to him was: Don't expect barfis and cashews with your tea. Amidst this tawdry bric-a-brac, the woman sit-ting before him on the divan looked quite glamorous.

Bakshi's roving eyes now paused above the TV cabinet to study a framed picture of an elderly woman smiling under a pine tree on a hilly road. "Is that Kamla Agarwal?" he asked, sitting down on a lumpy sofa with frayed upholstery.

The woman nodded. "My mother-in-law. That one was taken at Katra when she made a pilgrimage to Vaishno Devi last summer."

"Hmm." Bakshi stroked his well-trimmed mustache like a pet dog. He was pleased to note that the woman was nervously twisting a corner of her shawl. Did she have something to hide? Or was she just feeling uncomfortable in the presence of a beefy policeman when her husband wasn't around? Bakshi opened his notebook and plucked a pen from his breast pocket. "First things first," he said. "Your name?"

"Mukta Agarwal."

The inspector listened to Mukta's story while consuming a cup of tea and some namkeen. When he stepped out of quarter no. 761 half an hour later, he was inclined to believe that the deceased Kamla Agarwal was indeed just an unlucky woman who had visited Malai Mandir with her daughter-in-law to watch the evening aarti. Built entirely with blue granite stones in the hallowed traditions of Chola architecture, the temple was a south Delhi landmark that attracted thousands of devotees every day. After receiving prasadam from a priest, the two women had proceeded toward the back stairs of the temple for a quick exit. That was when Kamla slipped on a banana peel flung by a careless devotee and hurtled down ten steep steps, crushing her head on a massive boulder that awaited her like Yama, the god of death.

As Mukta narrated the incident, her face turned ashen, her eyes glistened with tears, and she finally broke down, gagging her mouth with her shawl. The woman either possessed the thespian talents of Meena Kumari or was an ordinary lachrymose housewife. Bad luck, Bakshi thought. If he could catch a whiff of foul play in her tale, he could find a way to squeeze her husband for a few thousand.

* * *

That evening, Mukta told her husband about the policeman's visit.

"And what did he ask?" said Ashok, masticating a matthi and sipping his tea with some relish. After his back-breaking eight-hour grind as a typist in the Ministry of Rural Industry, he didn't really want to be bothered with a detailed report of the policeman's visit. He had been a dutiful son and had already done enough for his domineering mother, who always treated him like a child. He had bribed the morgue assistant to jump the line for a quick postmortem, lit her pyre, consigned her ashes in the holy Yamuna, and, on the chautha, the fourth day of mourning, fed seven brahmins to ensure that his mother's soul speedily reached its heavenly abode without any interruptions from the dark creatures of the netherworld. Let his robust wife now handle this police inquiry, which, he believed, was just a routine exercise. She wasn't a weakling, after all. Didn't she once tell him that she had played on her school's kaabadi team?

Still, he nodded perfunctorily when Mukta detailed the day's proceedings. "He asked me how it happened and who saw it," she said. "I rattled off the same story I've told the whole world a hundred times. He also asked for a recent picture of Mataji and one of me too." Mukta sighed. "I'm tired of all this."

"So am I. I wish you hadn't taken her to that temple."

"Why blame me when it was *your* mother who wanted to see the evening prayer?"

"I'm not blaming you, dear," Ashok said, trying to mollify his wife. "Look, I don't think they'll bother us about this again." Like his late father Ramlal, Ashok was a quiet, peace-loving clerk who avoided trouble of any kind, so much that he wouldn't take a crowded bus if he found the conductor badmouthing a passenger traveling on the footboard.

Less than forty-eight hours had passed since he'd met Mukta Agarwal when Raghav Bakshi received a second anonymous call from the same woman. "Have you visited quarter no. 761?" she asked, sotto voce.

"Yes, but I found nothing suspicious there."

"So you too have been taken in by her cock-and-bull story? Slipping on the banana peel and all that bakwas."

"Look, if you want us to dig deeper, you have to come out in the open and give us a written statement."

"I can't do that. But do you know about her affair with one of the neighborhood boys—a jawan?"

"I think you're digressing," Bakshi said, feigning disinterest. But he had already pressed a button on his telephone that would record the conversation. Mukesh the techie might even be able to trace this elusive caller.

"Tell me your name," he said.

"Anamika."

Bakshi was about to needle her with more questions, but Anamika—or whoever she was—had hung up. As he sat there twirling the ends of his mustache, his lips slowly spread into a smile. The information he'd just acquired could be valuable. He briefed Mukesh and then summoned Ram Bhaj, a freelance informer who was his man Friday. A three-day watch on Mukta Agarwal would be good enough to ferret out her little secrets.

Mukta knew she was under watch, but she ignored her stalker since she had other things on her mind. She felt sick one morning, vomiting twice in ten minutes. Having missed two consecutive periods, Mukta knew those passionate afternoon sessions with Rakesh had given her something more tangible than orgasmic delight. The young soldier and the distraught housewife had consummated their relationship, built clandestinely over a period of six months, during one opportune week in October. Rakesh was on leave and Kamla was away at her daughter's place in NOIDA. What Ashok couldn't achieve in three years, even with the help of those exotic medicines prescribed by a renowned "sexologist" of Daryaganj, Rakesh did in seven days flat. Impressed by his performance in bed and assured by his declarations of unending love, Mukta had told her new lover she wanted to divorce her husband. Rakesh promised to marry her once he was posted away from the killing fields of Kashmir.

Bakshi hadn't been very happy with Ram Bhaj's initial report, which contained nothing more than Mukta's haggling with the greengrocers at Indira market and buying muffins and cheap noodles from Supreme Bakeries in Sector 8. Mukesh the techie wasn't very helpful either. All his efforts revealed was that Anamika, literally "Lady Anonymous," had called from a PCO in Sector 18 NOIDA.

"Dig deeper," Bakshi hectored his minion, "or you'll get a mighty kick on your gaand."

The threat of an immediate sack worked wonders on Ram Bhaj. He quizzed, cajoled, and threatened the Sector 7 women into revealing Mukta's secrets, which, he knew, would put his demanding boss in good spirits.

"Mukta has a lover called Rakesh who is a fauji," Ram Bhaj reported to his boss.

"Good," said Bakshi, reaching into his drawer for a sachet of paan masala. He had just returned to his seat after beating a confession out of a suspect. Punching and whipping suspects gave Inspector Bakshi the same thrill he felt when fucking a woman who wasn't his wife.

"The lover's parents live in quarter no. 353, directly opposite the CPWD Enquiry office," Ram Bhaj continued. "They'd been meeting on the sly since May this year but it wasn't until October that they actually shacked up. Rakesh had come home from Kashmir on a week's leave and Kamla Agarwal was away at her daughter's."

"Great," Bakshi grinned. *This* was what he called Class A material. "Who served up this chaat-masala?" he asked, just to make sure he wasn't being fed bazaar gossip.

"Two elderly women who knew Kamla Agarwal."

"And what did the young women say about Mukta?"

"A lotus in a dungheap."

"Really? How fascinating! And what did they say about Kamla?"

"She was a tyrant. She treated her bahu like dirt, even worse because Mukta didn't bring any dowry and couldn't conceive after six months of marriage. They said Kamla made three attempts on Mukta's life within the past year: The first time it was poison, dhatura seeds, then she tried pushing her daughter-in-law over the terrace. The last time she sprinkled kerosene on Mukta's clothes and tried torching her."

"Lucky woman, she's still alive and kicking after all that! Why didn't she run away to her parents?" asked Bakshi.

She went to her parents after the poison, Ram Bhaj explained, but they sent her back saying they already had too many mouths to feed.

"What about her husband?"

Ram Bhaj curled his thin lower lip in disdain. "He's a weakling, a coward who slunk away to the terrace when his mother turned the heat on his wife."

"You haven't told me the whole story, Ram Bhaj." Bakshi was stroking his mustache again. "Am I right?"

The lackey grinned. "Your brain works like a computer, sir. I am sure you will get the ACP's post very soon."

"Stop oiling my butt and spit out the gem you're holding in your gullet."

"He is impotent, sir," the informer whispered.

"Who told you this?"

"Neela, Mukta's close confidante."

"Hmm." Bakshi wanted to whistle, but he straightened himself up in his chair and assumed an official air to indicate that their meeting was over. "Good work, Ram Bhaj. Keep it up."

Bakshi pondered the case before him. If Kamla's friends knew about Mukta's affair with the virile fauji, Kamla herself must have known what her bahu was up to while she was away. Bakshi needn't be Sherlock Holmes to deduce that upon discovering Mukta's adultery, Kamla must have taken her tyranny to new heights by the first week of November, around the time when she had her great fall from the temple top. Perhaps the tortured bahu had pushed the tyrannical saas down the stairs after all.

The next day, Bakshi received yet another phone call regarding the Kamla Agarwal case, but this time it was from a man. "My wife has been making some wild allegations against Mukta Agarwal on telephone," said a phlegmy voice. "Please ignore them."

"Identify yourself first." The cop pressed the record button on his telephone and then looked at the crime chart on the wall. It showed that two suicides, one murder, and three burglaries had occurred that week. Not enough work for a proactive police officer like Bakshi.

"My name is Anand Bansal, I'm Ashok Agarwal's brother-in-law."

"Your profession?"

"I run a courier service from Atta Market, NOIDA."

After he had collected the address and telephone number of Anand Bansal, Bakshi threatened that he'd file a case against the man's wife for making unsubstantiated allegations against Mukta Agarwal and interfering with a police investigation. When Anand seemed sufficiently brow-beaten, Bakshi suggested they could settle the matter at 6:30 that evening— not at the police station, but in the Sector 9 park, near Sangam Cinema.

That evening, Bakshi not only collected ten thousand rupees from Anand Bansal to exonerate his wife from a police case—enough money to splurge on drinks and kebabs for a week—he also gathered a few nuggets on Mukta Agarwal that Ram Bhaj, his dogsbody, had failed to unearth. Nugget no. 1: Anand, who hailed from Meerut, was Mukta's former lover, and it was he who had persuaded Kamla to get Ashok married to his old flame. He'd wanted to see the poor shopkeeper's daughter happy and well-settled, but he had no idea that Ashok was a "nonfunctional male" or that his mother would be so hard on the poor girl. Nugget no. 2: Even though she'd denounced Mukta as barren, Kamla had let Anand know in a roundabout way that for the noble cause of perpetuating the Agarwal clan, she wouldn't mind if her virile son-in-law, who had already fathered three healthy children, inseminated Mukta, as long as it remained a family secret. While Anand was willing to oblige his mother-in-law, Mukta rejected her former lover's advances. Nugget no. 3: Savitri, Anand's wife, hated Mukta because she knew about her husband's premarital affair with the woman. Anand had no idea why his wife would allege foul play in her mother's death, other than a perverse wish to see her enemy incarcerated in a dark Tihar cell.

As Bakshi's visits to Safdarjung Hospital and Malai Mandir hadn't unearthed any substantial evidence, he was inclined to believe that Mukta had no hand in Kamla's death. Nonetheless, he couldn't get his mind off the woman, particularly after the new masala that Anand had provided about her. Ah, those lucky bastards, Rakesh and Anand, he thought wistfully.

On a chilly December afternoon, Bakshi pressed the bell of quarter no. 761 for the second time. He was clutching a slim gray police file. Mukta saw him through the peephole and rearranged her shawl to cover her bosom before opening the door.

"How are you, Mrs. Agarwal?" asked Bakshi. He stepped in without waiting for an invitation.

"I am fine, inspector saab," Mukta said, edging away from the path of the hulking policeman to avoid any accidental contact.

"You haven't told us the truth, Mrs. Agarwal," Bakshi said, settling down on a sofa.

"What truth are you talking about?"

"You had a very strained relationship with your mother-in-law."

"That's not true. We had a few saas-bahu spats in the past, but in the end we got along fine."

Bakshi guffawed and shook a few grains of paan masala into his mouth. The tang of lime and tobacco often fired his imagination. "A mongoose waltzing with a snake, huh?" he said with a sly wink. The inspector then tensed his facial muscles to look serious and slightly intimidating. "You haven't told me the true story, Mukta Agarwal."

"I told you everything I saw," Mukta maintained.

Bakshi held up his file, frowning. "Here I've got statements from three witnesses who saw you from the circular path that goes around the base of the temple. They identified you and your mother-in-law from the photographs." Bakshi studied his suspect's face to assess the effect of his words before opening his file. "Here we have Mrs. Natarajan of Saket telling us that she saw you arguing with the old lady."

"That's not true . . . We didn't have any arguments that evening."

"And here's Mr. Nair, our second witness from Moti Bagh, who saw you smiling while Kamla was still tumbling down the stairs and shrieking."

"That's totally absurd! I'm not mad, inspector."

"Of course you aren't; you just couldn't help rejoicing the death of a person you hated. You are a clever woman, Mukta Agarwal: You foiled three attempts on your life."

Mukta gave a start at this sudden disclosure which she had thought was known only to Neela, her best friend in the neighborhood.

"I can see that slimy spy of yours has filled your ears with rumors," she said, recovering quickly. "We have neighbors with old scores to settle with the Agarwals. Why don't you talk with my husband about this?"

"Let's forget the poor babu for the time being." Bakshi flipped through his papers and then looked up as he located the next piece of incriminating evidence against Mukta. "The temple management claims they keep the stairs clean by hiring a dozen sweepers. The banana peel that Kamla slipped on has to be a figment of your imagination."

"I haven't invented the banana peel, inspector saab," Mukta said. "How could the management expect to keep the staircases clean with a few sweepers when thousands of visitors are going up and down the stairs throughout the day? Many of them are from the villages and don't even know where to throw their garbage."

Bakshi ignored the rebuttal and looked sharply at Mukta. She no doubt had a point, but he wasn't going to allow her to debate her innocence. "You have a motive, Mukta Agarwal. You planned to eliminate your mother-in-law because she would not tolerate her bahu having an affair with a neighborhood boy and bringing shame to the family. Well, you got your chance when you accompanied Kamla to Malai Mandir, and you acted fast, like a pro. It just took one good push of your strong arms to get rid of your enemy." Having proclaimed his verdict, the inspector now indulged in his hobby of the month, ogling Mukta Agarwal's bosom.

"May I have a look at those statements?" Mukta said.

Bakshi shook his head. "Your lawyer can see them when we produce them as evidence before a judge."

"So you're dragging me to court?" Dodging a murderous mother-in-law was certainly easier than coping with a vindictive policeman, Mukta thought.

Bakshi nodded. "The Patiala House criminal courts. In the meantime, we'll have to arrest you, Mukta Agarwal. Here's the warrant." The inspector brandished a smudgy printed form made impressive with several signatures and rubber stamps. So, the inspector had come well-prepared for a real showdown. This must be the handiwork of Savitri, she mused. The inspector now took out a pair of handcuffs from his pocket and dangled them before her eyes. Mukta visualized the shocked women of Sector 7, even her best friend Neela, watching her from their verandas and balconies as the inspector frog-marched her to his jeep, her head bowed in shame.

"I have to inform my husband," she said, flicking away a teardrop from the corner of her eye.

"Of course. But before you do that, I can offer you an option to postpone your arrest."

The inspector's eyes were contemplating her thirty-eight-inch bust. Mukta got his drift. She was not surprised since she remembered that even on his first visit he had ogled her with his piggy eyes. He could in fact be blackmailing her with a few incriminating documents collected from dubious sources. But she knew she was powerless against him. Neither Ashok, her husband, nor Anand, her ex-lover, would come forward to get her off the hook. If only Rakesh, the bold, sinewy jawan, were by her side. He alone had the guts to call the inspector's bluff.

"I am a married woman, inspector," she said. "My husband—"

"You needn't worry about him," Bakshi cut in. "He is impotent, after all, and you have taken lovers from time to time to fulfill your needs. Haven't you, Mukta Agarwal?"

Mukta winced. That snooping bastard had dug out all her secrets. She stared hard at Kamla Agarwal's beaming likeness, which seemed to be jeering at her from the wall.

"I know about Rakesh, and Anand too," Bakshi continued. "I can produce a couple more names from your past, your glorious Meerut years, if you'd like. Why not add one more name to your list of lovers, eh?"

"I am not a veshya, you loocha-lafanga shaitan!" Mukta hissed. "Go and mount your sister if you're so horny."

Bakshi smiled at Mukta's outburst. This was the right moment to plunge the knife deeper and twist it a little for greater effect. "I like spirited women," he said airily. "Look, I have twenty-one incriminating documents in this file. Each one of them is a hissing cobra that can raise its hood and strike you dead when you are on trial. Unless, of course, I kill them. The question is, do you want me to destroy these hissing cobras?"

In spite of herself, Mukta began to nod.

"Good. You are a sensible woman, Mukta. Shall we start our first session right now? This divan looks pretty good for a roll."

"When are you going to destroy those papers?" Mukta asked, realizing she was stepping into a dark tunnel without a torch.

"I will kill one cobra after each session."

"Impossible!" The very idea of being ravaged by this gorilla for three weeks nauseated her. "I'd rather go to jail."

Bakshi didn't like negotiating terms with victims, be it over money or sex. But he also understood that what was most important in this delicate situation was a good beginning. More hissing cobras could eventually slither out of their holes and crevices, ensuring the continuance of his pet project until he discovered a new and more appetizing female suspect within his fiefdom. "Well, if you are so fastidious, dear, I will destroy three cobras after each session. Right?"

Mukta wanted to shout, *Wrong!* But she knew she couldn't stop this randy bastard from molesting her.

It was when the inspector had gone to the bathroom after his third rape session that Mukta managed to take a peek at the nest of hissing cobras. The papers the inspector had been blackmailing her with and destroying so scrupulously at the end of each encounter, she discovered, were actually pages from a recent police report on cybercrime. Mukta covered her face with her palms to hide her pain and fury when Bakshi returned, whistling "Crazy Kiya Re" from *Dhoom 2*, last summer's chartbuster. He'd presumed that with her big bindi, voluminous sari, and other signs of backwardness, Mukta was a perfect specimen of "behenji," a woman from one of the Hindi-speaking states where English wasn't a compulsory subject. But Mukta had studied up to class eight, and in addition to showing her prowess in the school's kaabadi team, she had also learned just enough English to read the newspaper headlines and understand what they were all about.

"Don't worry, sweetie, we just have a dozen cobras to destroy," Bakshi said, squeezing one of her ample breasts.

"I'm not worried," Mukta said, removing her palms from her face. "I was just wondering how many women suspects you're helping out these days."

The inspector tweaked her nipple and winked. "Jealous, huh? Well, at the moment there's just one, but she's not as young and sweet as you." He kissed her and then looked at his watch. "Got to rush back to the office for an important meeting with my subinspectors. See you next Monday."

Mukta didn't tell Ashok about the inspector's biweekly visits because he'd just throw a tantrum without actually offering to protect her. If—and it was a big if—the inspector kept his word, her suffering would come to an end in another two weeks. She couldn't, however, withhold her other secret from Ashok. Her vomiting had stopped but her small bump would soon be visible.

"Do you really love me, Ashok?" It was a Saturday night, they were in bed, and he hadn't started snoring yet.

"Of course, Mukta. Haven't I snapped my ties with my sister Savitri for you?"

"I am sorry for that," she said, and pecked him on the cheek. After all, until Rakesh rescued her from her dud marriage, Ashok was definitely her best bet. He had never joined his mother or sister in humiliating her. And since Kamla was no longer around to complicate matters, Mukta could now afford to be brutally honest with her husband. If he insisted on a divorce, so be it. "I'm going to be a mother, Ashok."

Her husband sat up bolt upright on the bed. "You aren't joking?"

"Are you blind or what? Haven't you seen me puking almost every morning?"

"Yes, but I never thought . . ." He broke off and looked searchingly at his wife's face. But Mukta couldn't meet his gaze.

She lowered her eyes and whispered: "You aren't the father of my child."

"Oh!" Ashok clutched his throat as if he wanted to strangle himself. His jaws hardened, his eyes became flinty. "Who's this lucky guy, may I know?"

"Rakesh, the fauji from quarter no. 353. We met—"

"Bas!" He snatched a pillow from the bed and dashed out of the room to spend a troubled night on the divan.

But Mukta knew Ashok would eventually cool down. He wanted to be a parent as much as she did. He would soon realize that what happened between his unsatisfied wife and the hot-blooded jawan was inevitable, if not providential.

And she was right. Ashok returned to his wife in the wee hours and quietly lay beside her. She turned and drew him to her bosom as if he were a child.

"Kamla is haunting my dreams," Mukta said when Bakshi visited her on Monday afternoon. "She looks so horrible, with blood dripping all over her face. And she stares at me as if I were responsible for her death. I can't eat, I can't sleep." Mukta started crying. Sex with a crying woman could be disastrous, so Bakshi stroked her head and made some soothing noises. Ah, these chicken-hearted middle-class housewives. Whether they lived in R.K. Puram, Sarojini Nagar, or Lodhi Colony, they were all the same. Even before the police had filed a First Information Report, they rushed to the nearest thana to spill their story. How boring! A woman from Vasant Vihar or Greater Kailash would strangle her husband in the morning and dance the night away with her boyfriend at Athena or Climax, one of those thousand-rupee-a-drink nightclubs. And if the law finally came knocking at her door, she'd just throw wads of five-hundred-rupee notes at everyone concerned, even the lowly chowkidar. Bakshi wanted to work among these smart, filthy-rich people, who drove BMWs and Benzes, carried BlackBerrys, and attended glitzy parties at the Hyatt or Maurya Sheraton. But till that prize posting came his way, he'd have to make do with the whimpering Mukta Agarwals of the babu colonies.

"I want to visit Malai Mandir and pray for Kamla's unhappy soul," Mukta declared, sniffing.

Bakshi grimaced. This woman was really going too far. She needed a little roughening up to clamp her mouth shut and spread her legs wide open. Harita, his reedy wife, also needed a mild thrashing now and then, especially when she complained too much about his philandering. The whining bitch had run away to her parents with their two daughters after he'd given her an egg-sized bump on the forehead and a few welts and bruises on her back. He normally would have kept her home with just a hard slap, but then Harita threw a vase at him and accused him of fucking their fifteen-year-old daughter on the sly, buying her silence with a sumptuous allowance.

"You've already performed Kamla's shradh ceremony, honey, so you needn't worry about her soul. Now peel off your sari and . . ."

But Mukta was adamant. She threatened to scream and alert her neighbors if she wasn't allowed to do her penance at the temple.

This woman was a pain in the ass, Bakshi thought, but she was good in bed. She had ample flesh in the right places, and he loved kneading her dough. And, like a good whore, she also knew how to fake an orgasm. In fact, she was better than his skinny wife and the other women he'd molested, threatening them too with his hissing cobras. One has to suffer the kicks of a cow if it yields milk, he thought. If a brief visit to the temple would stop her sniffing and make her bedworthy, so be it.

The evening aarti had just begun when they entered the temple. A bare-bodied priest was rhythmically waving a flickering brass lamp, revealing the immaculate stone idol of Lord Swaminatha carrying his mace. Like the other devotees, Mukta joined her palms and chanted paeans to the Lord. Earlier, as they had climbed the stairs, she had explained to her companion that in the north Lord Swaminatha was worshipped as Kartikeya, the handsome warrior god who was the son of goddess Durga, the destroyer of Mahishasur, the demon. Bakshi was not a religious person, so after Mukta had bowed before the idol for the umpteenth time, he whispered in her ear that she had done enough penance for the day and now they should return to her house and eliminate three more hissing cobras. Mukta sighed and allowed him to gently push her through the crowd of devotees toward the exit.

But when they were outside the temple, Mukta stopped short as if she remembered something.

"Now, don't tell me you have to complete your thousandth bow before the idol to complete your penance," Bakshi said.

"I won't tell you that," Mukta assured, looking very solemn

and contented. "I only want to stand and pray for my mother-in-law on the spot where she spoke to me for the last time."

"I don't give a fuck about that evil woman."

"Mind your language, inspector," Mukta frowned, even though she was amused by his unexpected surge of hatred for Kamla. "I wonder, have you really fallen in love with me?"

Bakshi squeezed her shoulders and whispered: "I have, darling. You are *so* special to me."

"Then come with me for just one minute. Once I have offered my prayers for Kamla's soul we can go back to my house and have some fun."

Bakshi felt elated. So, she had finally accepted him as a lover. Wow! He had fortified his virility with a Penagra tablet before mounting her each time, and his performance must have favorably compared with her previous lovers. Whistling "Crazy Kiya Re," he followed his ladylove to the back of the temple and then skirted a huge PVC water tank mounted on a stone platform. Away from the traffic of devotees, this was a desolate area used only by the temple staff and the priests. A faint light from a distant lamppost illuminated the staircase.

"So this is the spot where you stood that evening with your beloved mother-in-law?" Bakshi said.

Mukta nodded. Then she told him how, after finding out about her affair with Rakesh, Kamla had tortured her. Hadn't he noticed those scars on her body, the branding mark on her pubes?

Of course he had, but . . . well, married women were prone to getting a few bruises due to their obstinacy and unwarranted intrusion into the male zone. He'd actually found Mukta's bruises cute, even aphrodisiacal. "You should have filed an FIR against her," Bakshi said, squeezing her arm just to show that he was a sympathetic male.

"But the police don't take notice of domestic violence unless it's a murder or there's some pressure from someone powerful." Mukta looked up at the inspector and whispered: "So I decided to take things into my own hands."

Bakshi grinned. A confession at last! It was a nice jolt, like the one he often got from a big shot of whiskey. The oppressed had finally turned the tables on the oppressor. How fascinating! How filmic! The very idea of fornicating with a murderess gave him an instant hard-on.

"So you bumped Kamla Agarwal?" Bakshi said. "Wonderful!"

"Are you surprised?"

Bakshi nodded. Indeed, in his twenty-odd years in the profession, he was yet to come across a single case of a tortured wife liquidating her mother-in-law. "I guess you gave her a mighty push with your hands?"

"No, actually, I used my leg." She smiled and hitched up her sari.

His hard-on still intact, Bakshi was staring at Mukta's thunder thighs and imagined having a quickie right there behind the water tank. But a sudden shooting pain ended this fantasy. With all her might, Mukta had rammed the heel of her right foot into his crotch. Bakshi screamed as he keeled over clutching his balls. In the semidarkness, the inspector's left hand desperately groped for the iron railing. But Mukta, the veteran kaabadi player, was quick enough to land another kick on his flank. Bakshi fell like a ton of bricks and hurtled down the steep stairs. Then there was that stomach-churning sound again—a cranium cracking on a big boulder. She took a peek at the bloody mess sprawled on the massive stone on which someone had chalked *Om Shanti Om* and then returned to the temple. She bowed deeply before Lord Swaminatha, whose aarti had just reached its crescendo, and then weaved through the crowd of devotees to make a quick exit by the main door of the temple.

PART II

YOUNGISTAN

THE RAILWAY AUNTY

BY MOHAN SIKKA

Paharganj

I lay in my dark little veranda, the space I occupied in my bua's Delhi flat. The windows were open to the nonstop honking from Panchkuian Road. There was no breeze. The cool weather hadn't arrived and the sulfurous smell of popping fireworks made breathing difficult. I remembered how, in our old house in Jalandhar, my sisters hid behind each other as I lit bottle rockets on Diwali. Ma gave us sweaters and woolen socks she'd knitted herself. This coming winter, my sisters would even be lucky if their old sweaters were darned. The middle one was in a boarding school for orphans, the youngest with my frail grandfather.

I woke up late the next morning with a sensation of suffocation. I left the flat without breakfast and walked to Paharganj. I bought a cup of tea and sought out the quiet of the large Christian cemetery by Nehru Bazaar. Putting down my satchel under my favorite neem, I took out my chess set and my bitten paperback of the champion Kasparov's classic matches. I drank tea and practiced the grandmaster's moves. Worn concrete graves surrounded me on three sides.

I didn't see Johnny, the caretaker with the salt-and-pepper hair, until he was standing next to me, his stocky arms folded. With a grin on his long, craggy face he said, "Didn't you know an open chessboard attracts spirits with scores to settle?" I packed up my things, thinking he was going to escort me out.

But instead he took me to the workshop by the main gate. Workers inside were sawing and hammering wooden planks for coffins. Johnny ushered me into the cemetery office at one end of the shop. He fumbled in a drawer and took out a book, as beat-up as mine, about grandmaster Karpov, my hero Kasparov's archrival. "Kasparov played like a bull," he said, making a meaty fist in the air, "but Karpov was the wily fox." When he asked me to take out my chessboard, I knew I'd made a friend.

When I got home from college that night, my bua said: "Sarika called to remind you. Go pick up the apples." The next afternoon, fearful but of course intrigued, I made my way to Sarika Aunty's flat. It was in another building in Bua's colony. Growing up, any boy who teased my sisters in school knew he had a bloody nose coming. My mother would scold me but was secretly proud. Deflecting an aunty's advances was a lesson I hadn't learnt though.

Sarika's door was opened by a wrinkled woman in a gray sari and, despite the weather, a thick sweater-blouse. Her eyes were opaque with cataracts. She stood there like a sentry, and I could barely catch a word of her rustic Punjabi. "Mataji, I am Mrs. Verma's nephew," I kept saying in response to her soft, toothless mumbles. "I came for the case of apples." Finally, she cracked the door wider, and I bent forward to better understand what she was saying.

"Demon's daughter . . ." she muttered, "a snake in human form. Keeps me locked up." She grabbed my arm so tightly it hurt. "Poison. Careful of her poison."

I was about to leave when Sarika Aunty appeared. She was dressed in a loose, translucent salwar kameez which suggested that no special company was expected. The outline of her taut, shapely figure was noticeable even though she wasn't in the form-fitting clothes she wore to my bua's house. Her hair, black with streaks of brown, was tied in two thick braids. This gave her fair, oval face a pleasant expression. Around her neck were rudraksha prayer beads. Her feet were bare. She looked relaxed, glowing. Perhaps my unease was misplaced.

"You're not to open the door, Bibiji," she said sharply to the old woman. "What if some Nepali slashes our throats?"

I remained standing in the living room while she escorted the babbling Bibiji inside. The flat's layout was like Bua's, but the furniture was grander than Bua's practical, well-worn things. A carved-wood sofa with silver cushions sat on a plush carpet, flanked by wide lounge chairs. In the center was a marble-topped table. Ornate brass lamps stood in the corners. I thought: Sarika's husband must be the type of railway officer my father resented when he was alive—the kind who demanded "sweets" for his children from contractors. My inheritance had been gnawed away by such officers.

But there were no pictures of children here. The only item suggesting a child's presence was a tall glass cabinet. Inside were displayed rows of dolls—circus dolls in costumes, dolls with fancy hats wearing party dresses, dolls with startling green eyes. They were so well made, they didn't seem like toys. The large ones had realistic facial expressions; one had a sly, sinister look that followed you around.

Sarika returned. She saw my gaze. "My father was in the foreign service," she said proudly. "This is my collection. We traveled everywhere when I was a girl." She pointed to the sofa. "Sit."

I had picked out my best shirt and ironed it myself. But now I felt like a peon offered a seat in an officer's house. "Aunty, my bua said you called," I ventured.

"I don't like this Aunty-vanty stuff," she broke out, sitting down barely two feet from me. "Call me by my name."

"If my mother were to hear me—" I stumbled like a fool.

"From heaven?" she snapped, and then caught herself.

We both fell silent. Her fingertips, I noticed, were trembling slightly. Her nails were painted a dark maroon. As we sat close, my eyes downcast, I felt her assess me from head to foot. A prickly sensation arose on the back of my neck, just like when she teased me at my bua's lunch parties. "Working so hard, Mukesh?" Or, "I need help around the house too. When can I expect you?" She spoke loudly while I served lemonade and pakoras, knowing all the ladies thought she was amusing, just incorrigible. The space between us began to stretch like an elastic band, until I was sure it could snap at any second. I shifted awkwardly and crossed my legs. Her forward manner disconcerted but aroused me. Barely lifting my eyes, I could see the shadow of her bra beneath her thin shirt, the way it lifted and fell with her breath.

She said impatiently: "Why are you always at your bua's? Don't you have college friends?"

I stayed silent. Those with cash to burn went to the movies with college yaars. I played chess in an old Paharganj cemetery.

She moved closer. "What's the matter? Are you scared of me?" She picked up my hand and casually placed it just above her knee. "A burly boy like you."

I was torn between giving in to the softness of her leg and the grave presumption of doing just that. I pulled my hand away. "Sarikaji, someone may think I am being impertinent."

"Who is there to think that?"

I heard a scuffling noise from inside the flat. "Bibiji," I said, my cheeks hot.

"Bibiji is resting. She can sleep through a bomb blast."

"May I have the apples?" I pleaded. "Bua will be waiting."

"You took your time coming. I gave away the last case this morning. More will come soon from my brother's orchard." She passed her slender fingers through my hair. Every sinew and tendon in my body tensed. "So thick, like a girl's. Comb it properly or get it cut," she added cruelly.

She took my face in her hands and turned it toward her. Then she kissed me. Her tongue reached inside my mouth and elicited reactions in faraway places—my toes, my stomach, my quivering thighs. My heart was beating so fast I didn't know how it would slow down. I didn't want it to.

She stood up and removed her prayer necklace. Then she pulled her kameez up and over her head. It billowed like a banner before falling in a heap on the carpet. Her salwar had a drawstring like a man's pajamas, but the shape at the hips and ankles was different. She loosened the string and the salwar dropped like a curtain. I remembered my middle sister Sonu's shapeless drawers hanging on the clothesline. Sarika's panties were small and dark and lacy, fitting snugly against her light skin. Other than the flare of her hips, her frame was slighter, more boyish than I'd imagined.

She turned her back to me. "Get up," she ordered, breaking the brief illusion that she was something frail. She reached her arms behind her. "Unclasp this." I fumbled with her bra hook as best I could. Even from her backward glance I could feel the derision from her face.

She commanded me to lie down, knelt over me, and began to undo my buttons and buckles. When my underpants were off, she said: "It seems you aren't *too* scared. For a minute I thought you weren't a real man. Now I see you are like most—overeager."

She guided my hands to parts I had only imagined with eyes closed on a woman. My trembling fingers outlined the orbs of her breasts. They were shiny with perspiration, and the way they rose and peaked made my jaw ache with craving. Her nipples weren't much bigger than mine, but darker and harder. In my mouth they tasted like stiff, salty rubber. A line of fine hair traversed down the center of her stomach to a different kind of darkness between her legs.

She was nice enough to let me make amends for my first, clumsy effort, but before that she called my bua. We were both naked. "Hope you don't mind, Pammi. I sent Mukesh to Paharganj for some groceries." She put the receiver to my ear as Bua was saying: "Any time. I've trained him into quite an expert shopper. Make sure he gives you a full accounting."

"Now," Sarika said, "I am going to show you how to curb your enthusiasm." I shyly followed her into the bedroom, but I must have shown potential because she left me a prize I kept for several days—her nail indentations on my back and buttocks.

As the weather turned cooler, I found some release playing chess with Johnny in his caretaker's office. I often wanted our matches to move faster, but I learned a lot by watching his methodical openings, his surprisingly lethal middlegame.

Sarika, I discovered, preferred a combination of fixed and variable routines. Before we began, she would ask me to brush my teeth and take a bath, even if I had already done so. I would come out in my towel to find her lying undressed smoking her pipe packed with ganja she procured from a discrete Israeli dealer in Paharganj. She insisted on initiating any kissing, which she liked deep and rough. If I tried to just hold her, she would whinny and thrash like a trapped mare. My chest became bruised from her teeth marks. As soon as one set of scratches healed on my back, she covered me with another. This is what I remember from those days: her kneeling against the side of the bed, goading me on as I crouched over her from behind, my legs open and half-bent and trembling, her neck craning back and her pretty mouth distended, her spine coiling and convulsing like it was a reptile trapped beneath her skin.

She wanted me to be just as rough with her. I struggled to comply. "Bite me. Harder. Didn't I say harder?" she would cry mid-frenzy. Once, approaching climax, she halted abruptly and changed positions. "Choke me. Do it. I'll tell you when to stop." I hesitated, but she pummeled me until I actually wanted to hurt her. Dark and angry urges rose inside me as I pressed my fingers around her supple neck. Fortunately, I soon lost control. Sputtering and coughing, she examined her neck in the mirror. Even from a distance I could see the bruises I'd left. The salty bile of shame rose up in my throat. "Now we're making progress," she said, eyes gleaming with strange pleasure.

I played chess with Johnny after that session. He frowned and stopped the game. "What's the matter, Mukesh? You're sacrificing pawns early and without a plan."

"I have one," I insisted, but my lie was soon exposed.

After I'd lost the next three games, he looked at me and said kindly: "I enjoy our matches, Mukesh. But it's not right that you come to this place so much. Go spend time with other young people."

With a curt goodbye I left his office. If he didn't want to play, I had other preoccupations: I could sit under the neem and read my notes from college.

In the bright, early winter light I walked up the cemetery's central path. The bustle of Nehru Bazaar was just beyond the high walls but here the only sounds were the cackling of crows and the dull whack of workmen breaking the hard ground with pickaxes. I stood beside the workers for a moment, nursing the thick sensation I carried in my chest these days, a sensation like hard-boiled phlegm. The hole the workers were digging appeared too small for an adult. Perhaps it was for a missing person's funeral. Only room to bury personal items was needed.

I began to dress in my bua's bathroom to avoid scrutiny of my wounds. She did remark on my new jeans and jacket. I told her I'd bought them cheap in Main Bazaar. Bua felt the jacket's lining and said: "Main Bazaar or Bandits' Bazaar?" In truth, Sarika had given me money for them, saying she didn't care for my dreadful clothes. She also paid for me to get my hair styled, causing my bua to say: "Delhi air is something. Look how city wiles have sprouted."

In addition to Bua's chores, I was now also on call for Sarika's household errands. Picking up her dry cleaning one Sunday, I saw her tank of a husband lounging on the sofa in a loose bathrobe. Bibiji sat on the floor shucking peas into a steel tray. Locked away during my other visits, the old lady had become a rare sight. She rose and creakily approached, shouting: "She puts chains on my feet, but I am not a fool, you hear?"

The hair on my arms stood up. What was she reporting to Mr. Khanna? But he only yawned and stretched where he sat. His wide, bushy midsection peaked out from underneath his banyan. "Bibiji," he barked without putting down his newspaper, "brake lagao, or you'll be sent to bed." The old lady shuffled back to her peas.

Sarika came out with the dry cleaning. Right under her

husband's nose she said: "Come back later. Mr. Khanna is going to the club by 1, and the peon is out today."

Bibiji's face twisted with loathing. Mr. Khanna raised his thick eyebrows, but the rest of his face stayed hidden behind the paper. As I shut the door I heard him ask Sarika something in a gruff tone.

She said: "No one. Mrs. Verma's nephew. A helpful boy."

My grandfather's heart stopped in his sleep in December. I could not see Sarika for some weeks and found that I missed her rough attentions. A council of uncles and aunts was held at Bua's flat, just like after my parents' accident. The agenda was my youngest sister Chhoti's guardianship. "Already we are barely making ends meet," Bua said grimly. Another aunt added: "Mukesh, finish your BA quickly, beta. Everyone is counting on you." I responded to such demands with a blank face, and silently cursed my parents for their ill-timed pilgrimage, which, like a bad investment, was bearing expense without end. The decision was made to send Chhoti to the boarding school for orphans that Sonu, our middle sister, attended. People thanked my bua for the sacrifice of keeping me. The indignity of being a charity case sat like curdled milk in my stomach.

In the New Year my liaisons with Sarika resumed. If she knew what was happening in my family, she never asked about it. After our third meeting in January, however, she handed me a slip of paper with a lady's first name and number. I looked at her, confused, and she said: "You want to make some money, right?"

I heard out her proposition. The aunty on the paper would pay for small but important errands. If I was reliable, there would be more jobs.

The aunty sounded pleasant when I called her from Sarika's phone. She gave me an appointment for the next day. Her bungalow was on Doctor's Lane near Gol Market.

Sarika smiled broadly. "Come by soon and tell me what happened." Then she took out some money and said severely: "Buy a new undershirt before you go. Are you using deodorant regularly?"

I laughed. This was how she spoke to me after we'd made hard, sweaty love for an hour. I tried to kiss her, but she cringed at my eagerness and pushed me back.

I was the opposite of eager when I returned with my report from Doctor's Lane. "Sarikaji," I said, lips trembling, "forgive me for misunderstanding. I'm not that kind of boy."

"Oh?" she said, lifting her brows. "What kind are you then?"

I'd come in with the intention of confronting her, but her haughty self-assurance washed away my resolve. "The aunty . . . she gave me the money first. It seemed like too much. When she told me what she wanted, I tried to give it back."

"She didn't report any problems to me."

"I was forced to stay," I said, shuddering at the memory. "She told me she would raise a noise if I tried to leave, have me beaten as an intruder." I held all the money before Sarika. "Take this. I don't want it."

She peeled out a few notes from the bundle. "That's my share, Mukesh. Think of this work as social service you get paid for."

"No," I cried.

"Then don't come back here," she said flatly. "I can't tolerate undependable boys. I give you a chance and you come back wheedling and whining."

"Don't say that," I said, almost hacking. My throat was dry, constricted.

"Imagine what you can do with the money," she said, and pulled me by the arm to the bedroom. Afterwards, she looked at the bites on her breasts. "I've taught you well," she said. "Luckily, Mr. Khanna doesn't like the lights on."

With my first earnings I bought a mobile and a diary to keep track of my appointments. If the person I called didn't recognize the name I asked for, the rule was to pretend I had the wrong number. Sarika sent me to railway wives, lady doctors, businesswomen, young managers in offices. Now I understood why she usually began texting the moment we finished in bed. I saw the insides of flats and bungalows from Gol Market to Bengali Market, and as far south as Sundar Nagar. Some aunties only wanted to meet in a seedy tourist lodge in Tooti Chowk after shopping at Connaught Place. Sarika's instructions were to accommodate every request.

I serviced aunties who were beautiful and bored, homely but adventurous, unabashed about their needs, or shy and self-conscious. One fed me afterwards; another threw money in my face as though I'd offended her dignity. Both asked for me again. I remember the aunty who liked to watch her favorite serial in bed. While I pleased her she delightedly gave me a rundown of the episodes I'd missed. One roundly cursed her husband while we made love; it drove her to heights of frenzy. Most never mentioned their husbands at all. They all appreciated that I readily agreed to their commands or requests. They all enjoyed the tricks with tongue and finger that Sarika had taught me.

I'd wake up on my hard cot in Bua's veranda, remember the day's appointments, and think my mind was playing tricks. Then I'd feel the soreness in my lower back and thighs. A few times I caught Bua watching me with narrowed eyes. I became convinced she could smell it on me—the disrepute, I mean.

Winter was almost over when I sent a package of clothes to my sisters' hostel. Sweaters, woolen socks, new shoes. Sarika gave me grudging advice on size and colors, calling me a simpleton. On an impulse I bought silver anklets and left them by Sarika's bedside with my weekly payment. She said: "Money is enough. No presents." She never wore the anklets.

For Johnny, the caretaker, I bought a chess set from a Janpath curio store, with pieces carved from dark and light wood. He was happy to see me once again. "I am in your debt for this," he said. To remove some of his obligation, I played our next match with great focus and beat him in a fierce king and pawn endgame. Any awkwardness from our last exchange was gone.

I wasn't surprised when Bua commented on my new shoes. I told her Sarika Aunty had given me some tuition referrals. "I see you've both kept me in the dark," she said. "Be cautious, beta, that woman is very clever."

As the days warmed, the wad of cash in my satchel grew in size. Its heft made me both excited and uneasy. I began to dream of renting a room in Paharganj. I'd bring my sisters to live with me. It would be tight at first. Bua would pretend to be upset, but secretly she'd be relieved.

I tried to open a bank account, but they wanted to know my source of income and see my guardian's ID card. Instead, I went to Sarika and asked her to hold on to most of my earnings.

"Don't trust me so much," she said, very seriously.

"I have nowhere else to keep it."

She was amused. "I will charge interest."

"I know," I said, defending myself with my arms as she tried to clutch and bruise my chest. "This is that kind of bank."

She'd tied me to the bedposts one hot afternoon when we heard footsteps followed by banging on the bedroom door. At first I thought Bibiji had escaped. Then the door crashed open, and Mr. Khanna stood before us in a brown safari suit. We had carelessly left the back door unlocked. I wrenched myself free of my restraints, chafing my wrists badly.

Panic flowered on Sarika's face, but only for a moment. With exaggerated slowness, she reached for her bra and bath-robe, while I stumbled into my discarded jeans and T-shirt.

"If you can't knock like a civilized person, at least have the courtesy to look away," she said to her husband. But I could see that her hands were shaking.

Mr. Khanna's wide, brutish face appeared paralyzed on one side. "All these years I thought the hag was half-mad," he said hoarsely. "Then one day I asked myself: Ashok, how long since Sarika nagged you for anything? She seems *content*. What has changed?" He licked his lips as if they were parched. "You were certainly clever, Sarika. It took my man quite a while to discover your tricks." He produced an envelope and threw it at her. Photos spilled to the floor.

"Get out," Sarika said, eyes looking down. It took me a second to realize she meant me. I was flustered, but worried for her safety. "*Now*," she hissed. "I'll take care of it."

"Sorry, Uncleji," I mumbled stupidly as I passed Mr. Khanna. The thick, stubby fingers of his right hand were clenched as though around an invisible club.

"Beta," he said, "ask your bua to arrange your funeral party."

I grabbed my satchel from the dining table and fled. Bibiji, let free, was shucking peas on the floor. She rocked back and forth and chanted noisily.

Later that night, I climbed up to my bua's flat, my heart flapping like a wild bird in a cage. Everyone was watching TV with blank expressions. *Nothing has happened,* I thought. *Sarika has managed it.* Then Bua rose and asked me to follow her to the veranda. I saw the smirks on my cousins' faces and my legs turned to leaden weights.

Mr. Khanna had been over. He claimed I'd dropped in on Sarika asking for more cash. I'd complained that my bua withheld food and money. Sarika had listened because I'd been so respectful in the past. Then, in full view of Bibiji, I'd tried to give Sarika a hug. She had smelled cheap liquor on my breath and gently pushed me away. I was a boy, and boys can get stupid ideas when they have a woman's attention. But I had been insistent. I'd demanded a kiss. I had pulled so hard on Sarika's arm that I had badly bruised her.

I flinched. I knew who had caused that injury. Then I saw how red Bua's eyes were.

"You have one hour to pack your things," she said.

"Where will I go?" I said, becoming angry. My college exams were a week away.

"I don't know. Stay with a friend. Get a hotel with all the money you are making. Go indulge your new habits—fancy clothes and, now, drinking."

"What Mr. Khanna told you wasn't the truth," I said quietly.

"Sarika has a known reputation, beta. But this is a public shaming. Whatever his reasons, Khanna will make trouble if he sees you here."

As I was leaving, she stuffed some hundred-rupee notes

into my hand. I didn't refuse, but once outside I dropped the notes in the mail slot.

I camped outside the graveyard gates with my bags. There were any number of cheap hotels in Paharganj, but I was in the mood to see what destitution felt like. The air was dusty and full of exhaust fumes. Till midnight, traffic was brisk on Ramdwara Road, with people buying vegetables by the hiss of gas lanterns and groups of raggedy foreigners stumbling to their hovels, high on hashish. Soon, the market began closing down. A number of vendors put out their bedding right on their stands and carts. The smell of rotting vegetables hung like an unwelcome blanket in the night heat, the quiet broken by snatches of disco music blaring from hotel rooftops.

I was jostled awake during the night, I thought, by someone brushing against my luggage with evil intentions. But it was just stray dogs chasing enormous rats.

In the morning, Johnny took me to his bachelor abode. It was what I'd imagined for my sisters and me—one room in an alley not far from the lodge where I met some of my aunties. It overlooked a shared courtyard with a peepal tree. Johnny owned a kerosene stove, some aluminum pots and utensils, one wooden cot, and a trunk. There were no family photos. The solitary bright spot was a postcard taped on the wall showing blue skies over a white sand beach.

"My cousin in Mauritius," he explained. "He says I should emigrate, but I'm too old."

"Thank you, Johnny," I said. "As soon as my exams are over I'll find another place."

"Play chess with me every night, and you can stay forever."

That evening the power went out while I was studying,

and, with a hand on my thigh, he made a very different request of me. It was put gently, but with a clear expectation. Initially I was anxious, even fearful. But unlike my last lover, Johnny was tender in his attentions before he was forceful. Later I realized I enjoyed being held in the safety of his short, burly arms.

I knew Sarika would be waiting for a message so we could settle accounts and discuss the future. If she was aware how close I was, we could find a way to meet. I was sure even she was feeling badly about turning me in.

Meanwhile, I had to resume business on my own. I phoned an aunty by the alias of Devika. This lady, whose voice I knew well, said, "Wrong number." I wasn't concerned; it only meant I'd called at an inconvenient time. But two days later, the number was cut off. In this way, one by one, the numbers in my diary disappeared from service, snuffed out by an invisible hand.

I went to see the aunty on Doctor's Lane, and another bungalow I'd visited many times near Bengali Market. I rang and knocked in both places, but no one answered.

"Friend," I told Johnny one morning during these harrowing days, "one more favor from you. Please take a message to a lady in Basant Lane. Tell her I need to settle my tuition account." I'd told Johnny I'd fought with my bua and it was awkward going back to the railway colony. For his trouble, I put money into the pocket of his shirt hanging on a nail.

"I am a bachelor," he protested. "What use do I have for that?" But I didn't listen; I needed as little charity as possible. As he dressed to leave, I wrapped what was left of my earnings inside my underwear and locked them in my suitcase.

All day I paced in his room. As the sun got stronger, the walls heated up, until I felt I was being slowly cooked. In the late afternoon I must have fallen asleep. When I awoke, my half-shirt drenched in sweat, Johnny was priming the kerosene stove in the dark, the blue flame lighting up his creased face. The way he crouched on his haunches, his compact upper body folded over as he worked, made me feel a pang of affection for him, my one loyal friend.

"I met your lady friend in the railway flats," he said. "She wouldn't let me in. She said no one needs a tutor now."

"What about settling what she owes me? For her nephew's tuition?"

"She got angry. She said: 'We've paid our dues. Tell the tutor to keep what he has. But there is no more work.' Then she shut the door in my face."

It was as though someone had shot me point-blank through the heart. In bed that night, I turned away when Johnny reached for me. He was silent for a while. Then he said, in his somber way: "I don't know all your troubles, Mukesh. But if you've been treated unjustly, you must stand up for yourself."

Over several mornings I wandered down Basant Lane with a dark umbrella over my head, looking over the boundary wall at the buildings rising in staggered rows. Days of punishing sunlight had unevenly bleached the pink distemper on the outside of the buildings; to my eyes they had a mottled, diseased appearance.

I was sure Sarika was padlocking her doors now. I noticed that adjoining flats on each floor shared the narrow servants' balcony, with just a wall dividing it into two parts. A plan took shape in my head.

I knew Sarika headed to her gym and beauty salon on Monday mornings. I waited with my umbrella outside the colony gate to see if this ritual had changed, and, indeed, it had not. I followed her as she walked to the taxi stand on the main road. Her slender profile from the back, the sight of her pert shoulders in a T-shirt, made me melt through the center of my body.

By the following Monday my preparations were complete. I bought a length of strong rope, a crowbar, and a switchblade, and I put them inside a backpack. I got my hair cut with a quarter-inch clipper. Johnny said I looked different, tougher.

I shaved closely and wore dark glasses and clean pants, shirt, and shoes. "Soon I'll stop being a burden on you," I told my friend. He shook his head at me indulgently, but I knew what I had to do.

I walked one last time toward Basant Lane. I entered the colony compound with confidence, my backpack over my shoulder. The guard at the gate saluted smartly. I climbed up the stairs in Sarika's building two at a time.

As I had expected, the front door of her flat had a large lock on the outside. The servant's door appeared bolted and locked from the inside—Bibiji was trapped. But the neighbor's service entrance was open; they illegally sublet their quarters and people always went in and out. I stepped through and walked along the servants' balcony toward Sarika's side. It was quiet. If anyone saw me, I would say I was Mrs. Khanna's nephew, locked out by my aunt.

I straddled the dividing wall between the two flats, hanging precariously off the parapet as I crossed over. A vein in my temple throbbed. I found the door to Sarika's kitchen latched from inside, but I was a contractor's son and knew railway construction. I cracked open the foot latch with a few kicks, then leaned against the lower part of the door. It strained open a few inches. I reached into the gap with my crowbar and pried down the top latch.

I found Bibiji cowering on the living room floor. She hic-
cupped and gurgled as I tied up her hands and wrapped a strip
of cloth around her mouth. Her eyes widened when I used my
knife to cut the rope. She fell down as if dead. I picked her up
and took her to her room.

For an hour I examined every item in the household: re-
frigerator magnets, ashtrays, the doll case, confidential files in
Mr. Khanna's desk. I lay on Sarika's bed, but it felt strange and
unfamiliar somehow. I searched through open cupboards for
money, though all I found were bedsheets and pillowcases.

I heard the front door open and close, and then the squeak
of the inner deadbolt being drawn. If only we had taken such
precautions before. I waited in Bibiji's room, where the old
woman lay facedown, groaning occasionally.

Sarika screamed once, seeing Bibiji trussed up like a goat,
but I had my knife out and Sarika was a smart woman. I made
her sit down in a chair and tied her hands and ankles. She was
wearing a polo shirt, light jeans, sneakers. She had cropped
her hair below her ears. It made her look even more like a boy.
Her hands smelled of fresh nail polish. Her left eye twitched
and she cringed at my touch, but she stayed quiet.

"I came to settle our business," I said, keeping my voice
steady even though my temples were pounding hard.

"The network is gone," she replied, leaning forward. "I
told your friend with the long face."

"Mr. Khanna shut it down?" I said, trying to sound rea-
sonable.

"I did," she shot back. "Ashok knew about the boys, but
not yet all the ladies."

"There were other boys?" I burst out without thinking.

Contempt flashed across her face. "Poor Mukesh," she
said, despite her position. "You were only the cheapest."

I winced and shut my eyes. I clenched my aching head between my fists, the knife in my hand. When I opened my eyes, she was attempting to rise.

"Don't move!" I shouted. I was finished with her indignities. "I'm only asking once: Where is the money?" I held up the knife.

"There is two thousand in the almirah. Untie Bibiji and I'll get it. But if you ever return, my husband will be waiting." Was it fear or amusement in the curl of her lips?

"I'm not a thief who needs to hide. I came for my due, not charity."

She looked at me as though I were an exasperating child. "Then why threaten *me* with this bandit act? Ask the one who has it."

"Mr. Khanna?"

"My husband doesn't need your money," she said scornfully. "Your sad-faced friend. I wondered why you sent him. I could tell he was unreliable with just a glance."

I felt punched in the gut. My legs became unsteady. "Why would you lie?" I cried hoarsely.

"What kind of company are you keeping? You've forgotten everything I taught you." She'd risen to her feet despite my admonition. She held out her hands in a wordless demand to be untied. She was commanding me, just as she always had, from the day we met in her flat to the last time she farmed me out as her bull.

I stood staring at her open-mouthed. I should have known she'd efficiently neutralize my threats. Cornered and defeated, I raised my knife to slash her ropes, but just then, a sharp knock on the front door startled us both.

"Sarika," a gruff, familiar voice called out. "Open the door. Are you alone?"

For a moment I thought time itself had unwound—a strange, sick sensation.

"Good work, Mukesh," Sarika said. "Did you alert him before coming?" But there was a false note in her bravado now.

"What is he doing here?" I hissed, as the knocking changed into banging. The room was beginning to spin.

"He must have posted his man outside. Did you think of that when you made your plan?"

The pounding grew insistent. Bibiji groaned. Mr. Khanna was making loud threats that he'd break the front door down, that no barrier could keep Sarika from him. The bolt on the door, though strong, couldn't hold him out indefinitely.

"What should I do?" I asked, my gut in my throat. I was completely in her hands once again.

We heard the cracking of wood and metal. But instead of panicking, Sarika grew thoughtful. Slowly, her face took on an expression of perverse satisfaction, like those moments when she would examine her love bruises. "Stab me," she whispered, like an endearment.

I looked at her in fear and disbelief.

"You have to," she said calmly. "Remember, the ropes won't convince him."

"I couldn't," I said, trembling like a man with convulsions.

"Do it," she ordered. "Now! Quick." And she smiled the most chilling smile I have ever seen. "Bring it here, I'll help you."

I ran back to Paharganj. I kept waiting for shouts from behind me, a crowd chasing me down. Instead, people backed away when they saw the blood on my shirt. A foreigner with matted hair, wearing a torn shirt and lungi, said, "Man, are you okay?" but I brushed past him. When I got to Johnny's, my luggage was lying outside his door. My clothes were there but the money was gone from my suitcase. The lock on the door had been changed. I peered inside through a crack in the courtyard-side window. The room was empty. I pulled out a fresh shirt. My fingers were so rigid, my hands shook so hard, unfastening and fastening buttons took an eternity.

I abandoned my luggage and went to the cemetery. The workers grinned and told me Johnny Sahib had already left on a holiday. I came out in the bright, hot street and wanted to find a place to lay my head. There was so much time till nightfall. I stopped by an open gutter and heaved. Sarika didn't have to help me in the end; the knife had slipped into her side with effortless satisfaction. "It feels like heaven," she'd said, her fair face twisted in pain. She had fallen in an awful corkscrew motion, on her knees then her hands. "First-class first," she'd said, before she closed her eyes. Did she know it felt good to me too? Hell was the look on Mr. Khanna's face as we passed each other in the living room, my bloody knife in my hand.

I wandered through the alleys and byways of Paharganj for hours. I ventured by New Delhi Station but there were too many police cars. Eventually, it was dark. I knew I had to run but first I needed to rest. I scoped the cemetery perimeter until I found a place I could clamber over. With difficulty I scaled the wall and jumped inside. I found a freshly dug grave and crawled in. The earth was cool as I lay on my back. I stared at the inky sky and waited for dawn's unforgiving light.

HOSTEL

BY SIDDHARTH CHOWDHURY

Delhi University, North Campus

T he first time I saw Zorawar Singh Shokeen was
through the small gap between the doors connecting
my room in Shokeen Niwas to the adjoining one. He
sat astride a large, naked Punjabi woman in her late thirties
who had buttocks that even film star Asha Parekh would be
proud of. She was on her knees, at the edge of Jishnu Sharma's
cot. Jishnu da (MA, Previous, English, Ramjas), meanwhile,
was in my room looking as usual philosophical and tragic. His
left hand was buried in his loose, discolored Tweety Pie Ber-
muda shorts which he never washed. In fact the shorts were
so stiff with profligacy that the story went that once during
an argument in the hostel over who was supposed to pay for
the Old Monk khamba that Friday night, Jishnu da in anger
had taken off his shorts and thrown them in Farid Ashraf's
face. Though Farid managed to turn his head in time, he cut
his fingers on the razor-sharp edges of Jishnu da's shorts. The
next day Farid (third-year History Honors, KMC) had to get
a tetanus shot.

So right now, with his left hand Jishnu da was "making
baingan bharta," in his own immortal words. Eight or ten boys
from the neighboring rooms were clustered in mine, their faces
shining with barely repressed lust, the air dank with sweat and
Navy Cut smoke. It was 2 o'clock in the afternoon on a hot
July day in 1992 and I had just returned to my room after

my first day at Zakir Husain College. A week earlier I and my friend Pranjal Sinha had arrived in Delhi from Patna and landed up at Shokeen Niwas. Pranjal had taken admission in Hindu College reading Economics while I got English at Zakir.

"He has taken her once in the chut, then in her mouth, now he is doing her ass," Pranjal informed me in a cool matter-of-fact way, after taking a long drag from his cigarette. He added as an afterthought, "Jishnu da too is on his third shot." Then he bowed and beckoned me to the slightly ajar door.

Zorawar Singh was holding onto both of "Madam's" breasts with their large purplish nipples for balance, and was anally fucking her with much gusto. Her real name was Mrs. Midha and she was a section officer at Delhi University but everybody called her "Madam" because a few weeks back, Jishnu da, along with Farid Ashraf and Ramanuj Ghosh (second-year BA, Pass, Ramjas), was standing outside Shokeen Niwas when Zorawar Singh drove up with Mrs. Midha in his white Gypsy.

Zorawar had stopped the car and asked Jishnu da whether he had gotten admission for one of his candidates in Ramjas College, which he had asked him to follow up on.

"Uncle, you don't worry. The boy will be taken in through the sports quota after the third list. I have spoken to the teacher in charge. He was being uncooperative at first but I 'convinced' him in the end."

"Very good. Keep following it up though. These Ramjas people are bastards. Remember, this is for the Kaana."

"Uncle, it looks like it will rain tonight. We are all feeling a bit chilly." Jishnu smiled ingratiatingly and pointed to Farid and Ramanuj.

"Toh, madam ki le le." ("Here, screw the madam.")

Zorawar Singh had pointed toward Mrs. Midha, who was looking stonily out of the other window through her white plastic–framed sunglasses. To emphasize his point, Uncle gestured with his fist, moving it back and forth rapidly. Jishnu and the boys didn't know where to look. Then Zorawar Singh, laughing at their discomfort, had taken out two hundred-rupee notes from his shirt pocket and given them to Jishnu da. "Buy a bottle of Old Monk rum. You know what rum is, don't you? Regular Use Medicine. It will take care of the chill."

So from then on, Mrs. Midha was universally known as "Madam" in Shokeen Niwas.

Zorawar Singh looked as if he was concentrating hard on some faraway problem. His eyes were closed. From time to time Madam would turn her face away from the pillow and look back and call "Oye" as if she was hailing someone from the balcony. She too was concentrating hard it seemed. After five minutes of this, Zorawar Singh suddenly opened his eyes and shouted, "Jai mata di!" From the bed Jishnu da commented, "Game over." Now his eyes were closed. With a loud *plop*, Zorawar withdrew his dark, rapidly shrinking cock that a donkey would be proud of, and Madam slumped to the bed with a last feeble "Oye." A thin watery stream of semen trickled out of her anus.

Zorawar Singh Shokeen, mid-level political broker and property dealer, was our landlord. A strapping six-foot-two half-Jat half-Gujjar from Chandrawal, full-bearded with a dandy's taste in clothes. He usually wore deep pink or lemon-yellow silk shirts with gold cufflinks that brought out his peaches-and-cream complexion. His eyes were light brown and matched his beard. He was forty years old and for the last ten years had been the terror of Chandrawal, Shakti Nagar, Roop Nagar, Kamala Nagar, Vijay Nagar, Mukherjee Nagar, and other areas adjoining Delhi University. He was rumored to be close to H.K.L Bhagat, still then the undisputed New Delhi Congress boss and whom Zorawar called "Kaana" with the proud con-tempt that only close familiarity breeds, an obvious reference to the vain Bhagat's damaged eye.

Sometimes Zorawar would be picked up from Shokeen Niwas in a white Ambassador car with a red flashing light on the top, tinted windows, and a Black Cat commando in the front seat. Zorawar would quickly slide in back beside a small gnomelike silhouette and then the Ambassador would reverse at full speed and turn toward Bungalow Road.

Jishnu da was the de facto caretaker of Shokeen Niwas. In his first year he had endeared himself to Zorawar Singh, show-ing great presence of mind one evening when an enraged Sikh husband of a woman Zorawar was screwing arrived at the doorstep of the hostel with a Matador van full of sword-wielding Sardars. Zorawar was at the time doing his thing to the lady, who was on her knees at the edge of the bed with a mouthful of pillow. In Jishnu da's room, of course. Hear-ing the commotion, Jishnu da peeked out from the balcony and, gauging the situation correctly, promptly locked his room from the outside. He then gathered a couple of boys from the other rooms and headed downstairs to meet the Sardars who were trying to break open the front gates.

After instructing the boys, young kids from Chapra who had arrived only a week earlier, to just stand behind him coolly and not say a word, Jishnu da draped his cotton check-towel over his shoulders like a warrior's mail. With enormous pluck, he then opened the front gate, yawned, rubbed his eyes, and demanded quietly, "Madarchod, what the fuck do you want?" or something to that effect, to the Sardar who was banging on the door with the steel hilt of his sword. Taken aback at the sight of this emaciated five-foot-five rangbaz in a sandow ganji of indiscriminate color and Tweety Pie Bermudas, not to mention the towel over his back, the Sardar replied, "Where is Zorawar Singh Shokeen? He has kidnapped my wife."

"Is that the problem?" Jishnu da replied indifferently. "Rest assured he isn't here. Haven't seen him here for weeks. Actually, no, come to think of it, he did come here with a Sardarni a couple of weeks back but she was very friendly with him. Couldn't have kidnapped her. Probably some other Sardarni, not your wife." He rubbed his eyes and yawned.

Unable to contain his rage, the Sardar slapped Jishnu da, who in turn latched onto the Sardar's luxuriant beard with all his strength. Farid Ashraf and Ramanuj Ghosh, who had been standing behind Jishnu da, joined the fray along with the other Sardars. There was a lot of wild shouting and murderous threats but very little actual violence.

"I'm telling you," Jishnu da shouted, still hanging onto the Sardar, "Uncle is not here screwing your wife! If you don't go away, all twenty-five boys I have upstairs will come down and break your asses." He then called to the only boy upstairs, looking down from a balcony, "Tell Panday and Mumtaz to get the kattas."

The Sardars, confused by all the bluster, slowly retreated. After the van had backed out of the lane, Farid and Ramanuj almost collapsed with relief at the doorway. Jishnu da wiped sweat from his armpits with his towel and then dramatically tied it around his head like a peasant and lit a Navy Cut.

"Boss, what were you trying to do, get us killed?" Farid Ashraf inquired after a while.

"Never under any circumstance back down in a fight or have a dialogue or compromise. No fight lasts more than five minutes. Remember that always. Never try to have a rational conversation with anyone who is trying to fuck you. He will then fuck you. But if you call him a motherfucker and offer to cut his throat, he will respect you. When you say those words you must mean them from the bottom of your heart. Just like in the song."

Farid and Ramanuj looked at Jishnu da with profound incomprehension but nodded their heads in agreement.

"Both of you did good." Jishnu da passed the Navy Cut to Ramanuj. He then went upstairs and opened his locked room. Just as he triumphantly pushed open the door, a deafening roar erupted from inside the room. Zorawar Singh had opened fire from the Mauser 80 that he always carried in his trouser pocket. Though the bullet just grazed his hair, Jishnu da fainted and collapsed to the floor.

A close bond was forged that day between Zorawar Singh and Jishnu da, which continues unabated to the present times. From that day onwards, Jishnu da had lived rent-free at Shokeen Niwas and was given carte blanche as to the running of the place, the vetting of tenants, the collection of rents. He was the hostel president for life, so to say.

"Uncle has just one condition. The boys should be primarily Biharis. He seems to think that we are just like Gujjars. Tough and callous. No need to contradict him. So never under any circumstance prove yourself to be otherwise. Be tough, stupid, and callous always. Once in a while a Matador will come and you two will have to accompany the rest of us to some colony somewhere in Delhi where you just stand outside the van for an hour or so, smoking cigarettes or whatever. Usually a property dispute somewhere. Nothing major. It's just a show of strength, then you can go home."

This was one of many things that Jishnu da had told Pranjal and me during our first week at Shokeen Niwas, and I had solemnly promised him that we would do him proud.

After he finished his story about the Sardars and their swords, Jishnu da took us out to the balcony, where a hideous framed painting was hanging on the wall that showed Hanumanji on one knee baring his heart with both hands to reveal embedded images of Lord Ram and Sita. Pranjal and I both thought that Jishnu da was going to ask us to seek Hanumanji's blessing as another rite of initiation into the rarefied world of Shokeen Niwas. But no.

Jisnhu da simply removed the painting from the wall and showed us the round smooth hole made by that Mauser bullet. The bullet itself could be touched by wriggling in one's little finger.

"It is just like a chut, it gets bigger as you go deeper," Jishnu da said philosophically as he filled ganja into an empty Navy Cut cylinder.

It was whispered among the boys of Shokeen Niwas, usually the senior ones like Jishnu da, that at the age of twenty-five Zorawar had committed his first murder. He was then a student of Satyawati College in Ashok Vihar and in the evenings he would visit Kamala Nagar from Chandrawal, where he lived with his widowed mother.

One day while having tea near Hans Raj College, he saw a very pretty girl come out of the mandir across the street. (It was the same mandir where every Tuesday Jishnu da and Ramanuj Ghosh would go to offer their prayers. Ramanuj always carried a large cotton check-towel draped around his neck and the joke was that after offering prayers at the mandir, he would come outside, wrap the towel like a shroud around himself, and sit with the beggars lining the boundary walls. Come to think of it, he always did pay for his share of the Old Monk khamba with twenty-five and fifty-paise coins.) Zorawar, totally smitten, left his friends and followed the girl home. I like to imagine that Zorawar was perhaps intrigued by her bare feet, the delicate arch of her ankle partly uncovered at the bottom of her petticoat. He did this every day for fifteen days. The girl had noticed him and once or twice while coming out of the mandir had smiled at him. On the sixteenth day, just as she unlocked the latch of the front gate, Zorawar caught hold of her from behind and, slowly tilting her head, kissed her full on the lips.

"I am married," she is said to have whispered to him. "I know," Zorawar replied before parting her lips with his tongue again. The girl's name was Sunita Khandelwal and her husband worked as a lower division clerk in the Shakti Nagar branch of the Punjab National Bank.

I visualize Sunita as short and delicately built, in American georgette and leheriya-print sarees, with straight hair and the pallu wrapped tight around both shoulders, like many bania girls before the fat finally catches up with them.

Each afternoon after lunch, when Suresh Khandelwal returned to his bank, Zorawar would join Sunita in her marital bed. After a couple of months of this, Suresh comes home early one evening and his fourteen-year-old saali, Lado, lets him in and leads him straight to the bedroom, where he catches his wife sucking Zorawar's cock. Such is their passion that they continue with their lovemaking even though poor Suresh is right there, one foot on the wooden choukhat, poised to enter his own bedroom, watching his young wife's mouth fill with semen. Zorawar takes a hand towel and wipes the edges of Sunita's mouth, all the time smiling at Suresh Khandelwal. A mild-mannered man, Suresh then turns, retraces his steps to the front door, and carrying his rexine-lined briefcase walks off into the sunset. The next afternoon his body, cut in half by a freight train, is found near the Sarai Rohilla station. Suresh's father and younger brother arrive from Sikar to arrange his funeral. Within a month Zorawar moves in with Sunita. A couple of neighbors who object have their faces rearranged and their windows broken. No one complains to the police. Zorawar Singh Shokeen settles in. He loves the house. Sure beats his narrow two-room heat-trap of a hovel in Chandrawal. He enjoys the old-style expansiveness of the courtyard and the high-ceilinged rooms on three floors that surround it. He especially loves the dark-red flooring from which intricate patterns made with bits of broken china float up.

A true bhumihar if ever there was one, Jishnu da described Zorawar's love for his new acquisition, his joy at being finally a man of property, with great detail. From the top of the terrace Zorawar can see all of North Campus and the areas adjoining it. Kirori Mal and Hans Raj College at a stone's throw; beyond looms the dense kikar-encrusted Delhi Ridge, Bara Hindu Rao, Hindu College, St. Stephen's, and the back gate of Miranda House. The teeming Bungalow Road is just outside the lane, with its bookshops, cafés, juice corners, and glittering shops catering to all the needs of students who come to the university from faraway places and bring to it their own tribal customs and rituals. If Zorawar turns his head he can see Roop Nagar, Shakti Nagar, Amba Cinema Hall, and, finally, Malka Ganj, where Mrs. Midha, his future paramour, lives with her ho-meopath husband and thirteen-year-old daughter who bears a striking resemblance to the Bollywood starlet Divya Bharti, complete with round apple-fed cheeks and rounder tits. If he strains his eyes he can also see the vast spread of Chandrawal. But try as he might, he can't locate his own house where his mother still lives. It is too small. Too insignificant.

Six months pass. For Sunita it is a blissful time. A period of full sexual awakening. She never realized the amount of pleasure that can be had from the male body, to say nothing of her own. She constantly surprises herself. She forever wants to keep looking at Zorawar, keep touching him, have him three or four times a day, anywhere, anytime, if he is willing. "Uncle is a heavy choder," Jishnu da explained. Sunita can't have enough of her Zorawar. She doesn't care for household chores anymore, nor for the views of her neighbors. She realizes that Zorawar is a criminal of some kind but she can't care less. She would gladly give up a hundred Suresh Khandelwals for one Zorawar Singh Shokeen, every time. Meanwhile, it is Lado who cooks and takes up housekeeping. She stops going to school and Sunita and Zorawar do not force her to. Lado has always hated school and for her, too, this is a time of liberation. Sunita and Lado have money of their own, provided by their father, who was a prosperous Kamala Nagar cloth merchant before his death. Their mother had died during Lado's birth. It is Sunita who has brought Lado up like a daughter, and now Lado at fourteen has finally come of age.

One night around 3 a.m. Sunita wakes up languorously, wants to curl up into her gorgeous Zorawar, but there is no Zorawar anywhere. Her bed is empty. Mildly alarmed, she pulls on her black kaftan and leaves her bedroom to look for him.

"Black kaftan? How do you know it was black?" I interrupted Jishnu da's narrative flow but he didn't mind.

"Would you rather it was pink, Hriday?" Jishnu da lit a Navy Cut spiked with prime Bhagalpuri ganja and carried on. Stepping outside her room in her black kaftan, Sunita finds the door to Lado's room ajar. Even before she enters the room she knows in her heart what she will find there. Her fate is sealed. She can turn back, return to her room, pull off her black kaftan, and wait for Zorawar to slip back beside her and all will be fine. But she does not do that. Mesmerized by fear and loathing, Sunita walks into her sister's bedroom and is assailed by the very scene that led Suresh Khandelwal to kill himself. With a slight role reversal: This time, Zorawar is between the girl's legs.

Sunita screams, rants, and tells Zorawar to clear out of her house. Right then, in the middle of the night. Then, with tears streaming down her face, she runs to her bedroom and bolts the door.

Her charred-to-the-bone body, to which flesh still clings in spots like sludge, is recovered by the police the next morning. The entire room reeks of kerosene for years afterwards.

"If you inhale deeply, you can still smell Sunita off the walls," Jishnu da said, and took a deep breath.

It is true, the room had a funny smell that no amount of distemper and room freshener could do away with. The room which was once the pride and joy of Sunita Khandelwal was now mine and Pranjal's for the rent of 900 rupees a month.

Within a month of Sunita's death, Zorawar married the fourteen-year-old Lado and the house was finally his. He named it quite expectedly Shokeen Niwas. He was finally a man of property. Full and proper.

About seven years back, Zorawar moved out of Shokeen Niwas with Lado and his two daughters, Goldy and Shiny, to a plusher house in West Patel Nagar that he had captured from a Sikh major in the aftermath of the 1984 riots. He then converted Shokeen Niwas into a student lodge. There were twelve rooms, four on each floor. Usually two or three boys in each room. On weekends more, as friends would join in for drunken revelries from Ramjas, Stephen's, Hindu, Hans Raj, SRCC, and KMC hostels. Across the street there was a small grocery store run by a man called Mehendiratta who also lived there with his family. Mehendiratta catered to all our needs.

Even though Zorawar had left Shokeen Niwas, he still liked it for his romantic trysts, about once every fortnight. He often used Jishnu da's room, as it had been Lado's bedroom in the early days.

"You and Hriday do not have to worry at all. He usually walks right by your room. He would never barge into it with a randi," Jishnu da reassured Pranjal, who had deep misgivings about living in Shokeen Niwas and was thinking of moving out. But I, Hriday Thakur, had no such misgivings. I loved the wanton amorality of the place. Its chanciness, its far remove from respectability. I wanted to be a writer. It would be here, I knew, that I would start to truly become one. I had finally found my material, if not my voice. Even though Pranjal would later be proven right (as always), I was deeply grateful to Jishnu da for introducing me to the magical world of Shokeen Niwas and the kerosene-suffused bedroom of the late, lamented Sunita Khandelwal.

SMALL FRY

BY MEERA NAIR

Inter State Bus Terminal

There was this girl. The first time I laid eyes on her she was standing in front of the closed Himachal Roadways ticket counter, clutching a valise as if it contained her life savings. From behind she looked like a schoolgirl—her hair fell down her back in two long braids. But then she swung the valise down and turned around and that's when I saw her chest—straining to escape the tightest T-shirt this side of Bollywood. She was a real cheez, a top-class no. 1 item. Even in the sickly light of the fluorescent bulb that flickered above the counter, her skin looked like she bathed in milk.

I never learned her name, but I owe her my life. Sort of.

She was with a guy and they were arguing. He wanted to get the hell out of there and she wanted him to go to hell—only she said it in words I never imagined could come out of a movie-star mouth like hers.

I was lying under a cart parked in a safe corner of Delhi's Inter State Bus Terminal. I was fifteen going on hundred that year. A street kid who had seen everything. Still, I had never seen anyone like her. Smooth, rich, glossy from head to carefully painted toe.

I had taught myself to size up people, to spot the suckers and the desperate. In my line of work it was a survival skill. I quickly figured out that she was putting on an act. There was something a little too eager about the way she looked around, as if expecting someone to rush forward any minute and do her bidding. Three in the morning, not even a decent dog awake, and here she was, carrying on loud enough to excite every insomniac crook in the place. Obviously these two weren't from Delhi. No Dilli-wallah would venture into the bus terminal and yell at this time of night. The last bus had left hours ago and the earliest one was hours away.

After watching a few minutes longer I decided they were boyfriend and girlfriend, even though the chokra looked a good five years younger than Miss India there. The two of them must be off to someplace high in the hills for a week or two of fucking, I figured. Probably staying in some hushed hotel where no one would recognize them and report back to unsuspecting mamas-papas back home.

The boyfriend tried to put a hand on her shoulder and she shook it off. Now, he was a different breed altogether. Hrithik Roshan–style star stubble. Nike shoes. Leather jacket. Everything he had on was foreign, imported, no Palika Bazaar fakery for this one. I just knew she had bought his outfit. He looked like a kept boy, the lucky bastard. I hated him instantly.

Although just then he wasn't exactly feeling fortunate, judging by his swiveling eyes. Scared shitless more like it. The thought cheered me up a little as I sidled out from under the cart and went in search of Hoshiyaar.

Scalper, tout, scam artist, mentor, mai-baap, fathermother— Hoshiyaar Singh was the closest thing to family I had in that place. He, better than anyone else, would know how to take care of the loving couple.

Hoshiyaar was asleep on his blanket against the wall of the so-called waiting room of the bus terminal, his hands crossed neatly on his chest. Business hadn't been great tonight, and he'd stuck around in case I managed to reel in an extra customer or two. Fast asleep like this, his gray beard resting on his chest, Hoshiyaar looked like someone's kindly grandfather, a devout old man who made daily trips to the gurdwara to pray for his soul.

The streetlights outside shone dimly through the high windows of the room. Around me, strewn beside the broken plastic chairs, other men lay huddled on their sheets, hands clutched between their knees. The suffocating stink of urine pressed down on us all. A chilly little breeze had sprung up and it came in through the open doorway and twirled up the trash, yesterday's newspaper pages and plastic bags, toward the hapless sleepers.

These poor bastards hadn't managed to snag an official ticket in time for a bus to Karnal or Kullu or any one of the small towns the government buses jolted past. The men had probably stood in endless lines all yesterday. By the time they got their precious ticket the last buses would've been full. That's why they were still here, sleeping open-mouthed on the filthy floor—because they couldn't afford anything but a cheap ticket on a government bus.

But for the rich or desperate there were easier options: buses that parked with their lights and engines switched off in the dusty lanes behind Ritz Theatre or Mori Gate, or in front of the Tibetan refugee colony. Most of these vehicles were illegal, run by black-market operators without government permits. The bus mafia bribed local politicos, State Travel Association clerks, travel agents, the police—threw money all the way down the food chain to scalpers like Hoshiyaar. Who, in turn, sold tickets for whatever the going rate was that day.

The ticket counters wouldn't open for a few hours yet and the shouting, fist-waving crowds wouldn't be here until later, but I was dead certain Hoshiyaar had tickets to sell. I was also pretty sure that Miss India had cash enough in that bag of hers to buy a Volvo bus, never mind a ticket on one.

Now, standing next to Hoshiyaar, I shivered. His face, shadowed and cratered in the half-light that came in through the window, looked bloodless. Someone nearby sighed deeply in his sleep and I was suddenly frantic for Hoshiyaar to wake up, scared like a child alone in the dark.

"Chacha." I crouched down close to him, then remembered. I'd better make sure the couple was still there before I woke Hoshiyaar—otherwise he'd twist my ear like a bottle cap.

The couple was headed toward us looking around for someone to make them an offer. They knew the rules of the ticket game after all.

"Chacha," I hissed once again in Hoshiyaar's ear. The old man snapped awake and stared at my face fiercely without missing a beat, as if he had just closed his eyes a second ago.

"Kya bey, Ramu? What is it?" Even after all these years, his instant alertness unnerved me and I took a shaky breath before I stuck a thumb in the direction of the duo.

"Two bakras for you," I said. Sheep for the shearing.

He took a look then turned to face the wall. "You woke me up for *that?*" he said. "Go away, fucker, I'm asleep."

I couldn't believe it. Ever since I was a kid, washing used plates and glasses in a basin under the table at Sethi's food stall, it had been my job to spot the potentials, to alert Hoshiyaar or keep the suckers talking until he arrived and took over. This was the second time this month he'd chosen sleep over the solid dhanda I was reeling in.

"Acha, theek hai, I'll go tell Jaggu then," I said, naming a rival ticket tout. "He needs the business and that chick is dripping with cash." The old man sat up at that, hands smoothing down his beard, and I swear I could hear his mind click on instantly, I am talking *tchak*, like a pistol's trigger cocking. He flicked two fingers at my skull but I ducked.

"You do that and I'll break your legs." He wasn't kidding so I grinned to convince him that I was. He stood up, straightened his white kurta, still crisp after a full day's work, and waited until the couple came closer. Behind them, Jaggu and another ticket tout emerged, snouts quivering, but slunk back into their corners when Hoshiyaar sauntered toward them. No one who did any business in the terminal messed with Hoshiyaar. The few who did either left to find other turf fast or had nasty accidents. Once I saw him slowly bend a man's arm the wrong way until it jerked out of the shoulder socket with a soft pop. The sound kept me from sleeping some nights—nights I lay awake and thought of leaving Hoshiyaar.

The girl faltered when she saw Hoshiyaar, then continued walking toward us. He must have looked terrifying looming out of the dark like that—a tall Sikh made taller by his turban. A blanket was slung around his shoulders and underneath it was a belt strapped across his chest. It ended in a holster for his kirpan. The dagger was his most precious possession, and he checked now to see if it was resting against his thigh where everyone would notice. He'd said I could keep it when he passed away.

He liked to say I was the son he'd never have, especially after he gave me a pasting for something I had failed to do properly. A year ago, after he broke my nose and had to take me to the hospital, Hoshiyaar had started letting me distribute the hafta money to his network. Now I was in charge of weekly payments to the hotel receptionists, autorickshaw and taxi drivers, and eager little clerks in their ticket cages who funneled travelers to him.

I knew he also wanted me to slip secret packets to rich young men idling their motorbikes in a bylane near Kashmiri Gate, far away from the cops—it was a new sideline he'd started and he needed a runner. He'd asked me once or twice, pretending he was joking, but so far I'd found some excuse to sidestep him. Every once in a while some kid turned up dead or cut up by the drug dealers and I wasn't looking to lose any bits of myself just yet. But Hoshiyaar was a dangerous man to cross and soon his patience would run out. Then I didn't know what I'd do.

In return for my help with his ticket business, he gave me a small percentage of the profits and a corner of his room to sleep in and watch Zee TV. Plus he made sure I was safe from gangsters, homosexuals, and Sethi's rages, or the odd policeman looking to make an easy arrest. I was grateful for the protection.

Back then I was scrawny, with arms like sticks, no different than the other chokras who harassed passengers streaming through the bus adda, urging peanuts or shoe shines on them. As long as I had my tea caddy, no one paid me any attention a second longer than it took to buy a glass of chai. Since I was invisible to most people, I was able to hear conversations and pick up tips that were useful to Hoshiyaar. Sometimes I'd stand with my mouth slightly open, stupid expression firmly in place. Or hunker down and pretend to be heavily asleep, head lolling on my chest. I made up roles in my own little drama. Together we were a double-action pair. Hoshiyaar stood out, I did not. I bagged the customers, Hoshiyaar finished them off.

That night I must have done a good job of acting because Miss India didn't spare me a glance for the longest time, even though I was standing close to the three of them. She was busy frowning up at Hoshiyaar's face. He was playing Leather

Jacket like a ringmaster in the Apollo circus. *Here's the hoop, now jump, doggy!*

The two of them wanted tickets to Shimla.

"So I am getting tickets to you the moment it is morning," Hoshiyaar said, speaking English—the boyfriend didn't know Hindi. Perhaps he was from the South, a Madrasi. "You not pay single paisa now—only on delivery. Yes, I am doing under-table business, but bahoot clean dealings only, sir. I have to feed wife, four children, old mother. But I giving good customer service. You tell other people about Hoshiyaar, okay?"

His eyes twinkled when he raised his palms in front of his chest as if he was blessing the boyfriend. Or surrendering, like the gangsters did in the movies when the police arrived with guns drawn, I thought, suppressing a grin. Tonight Hoshiyaar was a harmless, jolly old fellow trying to make a living, getting by in his own fashion. The honest broker—Hoshiyaar, too, was good at his act.

"How much?" Miss India demanded. It was clear she was the boss. Hoshiyaar acted as if he hadn't heard and continued talking.

"We have to leave tonight," the boyfriend said, sealing their fate.

I stepped up from where I was making like a shadow behind Hoshiyaar and named a sum four times the official rate before the old man could hazard a price. Leather Jacket's mouth fell open a little. He was a got-to, must-have type—let him pay through the nose. I could feel Hoshiyaar staring at me but I ignored him.

"That's bullshit, yaar!" Leather Jacket finally bleated, his eyes skittering over Miss India's face. She made an impatient sound then raised her perfect eyebrows in my direction, noticing me for the first time. I forced myself to hold her glance.

"Can't you lower it a little? It's too much, bhayya—" Her voice went all breathy and pleading. *Brother*, she had called me. If only she knew. The things I wanted to do to her were far from brotherly.

"Not too much." I shook my head. "You want to go to-day night—that is rate. Tomorrow night different rate. You ask anyone, he and me are not like others, only less profit we are taking." I could feel Hoshiyaar beside me stiffening but I didn't look at him to see how he felt about my promoting myself to partner.

"Private superdeluxe bus—AC, semisleeper, free water bottle, free cinema," I continued, and I swear she was amused by my persistence. Not that she deigned to smile or anything but there was something softer in her look, something almost admiring, I thought.

I tore my eyes off her mouth and turned to the boyfriend. "Bus parked very close to here—you board without problem. Where you and madam are staying?" I asked casually.

"Anand—" Leather Jacket blurted out like the fool he was—and Miss India clutched at his arm in warning.

"We're checking out in the morning," she said quickly.

I glanced at Hoshiyaar. If he was as surprised as I was, he didn't show it.

One would have thought anyone who looked and dressed like these two would choose a better hotel. Anand Vikas was a low-class, dirt-cheap, zero-star cowshed on Chuna Mandi managed by a tobacco-chewing degenerate who sometimes let me go up to an empty room and watch a whore performing on her customer next door through a secret hole drilled into the wall. The manager charged by the hour—same as the whore.

Hoshiyaar jumped in: "We're giving good service. No

standing in line for you—we bring tickets to your hotel," he said. I'd asked where they were staying as a bluff. I was horny and curious and had some vague idea of stalking Miss India in the morning. But what was Hoshiyaar up to?

"There's no need—we'll come back. Just tell us where," Miss India said quickly. She sounded nervous all of a sudden.

"No tension, no tension—I bringing to hotel in Paharganj," Hoshiyaar insisted. Leather Jacket was shifting from foot to foot. "Ticket delivery only in hotel," Hoshiyaar repeated, his voice still silky-smooth.

She looked down at her high heels and my stomach clenched. Hoshiyaar had botched it—she was going to walk away from the deal and I wouldn't see her again.

"Don't worry, be happy," I chimed in, and her head shot up at that. A lopsided little smile came and went.

"When you come to the hotel, ask the manager to call the room and we'll come downstairs to collect. Understood?" she said finally, addressing Hoshiyaar, ignoring me once more. It dawned on me that whatever was waiting in Shimla for these two must be life-and-death. They were a little too desperate, too willing to pay the price. Miss India was mixed up in some shady number-two dhanda, the kind of rich-people's business that wasn't exactly legal but never got anyone marched off in handcuffs.

Hoshiyaar nodded with obsequious vigor and she turned, heading for the exit. Her boyfriend stared after her, perhaps surprised at her abrupt capitulation, threw an awkward smile at Hoshiyaar, and trotted off after her. She stalked past me behind my pillar and I got a whiff of her perfume, a scent of jasmine. A memory teased at the edges of my mind then drifted away, leaving only a feeling of warmth and softness. My throat began to ache.

"Tomorrow morning," Hoshiyaar called after her, winking at me. He jerked his head approvingly at her backside. I swear I would have laid my life down for a piece of that world-class ass.

Walking back, Hoshiyaar thumped my shoulder. "At that price I'm willing to arrange delivery on the moon!" he laughed. "You're getting balls, chotey!" I grinned back. Until tonight I'd never interfered in the bargaining.

"Give me a little extra cut then—" I said, getting the words out before I lost my nerve.

"We'll see," was all Hoshiyaar replied. Still, it had been a good night.

When we got back to the waiting room, Hoshiyaar lay down again. "Get lost! I'll see you in a few hours."

"Chacha, why are you delivering at the hotel?"

Hoshiyaar shrugged. "That bitch was talking a bit too much. I just want to scare her a little—have some fun."

Don't ask me how but I knew he was lying. I stayed put, staring down at him.

He turned his back. "Okay, okay. This place is crawling with sisterfucking cops—that Inspector Balwant is always sniffing around so it's safer to go to the hotel," he proffered. But I wasn't convinced. He was definitely up to something.

"Chacha, I'm coming to the hotel with you," I said. He pulled the blanket over his head and didn't respond.

The sky was lightening all around me as I walked away from Hoshiyaar. The terminal was slowly stirring to life. I could hear the deep roar of cars on Mahatma Gandhi Road, all those people rushing to beat the early-morning traffic. Passengers were streaming in through the main gate, many of whom would want tea.

I went into a PCO booth and made a local call. Outside the sweepers began their futile cleaning, scraping their stiff brooms through the trash. Farther away, the earliest buses started up with a rumble.

Sethi's food stall was already busy when I wandered over to pick up my tea caddy, my stomach gurgling at the hot smell of chole baturas frying.

A few hours later, at 8:30 a.m., Inspector Balwant turned up and parked his ample backside on the bench in front of Sethi's. I had come back for a refill and was waiting for the cook to pour the boiling tea into my metal caddy.

The inspector was an extra-large man with a hairy paunch that flashed through the buttons on his khaki uniform. He was the seniormost of the policemen that swarmed all over ISBT. He liked to make surprise visits to the terminal and, although he never bothered me, it was obvious he didn't like Hoshiyaar.

"A holy warrior meditating on money," he had characterized Hoshiyaar last week. "Who knows if he is even really a Sikh or just pretending to be one? Though his look is a smart move, sant aur shaitan—saint and devil at the same time. Must be good for business, eh?"

I had never seen Hoshiyaar enter a gurdwara in the years I'd known him, but I didn't give a damn. Anyway, I knew that the inspector was telling me that he knew what Hoshiyaar and I were up to—the cop wasn't looking for answers. So I'd said nothing, just made myself scarce.

Still, Hoshiyaar and every other tout at ISBT knew Inspector Balwant was after bigger fish and couldn't be bothered with our petty scrounging.

There was someone new with the cop today, a clean-shaven young man with glasses.

"Chole batura for my journalist friend here!" shouted the inspector. As if there was any other food choice. The cook rushed to comply, fishing the fried bread out of the huge kadai and artistically arranging raw onion rings and lemon slices on the plates.

"No, no, how can I? I already ate, sir . . ." the journalist demurred, but he wolfed the food down anyway, nodding with his mouth full, while the inspector held forth.

"As you can see, sir, this is the shithole of the world." He waved his hand in a circle. A family passed the stall—a man and wife with bundles on their heads, two ragged children dragging after them. The man touched his hand to his head in a salaam as they moved past the inspector. "Ten thousand people rushing about every day—and my bosses expect me to find one or two criminals." He shifted on the seat and his stomach jiggled on his thighs like an oversized baby.

"But sir, you caught Abdul Kadeer just recently. Then what about those fellows from the Tyagi gang your team stopped on the Chirag Delhi flyover?" A few months ago the inspector had walked up to a bearded man climbing into a bus near Jahanpanah forest and had drawn his gun on him. That's where men go to fuck other men, and who knows what that guy was really up to, but the next day it was all over TV that Balwant had caught some most-wanted terrorist type.

"Aah! Yes—you remember that? Very good memory. Yes, sometimes God is with me." The inspector looked pleased at the journalist's chamchagiri. Recently the government had designated Balwant to some big-shot post in the antiterrorism task force. The papers had immediately dubbed him the Don of Delhi. Maybe the journalist was here because he was hoping the inspector would fall over a terrorist or two right then and there in front of his camera.

"Get going, fucker," Sethi, who had appeared from nowhere, snarled at me. The inspector looked up from his plate.

As I picked up my full caddy and left I could feel his eyes following me.

The ISBT was roaring around me when I plunged back into the crowds. Dust rose in thick clouds and diesel fumes were everywhere. The place smelled of fried food—and nervousness. Everyone here was anxious to be gone, to be somewhere else. At least the ones who had somewhere else to go. As I passed, a flower seller I knew brandished her jasmine garlands in my face, teasing. Around me vendors shouted, babies cried, autorickshaws honked.

My mother had been a flower seller, Hoshiyaar said. I couldn't recall her face, though sometimes if I concentrated her smell came back to me. She'd been killed in a hit-and-run accident near our slum. I was five years old and would have been doomed to begging in the streets if Hoshiyaar hadn't taken me home, found me work at the stall, given me a life. He reminded me of his magnanimity often. On most days I believed him.

When my caddy was empty I went back to the stall. Inspector Balwant was still there declaiming to the journalist.

I had been out among the crowds five times already and I was tired. All I had eaten since last night was a slightly brown banana one of the vendors had given me. I slid to the ground and sat on my haunches.

The cook plunked another full caddy in front of me and I picked it up. Sethi would leave to check on his other business in an hour. I could go to Miss India's hotel then. Without waiting for Hoshiyaar.

"Oy, chotey! Naam kya hai tera? Come here," the inspector called out, waving his hand at me.

"Ji! Abhi aaya." I went around to the bench, stood in front of him. "I'm Ramu," I said. He knew my name. He'd asked me twice before. The inspector heaved himself to his feet. The journalist stood up too, and then at a word from the inspector walked off in the direction of the white Maruti Gypsy parked a short distance away.

"There's something I want to ask you, Ramu—so don't go anywhere," he said. I wondered what he wanted with me—I was small fry, insignificant.

I felt a cold little tickle start up in my stomach. These cops were always sniffing around for trouble until someone paid them to go sniff somewhere else. Hoshiyaar had said the inspector wasn't interested in our little sideline, but now I wasn't so sure.

Inspector Balwant's lips drooped. He sighed, his face comically sad. I shifted from one leg to the other. "Give me your hand," he said.

I hesitated, set the caddy down, and put my hand out. The cop took it in his huge paw and held it loosely, then covered it with his other palm, so my fingers were sandwiched in between.

"Where are those two going?"

"Who?" I said.

"The couple who wanted tickets from your Hoshiyaar last night," the inspector said, and pushed my fingers backwards so hard that the pain made me rise up on my toes.

"Shimla, sir," I said when I could speak.

"Are they coming back here to collect the tickets?" The inspector's hand moved up casually until his fingers circled my wrist, gave it a little experimental twist. I felt slightly lightheaded—this man was going to snap my wrist in broad daylight. Past Inspector Balwant's bulk I could see the journalist smiling at the sight of the two of us, from the window of the jeep. He took out his camera and snapped a picture of the celebrated inspector shaking hands with the lowly tea-boy.

"I don't know, sir," I said. My voice came out cracked and whispery like an old man's. The inspector's hand squeezed my wrist. Hard. "They arranged delivery with Hoshiyaar. They're leaving tonight—that's all I know. By private bus."

"Where's Hoshiyaar now?" He glanced toward the ticket booths, searching.

I didn't look up. "I don't know, sir." I could taste the sweat dripping off my upper lip.

"Tell him I am looking for him, okay?" The inspector released my hand and it flopped down to my side. "If they come back here I want you to call me," he added, then wrote a number on his notepad and pushed the torn page roughly into my shirt pocket before walking off.

Gaandusaalachutiyabenchodmaderchodbastardwhore-spawnmotherfuckingsisterfucker. My fingers hurt as if they were broken. Watch out for the ones who aren't on the take—they're the worst, Hoshiyaar always said.

I waited until the Gypsy, with the inspector squeezed safely inside, had driven off. Then I shoved my tea caddy back into the stall with my good hand and left for the hotel. I could hear Sethi behind me yelling for me to come back "right-now-this-minute or I'll skin you alive," but at that moment I didn't care. Miss India and her loverboy were up to something that was bad enough to get the police all excited. Perhaps I could do her a favor, warn her somehow.

"I transferred them to room 5-B this morning. You owe me," the manager said in answer to my panted question, pointing a finger to the ceiling. The room number was familiar. I had called him this morning, made him change Miss India's room. No harm in a little look-see, I'd thought. Coming here, the bus had gotten stuck in traffic a mile away and I had cut in front of Imperial Cinema to get to the hotel. As usual there was a big crowd of people chowing down in front of Sitaram Diwan Chand. These suited-booted types were crazy to come to the stall from faraway places to eat chole baturas of all things. As if there weren't a million other places in Delhi selling the same greasy shit.

Behind the reception desk was a glass mirror with the outline of the Red Fort etched in gold on it and I got a glimpse of my sweaty face. I pushed my hair off my forehead.

"You missed some top action, yaar. She was licking him like an ice-cream cone. Early in the morning they were at it—without even brushing their teeth," the manager said. He made an obscene sucking noise. I turned and bounded up the stairs two at a time. He called something after me but I didn't stop to listen.

When I put my eye to the hole in the wall, my view of the bed was partly blocked by Hoshiyaar. He had come without telling me and the manager must have let him up. He was standing quite still, his back to me. Beyond him was Miss India's smooth naked leg sticking out to one side.

I knocked on the closed door of 5-B and said his name twice before Hoshiyaar replied.

"Go home and wait for me," he growled.

"No. Inspector Balwant came after me—there's something going on with those two." Hoshiyaar opened the door and yanked me inside.

"And what did you tell him?" He grabbed my arm and shook it.

"Nothing. I didn't know where you were." I glanced at the bed and the words jammed in my throat.

Miss India lay on top of the blood-soaked sheet, arms flung wide apart, a stab wound to her throat. Her valise lay

open on its side next to her. Spilled out of it were three hand-
guns and bundles upon bundles of rupees wrapped in transparent plastic. The guns looked so much smaller than in the
movies.

She mumbled something indistinct and weakly moved her
fingers. My legs gave way under me and I stumbled to a chair,
held onto its arms. Her eyes were open and they locked into
mine as if she was trying to tell me something. My stomach
heaved and I swallowed hard, forcing myself to look away.

"We fought, struggled. Bitch pulled a gun on me—I lost my
head," Hoshiyaar said. "Her friend ran into the bathroom—I
locked him in. He was crying and carrying on—I couldn't
think." His eyes bounced around the room. "I need to think."
His turban had fallen off his head and his bald pate, barely
covered by his wispy topknot, shone with sweat.

Leather Jacket thumped on the bathroom door, yelled
something I couldn't quite understand.

It seemed important at that moment to find Hoshiyaar's
turban. I looked around until I spotted it fallen down behind
the chair. I picked it up carefully, dusted it off, and handed it
to him. "What the hell are you doing?" he said.

I heard sirens in the distance. They were coming closer.

"The bastard cops must have had you followed." Hoshiyaar looked toward the door. "Will the manager lie to them?
Go down and tell him I'll kill him if he opens his mouth."

"No—it's no good," I said. "He'll sell his own sister—and
then watch while they fuck her." I started to laugh and couldn't
stop. I felt unhinged by the blood, the dying girl.

Hoshiyaar slapped me so hard that my head snapped back.
I put a hand to my cheek, then drew a deep breath. The shock
steadied my head. Below us the terrifying *wow-wow* of the sirens drew even closer, then passed. Just some fat-cat politician

going about his dirty business. I looked at the money. Miss India was quiet now, her eyes closed.

"Did you bring their tickets?" The old man nodded. I walked to the bed. I couldn't make myself touch the valise, so I tore off a pillowcase and started shoving the money into it.

"Don't touch the money!" Hoshiyaar said. So that's why he had come here without me. He must have sensed that these two would have hard cash hidden in the room. If I hadn't barged in, if his plan had gone smoothly, would he have shared any of it with me, his so-called son?

I doubted it.

"We'll take the money and get out of here," I said, then resumed picking up brick after brick of cash and stacking each inside the pillowcase. It was all becoming clear to me. Our life here was over. "I'll go to Shimla—wait for you."

"Shut up! Put the money down and get out of here. I'll say she pulled a gun—I stuck her with the kirpan in self-defense. Lots of these cops owe me favors—I'll take care of everything. But you shouldn't be found here." Hoshiyaar was talking fast, almost babbling.

"But what about the manager?" I asked. The pillowcase was full and I put it down where he could see it. "He saw us, and you're going to have to take care of him."

Hoshiyaar turned away and picked up a jug and glass from the little table beside the bed. It took him a few tries but in the end he managed to pour himself some water without spilling it. He drank noisily. "Go down and get the manager," he said after a while.

I went down to the manager. There was no one else around. There never was—this hotel was probably a front for some other operation.

"You have to come and see this," I said, acting excited. "You can't believe what she's doing." I took him back to the empty room next door to 5-B. He was bending over to look through the hole when Hoshiyaar came in. I thought he was going to offer him money to keep quiet but instead he simply snapped his neck. "It was either him or us," Hoshiyaar said. I couldn't talk—what was left to say now? Hoshiyaar was taking me some-where I hadn't been before, a place I didn't want to inhabit. "Help me here," he ordered, and I got hold of the manager's arm and together we dragged him back to Miss India's room.

That's when I had my idea. "Shoot him with her gun," I suggested. "When the cops come they'll think they had a fight and he killed her." I pulled cash out of the pillowcase, tore the plastic off, and scattered some bundles on the bed. The manager tried to rob her and she shot him—that was the story here. It would save the old man, I thought. Hoshiyaar put a pillow over the gun to muffle the shot but it still sounded like an explosion. I could feel myself beginning to shake. Deep inside, not anyplace where it showed.

When Hoshiyaar went to wash his hands in the bathroom, I took three bricks of cash and dropped them down the front of my pants. My shirt was many sizes too big and I figured he had been too rattled to count the money.

When he came back, Hoshiyaar reached into the pocket of his kurta, fished out a bus ticket, and gave it to me. He talked fast, panting a little. "Get out of the city. Wait for me in Shimla, check in at the Satyam Chaat stall once in a while— I'll find you. I'll get out of here in a few days—I'll work as usual at the ISBT so no one gets suspicious."

"Give me the money," I said, pointing to the pillowcase. "You can't be found with it." He looked at me for a long time, his eyes hooded. I waited, testing him.

"Don't worry about it—I'll hide it somewhere and bring it with me to Shimla," he replied finally.

I nodded, then swallowed. My throat felt tight, squeezed shut.

"What about him?" I asked, to change the subject, indicating the bathroom door. Poor Leather Jacket.

"I'll take care of him," he said.

Then he grabbed me by the arm and marched me toward a door at the other end of the room. It led to a tiny balcony. "Leave from here so no one sees you exiting the building."

At the door he hesitated, then went back to the bed and returned with some cash and handed it to me. It must've been a couple of thousand rupees.

"That should be enough till I get there." He put out a hand and patted me on my cheek. His fingers were cold. "Don't be afraid, son, I'll be all right. We'll leave Dilli—disappear forever. You and I—we can do business anywhere. I'll phone Satyam—he'll be waiting for you." He pushed me through the doorway onto the balcony, then closed the thick wooden door behind me and latched it with a loud click.

Five stories below me was a gali filled with garbage. On the left side of the balcony, fat water pipes ran all the way to the ground. My heart jumped inside my chest as if it was trying to break free.

I took a deep breath and threw my flip-flops down before swinging my leg over the balcony ledge. My palms were wet and slipped on the pipe once or twice but I made it down okay. When my feet touched the ground I collapsed and sat legs splayed out in the dirt of the alleyway for a few minutes, crying and shaking. I thought of us in Shimla, me doing what I always did, living the life Hoshiyaar planned, stepping on the stones he laid down. I stumbled to my feet and started running.

At the ISBT there were no busloads of policemen, just the usual chaos. I grabbed two plastic bags off a cart selling oranges. At another stall I wheedled a bar of soap from the owner, a Bihari guy I treated to free tea once in a while. Inside the bathroom of the waiting room I washed my face, hands, and neck, combed my hair in the mirror. I took Inspector Balwant's note out of my pocket. On it he had printed his name and ANTITERRORISM TASK FORCE in spindly capitals. Hoshiyaar had taught me to read from the garish children's books the vendors sold. I put the money and Inspector Balwant's note in the bags, then walked into one of the stores near the terminal and bought some jeans, a long-sleeved white shirt, cheap dark glasses, and a pair of fake Nikes. After I put them on I looked like a new person—even Hoshiyaar would have trouble recognizing me. I threw away my shirt and shorts. Afterwards, I went into the Ritz Theatre and bought tickets for all the films and watched them one after the other, staring blankly at the screen until it was time for the bus to leave.

I looked out of the window at the busy street as the vehicle turned away from Kashmiri Gate. The monument itself was now behind grating, locked away by the government. There were a few foreigners around it, mouths and guidebooks open as they squinted up at its massive curved brick doorways. I had lived my whole life in the city yet had never gotten on a bus, never ventured beyond this little world. Now Delhi was spitting me out. As we raced over the quiet highways I couldn't sleep. Miss India would have sat in the seat I was in, rested her cheek against the cool glass of my window. I imagined Hoshiyaar a week from now leaving for Shimla. I would go to the Satyam Chaat stall and there he'd be waiting, smiling faintly, ready to kick-start our life together again.

Sometime in the middle of that night, the bus driver

stopped on the outskirts of a small town to let passengers use the bathroom. I got off the bus, plastic bag in hand, and walked toward the blazing storefronts. There was a phone booth there and I told the operator I had never made a long-distance call and so he dialed the number on the paper in my hand. The inspector answered and I told him about the hotel and Hoshiyaar and the money he had taken and hung up before the cop could ask me a thing.

Next to the booth was a dhaba with a corrugated tin roof. A man in an undershirt was rolling rotis and pressing them onto the walls of a tandoor. I asked him to wrap up an order of dal-roti and stood there beside the glowing drum, breathing in the scent of toasted flour.

(Years after I had made myself into another Ramu, I went into a library in a big city far from Delhi and dug through old newspapers until I found the one I wanted. There was a picture of Inspector Balwant, another of Hotel Anand Vihar. It had been big news at the time because there was a woman involved. The couple had posed as tourists but the police had credible information that they were aiding and abetting terrorists from the northeast, one of the many separatist groups fighting for their piece of the homeland. The woman killed in the hotel room was beautiful, the writer noted. I searched hard but there was no mention of Hoshiyaar. Yet on the inside pages there was a fawning profile of Balwant as the "people's cop" accompanied by a picture of him shaking hands with a tea boy—me. It set me trembling and I tell you I quit that library fast.)

When the man handed me my food, I asked and he told me—but I have forgotten—how many miles we were from Shimla.

The bathroom was a shed in the back of the building, set

at the edge of sugarcane fields that stretched out into the distance. The moon was large and round in the sky and the little crooked trails that ran between the fields were full of light and shadow. I waited till the rest of the men had zipped up their flies and left. Then I stepped down into the dirt of the pathway in front of me and started walking without glancing back. Someone did come search for me and shouted my seat number a few times. I could see a glimmer of his shirt as he stood at the edge of the fields searching the darkness. But the cane was tall on both sides of the path and I stayed still. Finally he left and a few minutes later the bus started and drove off. After that it was just me. As for Hoshiyaar, I couldn't give a fuck. Really.

FIT OF RAGE

by Palash Krishna Mehrotra

Defence Colony

I sit on a blue plastic stool outside the Mother Dairy booth in Def Col Market and do nothing. It's the end of another gray and cloudy August day. The monsoon has yielded little rain. Even though it's evening, I'm sweating. The humidity makes me feel like a squeezed sponge.

I should be at home. I really don't know what makes me leave my room. These days I am pushed along by forces not in my control. One day slips into another. Every night is a silent dark space that swallows me whole. I squat inside her belly until she spits me out at dawn, covered in phlegm and bile.

Something happened a year ago. Arpita and I were living in Bombay then. We were locked in the missionary position when, suddenly, she pushed me off. She said, "Manik, I feel hemmed in. Every day it is the same damn thing. We've been together for five whole years and every night it's the same old shit. No new positions. No nothing. I don't want to spend the rest of my life like this. I feel my youth slipping away from me, Manik." She sat on the floor and glared at her toes. I smoked a cigarette. I felt deeply humiliated.

Then I did something terrible.

It's not very clear to me what exactly happened. I did what I did in a fit of rage. I remember a kitchen knife, I remember being seized by an uncontrollable urge and doing what had to be done. I recall a pair of dangling headphones playing tinny music.

Defence Colony isn't a completely new place for me. I lived here many years ago, when I was a techie with a dot-com. It was my first job.

In Bombay, I thought to myself: It's all over now, let me return to where I started my adult life. From twenty to thirty has been one long journey. I suppose you could say my life never really took off. Many strange things happened in those ten years. I try not to remember them but very often memories force themselves on my consciousness; they are like stubborn relatives who invite themselves over even when you've made it clear that they are unwelcome.

I have a room on the first floor, directly above the garage. The house faces a school. In the mornings I can hear the bell go off every forty minutes, signalling the end of one period and the start of another. Midmorning, at around 11, a drum starts its heavy pounding, probably a P.T. class. From my window I can see only a small part of the playground. The lot is dusty and shorn of grass. During the break the girls play a game where they run around holding each other's hands, forming a chain. When the girls stray into the corner of the field visible from my window, I back away or hide behind the curtain. I wouldn't want them to see me.

Defence Colony is a posh Delhi neighborhood, but in the afternoons it has the air of a small, well-planned town. The roads are narrow and quiet. Guards nap in their plastic chairs, their bottoms squeezed in at odd angles. Mongrel dogs give chase to each other, or join the guards in their siesta. A dirty open drain divides the neighborhood in two halves. Cows graze peacefully on the grass on both sides of the nullah. Abandoned bulls forage in overflowing garbage dumps. And cycle-rickshaws weave in and out of the lanes, obediently slowing down and pulling to the side in order to give way to passing SUVs.

When I arrived here four months ago in May, it was very hot. I would stay in my room all day long. When the landlady, Mrs. Bindra, asked what I did, I told her I was an online journalist. Delhi is a big city. People do all kinds of things. My landlady didn't ask me any more questions.

In the evenings I would go to the C-block market and walk around in circles. Sometimes I would hire a cycle-rickshaw and ask to be peddled around the various blocks of the neighborhood. That's how I met Sadiq. It didn't take me long to befriend him. He was a Bihari migrant to Delhi. He rented his rickshaw from a rich man who owned an entire fleet. He was also a smackhead.

Every other day he'd take a bus to Connaught Place and come back with small, innocuous-looking paper pellets. The pudiyas contained the deadly brown powder. He would do it all the time, in all sorts of places. Sadiq had a friend who lived in the Jungpura slums, near the railway tracks. He'd head over there often. I'd go along, not for the smack but for the ganja which his smack buddy also dealt.

When no one was looking, I'd get Sadiq to come up to my room. He always expressed amazement at the fact I lived on my own. "Don't you get lonely all by yourself? I just wouldn't be able to handle it . . ." Sadiq lived in a one-room tenement in Kotla, a poor neighborhood just around the corner from Def Col. His four children, wife, and younger brother all slept in the same room. And he alone wouldn't have been able to afford even that. His younger brother had been lucky to get a job in an electrical repair shop. When he rented the room he had felt obligated to ask his older brother if he and his family wanted to move in.

I am sitting in my room with Sadiq and Chotu. Chotu is the newest member of our two-person gang. Now we are a trio.

Chotu works at Mrs. Bindra's. He lives in a room on the terrace, surrounded by black Sintex water tanks. His room has a tin roof which heats up during the daytime. He has few possessions, all of which he keeps locked in his gray tin trunk. For furniture he has a bed, a mattress, a surahi, a small rectangular mirror, a noisy table fan. To liven up the walls he's cut out glamorous pictures from *Delhi Times*. Seminaked Bollywood actresses and foreign models smile and pout at Chotu. At night they go a step further. Some pop out of their frames and climb into bed with him. He says he has felt them touching him in all the right places.

Chotu is from Garhwal. He is fair-skinned, has shiny black eyes and big hands. He is moody and irritable when with us. In front of Mrs. Bindra he is subservient and self-effacing, always ready to please. He misses the rain and the mountains, the company of his friends. He's fond of his drink. We do a lot of that sitting in the park opposite the main market or in Sadiq's rickshaw while he peddles us around. Chotu stares at all the fancy women with their oversized sunglasses and opulent cars. He finds it strange that I remain indifferent to the sensual world around us.

We have another hangout—the first floor. The golf-playing Mrs. Bindra, wife of the dead Rear Admiral Bindra, owns C-47, Defence Colony. She lives on the ground floor. Between Mrs. Bindra's plush, dark home and the terrace lies a vacant first-floor apartment. A young woman committed suicide here several weeks before I moved in. No one has been bold enough to rent the place after that incident. Chotu feels her ghost is still around. He describes her as being very sexy, very aloof. She worked for a bank and lived on her own. At night she had boyfriends over. Chotu used to clean her apartment on Sundays. He had a key to the flat. He was the one who found her dead body dangling from an Orient ceiling fan.

The three of us go there sometimes, either in the mornings when Mrs. Bindra is playing golf or when she's out-of-station, visiting her only daughter in Bombay.

It's one of those weekends. Mrs. Bindra is in Worli, visiting her daughter who works for Hewlett-Packard. We have taken over the first floor. The curtains are drawn. The rooms are empty so our voices echo, bounce off the walls. In the vacant space our low voices acquire a rumbling, basslike quality.

Chotu and I are sitting on folding chairs. Sadiq is on the floor surrounded by the tools of his drug habit: silver kitchen foil, a new one-rupee coin which he uses as a filter, a mutilated Bisleri bottle serving as a spittoon. I use wax matches to light the foil from underneath while he chases the dragon. Afterwards, he lies down. Every once in a while he gets up and goes to the toilet to puke.

Chotu is drinking. He has finished half a bottle of country liquor and is ranting about his boss. There's too much work. He was initially hired to cook but now does a host of other jobs at the same salary: dusting, cleaning, driving, shopping for groceries, walking the dog, ironing the clothes, driving Mrs. Bindra around. She hasn't given him a raise in two years. He says he could kill her. I say I would if I were him. He tells me to watch out; he just might one of these days.

I am smoking thin joints of Stadium ganja. I'm only half-listening to Chotu. The more I smoke, the more I think of

Arpita. I'm fighting my memories but it's a losing battle.

We are like hikers, heading toward a common summit but from different directions. At the moment we are all trekking along on our solitary paths; very soon we'll be united at the summit. We will exchange high-fives, shake our fists, plant flags.

At around 3 in the afternoon I feel like eating. The ganja has made me hungry. Chotu is drunk but steady on his feet. He's willing to join me. Sadiq is lying on the bare floor with his eyes shut. When I poke him he doesn't budge. His clothes are so dirty I can't make out what he's wearing. His body is wrapped in rags. I realize I haven't looked at him much all these months we have been together.

Chotu and I decide to go to Sagar Restaurant in the C-block market. I'm wearing a green polo T-shirt and faded blue jeans. Chotu's wearing a plain red shirt and dark-brown trousers. The doorman at the restaurant hesitates for a moment, then decides to let us in. He bows and says, "Please," pointing toward the windowless ground-floor section. He knows me by face: I eat here almost every other day. Chotu doesn't cast his eyes around the other tables; he stares at the floor and follows me. We sidestep a couple of barefoot attendants on their knees in the narrow aisle between the tables. They have brushes and dustpans and are cleaning the floor. Not a single crumb will escape their deft hands and keen eyesight.

We make our way to the first floor where a group of Punjabi ladies are playing bingo: "Two-saven, twanty-saven, one-zero Downing Street." Their restless children sit at another table and order ice-cream shakes and kulfis. Some of the women cast suspicious glances at us when we enter.

We sit down at a corner table and place orders for Mysore

masala dosas. Chotu leans back and looks around in disgust as if we are sitting amongst mounds of smelly garbage.

After the late lunch, Chotu and I stroll around for a while: Chotu checking out women's feet, I staring vacantly at passersby. Fortunately, everyone comes to Def Col with their maids in tow so the two of us together don't attract much attention.

We find a cycle-rickshaw near Kent's Fast Food. We take him to the Flyover Market. We need more booze and cigarettes. Chotu is grumpy and disgruntled. He says he can see this life of slavery is not going to go anywhere. He wants money. His present job is not going to earn him that. "Seven days of nonstop work," he complains, "and at the end of the month a fuck-all salary. She gives me food and shelter. That's supposed to be enough. Whatever little I have left I send home. I never had any money I could spend on myself. I'll never have that." He wanted a motor scooter but Mrs. Bindra refused. Chotu claims it would make the shopping quicker and easier. "But no. She insists I do everything on my bicycle. This is no place for bicycles, brother. I am tired of cars honking me out of their way."

At the Flyover Market I take him to Nirula's for a drink of water. His lips are chapped and dry. He looks dehydrated. He is on his third glass when I notice one of the red-uniformed employees walking toward us. I asked Chotu to hurry. We leave before he can reach us.

We buy whiskey from the off-license under the dingy Flyover Market. The sound of the traffic is loud. Invisible trucks and buses roll past above our heads. We are the small fish covering the ocean floor while the big fish hunt closer to the surface. I buy cigarettes from a man sitting opposite Central Bank. We walk home in silence. Chotu has stopped complaining for the time being. While walking over the small bridge across the nullah, I see cows grazing in the grass down below. They look sluggish and bored.

When we get back, Sadiq is awake. He is doing a line. He seems happy to see us. He tries convincing us to join him but neither of us is interested. Then, turning to Chotu, he says, "So, are we doing it tomorrow or not?"

Chotu seems irritated. "For that you'll have to stay off the brown for a bit, you know. Finishing someone off requires brains and energy. You have neither in the state you're in right now."

Sadiq tells Chotu not to be deceived by appearances. He says he is ready, that he is an able and strong man—as a boy he fought a cobra with his bare hands; as a young man he fathered no less than four children.

Chotu says, "Okay, I trust you. We'll need some of that old vigor tomorrow. Not that Mrs. Bindra's a cobra, but still . . ."

By evening I had been taken into confidence. Initially I was a little apprehensive, even paranoid. Why were they sharing this with me? Had they stumbled upon something related to my own past? But that was impossible. As far as I knew they had no friends or acquaintances in Bombay. Had the police come snooping around then?

But as they talked amongst themselves I realized it had nothing to do with me: It was all about them and their plans for freedom. They just trusted me. We had been hanging out together for the last few months. They knew our backgrounds were different. Still, I didn't behave like other men of my class; I didn't even seem to know any. Chotu and Sadiq were fully aware that they were the only friends I had. No one came to visit me and I hardly left my room. I suppose a strange kind of desperation bound us together, gave us the illusion of belonging to each other's worlds.

The plan was simple. Mrs. Bindra was supposed to return from Bombay the next afternoon. Chotu would go to Palam and pick her up. He would serve her lunch, after which Mrs. B would lie down to rest. Sadiq was supposed to arrive around this time and park his rickshaw further down the road. When Mrs. B was fast asleep, Chotu would give the all-clear sign to Sadiq. He would then slip in through the open front door; together they would overpower and kill the old lady. They would break open the almirah in her bedroom—that, according to Chotu, was where Mrs. B kept all her cash and valuables. They would stuff the booty in two empty bags, get on Sadiq's rickshaw, and head up to the main road to catch a bus to New Delhi Railway Station.

They wanted my opinion. I said the plan sounded okay. They didn't tell me where they were going to go afterwards. I didn't particularly want to know. Servants murdered their masters all the time in Delhi. Every other week the newspapers carried stories of elderly couples being drugged and clobbered to death. I often wondered: If the motive was robbery, why kill? Why not steal and scoot? Anyway, this seemed to be how they did it in Delhi.

Later that evening we went to the Vaishno Dhaba in the A-block market. On the way back we stopped by a construction site. An old house had been pulled down recently and a new one was coming up in its place. The front stood in darkness. The roof had already been laid. A laborer's family was living inside. One could see a faint light in a back room. A transistor radio played film music.

Chotu seemed to know exactly what to do. He took us

toward the boundary wall to the left of the house. The ground was uneven and embedded with pieces of broken tiles and shards of glass. Some iron rods were lying next to the wall. Chotu picked up three. We walked back to the rickshaw, constantly looking over our shoulders, hoping no one had seen us.

Sadiq and I piled into the rickshaw, laying the rods flat on the footrest. Chotu wheeled us to C-47. They asked me if they could store the rods in my room for the night. I had no problem. Still, I was curious, so I asked Chotu why he didn't keep them in his room. He said he would but he didn't want to take any chances. The ironing lady across the road was a bitch. She was always trying to get him into some kind of trouble with Mrs. Bindra. She poisoned the old lady's ears with tales. Once she'd told her that each time she was away, Chotu had whores in his room. This had gotten Mrs. Bindra very exercised.

She had promptly marched up to his room for an inspection. He had been embarrassed by the pictures on the wall: Mallika Sherawat, kneeling on the ground in a red satin dress; Kareena Kapoor in white bra and denim microshorts, a basque cap on her head. Not finding anyone, she had asked him to take the pictures down: "Give these people a roof to live under and they turn it into a brothel." He'd taken them down only to put some of them back up as soon as she left. But the damage was done: Mrs. B's ears had been poisoned. Despite her age—she was seventy-six—Mrs. B was given to climbing the stairs all the way to the top of the house, especially when she returned from a trip.

Chotu slipped the rods under my bed. He had also procured a kitchen knife which he had sharpened at the Kotla market. He went and got it from its hiding place in his quarter. I kept it in a drawer in my wardrobe.

After this we said goodbye. Sadiq had to go home. This was probably the last time he was going to see his family. Chotu returned to his quarter and slipped into bed with one of his sexy, pixelated women.

The next day, Chotu returned from the airport with a very vexed Mrs. Bindra. I could hear her complaining about something. I could hear Chotu saying "Ji Madam" repeatedly, to appease her.

Gradually the sounds died down. Silence returned to C-47. The guards, mongrels, and lanes of Def Col returned to their customary afternoon stupor. At around 3, exactly three hours after Mrs. Bindra's return, Chotu knocked on my door. He seemed calm and distant. We didn't greet each other. He brushed past me and gathered the knife and the rods. We didn't exchange many words. He asked me to take care of myself and I asked him to do the same.

I went out on my cramped balcony. Sadiq was standing a little distance from the house, under a neem tree. I saw Chotu step out of the front gate. There wasn't a soul in sight. Even the ironing lady had closed shop, it being time for her siesta. A cuckoo bird sang doggedly and insistently. A parrot shrieked somewhere.

Chotu signalled to Sadiq. He threw away the bidi he was smoking and began walking toward C-47. I heard them shuffle in quietly. Silence followed. After a minute or two I heard Mrs. Bindra's raised voice. She sounded more angry than scared, but then again, I could have been imagining things. Her voice vanished as abruptly as it had started up. The sound of loud hammering followed: the sound of Chotu and Sadiq forcing a lock open.

I stepped back into my room and bolted the door from the

inside. Arpita was sitting on my bed painting her toenails. I had a knife in my hand. I shut my eyes for what seemed like a very long time, but it couldn't have been more than a few seconds. I missed her terribly. I desperately wanted to hold her and press my nose into her breasts. I wanted to fall at her feet and suck her freshly polished toes.

I stand by the window overlooking the school playground. It is empty at this hour. Babblers hop about on the ground. They look as busy as ants, pecking at random, immersed in their ceaseless chatter.

After about twenty minutes I catch a glimpse of Chotu and Sadiq walking down the part of the road that curves around the edge of the playground. They are on foot and carrying one bag each. They could be going shopping, getting Madam's mixie fixed. Within seconds they have turned the corner and are out of my field of vision.

I know I am never going to see them again. They are going to start anew. I wish I could do the same. Murder has liberated them but trapped me in this horrible prison. They have a plan; I don't.

Yet plan or no plan, things will take their own course. Mrs. Bindra's corpse will rot. There will be a smell. The ironing lady will raise an alarm. The police will knock on my door one of these days. I will tell them whatever I know about Chotu. I will give them directions to Sadiq's house in Kotla. Maybe I'll tell them what I did to Arpita.

JUST ANOTHER DEATH

BY HARTOSH SINGH BAL

Gyan Kunj

I t wasn't even supposed to be my first assignment. I was at the desk, working one shift after another at the *Hindustan Express*. A few years earlier, heralding the changes now underway, the hot metal setting of headlines had given way to the bromides printed out by the new machine installed two floors below. There in the basement, sweaty old men in banyans, their hairy arms retrained to the art of cut-and-paste, would follow our instructions while speaking of the girls on the floors above.

The editor, employed only because he had some shares in a publication the group wanted to take over, was no different. Rarely venturing out of his new glass-paned office perched above the open newsroom, he never managed to make the aphrodisiac of power work for him. Suspended between the desperation above and the lust below were men like me, somewhat more at ease with the women because of the English we spoke, the youth that we then took so much for granted.

The day I ran into my first story I was on the morning shift. I had loitered around to chat with friends who had come in for the later shift. By the time I started walking back the sun was already low on the horizon, barely visible through the exhaust from the half-digested kerosene-diesel mixture belched out by autorickshaws.

I was living across the bridge from ITO, unable to afford

the better-off localities in south Delhi. The walk back home led past the crowded narrow lanes of Laxmi Nagar. Even here change was in the air; cheap plastic digital Casio watches had started flooding the shops and Sukh Ram's PCOs were taking root everywhere.

At the very edge of Laxmi Nagar, just a few hundred yards short of the Radhu Palace cinema, was an enclave of upwardly mobile middle-class respectability—Gyan Kunj, the repository of knowledge. Decades earlier, retired college teachers had gotten together to form a society that had been allotted land at concessional rates by the government. Some of the old single-story houses that still survived on the large plots spoke of the difficulties of fulfilling the ambition of a home of one's own on an honest college teacher's salary. Their decades of labor had now liberated the next generation from the usual step-by-step pursuit of salaried respectability.

There were five of us staying in two rooms on the first floor of a house now managed by an architect. He and his wife lived with his aging parents, both retired college teachers. A side entrance led to our rooms, a large one with three beds lined up in a row and a smaller one that I shared with a Bengali. His excessive attachment to his mother and poetry would soon take him back to Calcutta. We had all been trainees together at journalism school—the Bihari thakur who had not made it through umpteen UPSC attempts and the two Lucknow Brahmans who were far more focused in their ambitions.

They had all gladly taken up offers from the financial newspaper in the Hindustan group. The economy was just beginning to open up and the salaries were higher. I thought I'd be better off editing copy from remote parts of the country, straightening out stilted language while I dwelt amidst books and the fond hope of writing one of my own someday.

The reality of the job turned out to be somewhat different. The first day at work I walked up to the horseshoe table at the heart of the newsroom and sat there for six hours with nothing to do. Over the next week the chief sub on duty would throw the most inane articles my way. Often enough he would crumple my subbed copy and drop it into the wastebasket at his feet without even a look. It took ten days before a brief I'd touched made it to the paper.

In the end it didn't take much to get more work. On a dull summer day with nothing other than a picture of a bitch wallowing in water for the front page, the chief sub warmed up to my suggestion of "Dog Day Afternoons." I was suddenly seen as a sub with promise. But it didn't dispel the tedium of the job, a tedium that would grip me each day as I walked back from ITO.

The day the tedium finally broke, I'd been thinking of a new girl on the desk, a welcome change from the tattered magazines lying under my mattress.

Barely a few hundred yards from the house, near the ramshackle jhuggis huddled together in a hollow by the sewer line, the traffic had come to a standstill. Long before I managed to make my way to the group of mourners blocking the road, I could hear them. They were gathered around a body that lay at the center of the street, covered with a sheet. As always, it was the women who were the loudest, each trying to outdo the other. Threading my way past them I was halted by a voice I recognized. It was the maid who worked at the house.

"Bhaiyya, Ekka ko mar diya." ("They've killed Ekka.") Ekka was her brother-in-law and would clean and cook for us whenever she took time off. A tribal from what was then south Bihar, Ekka was true to every stereotype, working only when he felt like. He would always turn up at our place thanks to the dregs of liquor he could find in the bottles we had tossed away under the beds. If he worked a few days in a row, he knew we'd hand him a bottle of Old Monk.

In a moment of weakness, late one evening as he fried some fish for us with our rum, I had even given him my business card. Thankfully, no such thing as a mobile existed then, but at times, as I struggled against a deadline on the night shift, I would get a call from Ekka. "Bhaiyya, yeh log mujhe maar rahein hain. Main bhag ke PCO me ghus aiya hun, kuch kariye nahin to meri jaan le lenge." ("Some guys are beating me up. I had to run inside this phone booth. Do something or they'll kill me.")

The first few times, I requested the reporter on duty to help him out. In turn I would insert a brief item to favor some official the reporter needed to placate. Once, as Ekka was putting the receiver down, I heard him tell someone, "Ab dikhata hun saalon, dekhna kaise police aati hai." ("Now I'll show you bastards, see how the police turn up.") I soon started hearing him out only to quickly return to the headlines awaiting me, the urgent need to get the pica count right for a three-column heading on the calming of Punjab or further strife in Kashmir. It seemed the night before his death Ekka didn't even have time to make that call.

Standing there amidst the mourners it was difficult to connect the man alive in my mind with the body that lay before me. The maid's voice, as she began telling me what had happened, was the only thing that brought the two together.

Today, as I quote her, there is a double deception involved, the first because I am recreating these events from an uncertain memory that cannot recall her name, and the second because she actually spoke in a dialect of Hindi that I cannot even begin to capture.

"We were given the body this afternoon at the police station. He had left home yesterday and we didn't worry about him till early this morning. It was when I woke up to his absence that we started looking for him. We thought we'd ask you whether he had called. Then, in the afternoon, a policeman came looking for us." I didn't interrupt her as she spoke. She was oblivious to the blocked traffic, the gathering crowd. I was hoping to get away as fast as possible.

"He took us to the police station. There we were made to put our thumbprints on several forms. No one told us anything. We were asked to pick up his body from the mortuary after the postmortem. That was when we realized Ekka was dead. Now they are telling us that he was a thief who died while trying to escape. You know the house behind the general store, the one where the Punjabi councilor lives? They said Ekka broke in, and when the people in the house raised an alarm, he ran up to the roof and jumped off the second floor onto a pile of wood lying at the back. But we saw his body, you look at him yourself."

And before I could say a word, she had thrown the sheet off his torso. His body was badly bruised but his face was untouched. He lay there in repose, his eyelids shut, no different from how he would have looked in his sleep.

"They beat him to death, bhaiyya. Look at him, look at him. He worked for the councilor's opponent during the election and all the basti votes went against the Punjabi."

She kept repeating—*They beat him to death, they beat him to death*—and the mourners picked up the chant, the uncovered body adding to their frenzy.

I called up the crime reporter who just said he had too much on his plate for the evening. In the morning I ran the story past the metro editor—he was a veteran who had made his peace with the new setup. He just told me to look around and see if anyone in the office gave a damn about a dead Bihari from a jhuggi.

He was right. The old man who had run the paper for decades was dead. His son was an MBA from Wharton, he wanted the paper to make money. This was no unreasonable demand but it required drastic changes in a newspaper so far shaped by his father's whims. There was little space left for dead Biharis from a jhuggi.

I just couldn't easily stomach the thought that a man could die such a death. It helped that for the time being the morning shift was sheltered from the cuts underway, and in the first few days after Ekka's death my afternoons were free. Outside the office, people had little sense of journalistic designations and the *Hindustan Express* logo on my business card allowed me to go around asking questions.

I learned on the job, there was no one around to tell me what to do. The first thing I did was contact the police. I was to learn later this was best left to the end. The SHO in charge of the local police station was also a Punjabi, fair and light-eyed, his tall frame now putting on bulk, his face sagging with the weight of two decades of free alcohol.

He made me wait a few minutes in the large hall where the FIRs were registered. Three other policemen sat around sipping the tea that had been sent for on my arrival. A suspect was seated in a corner, manacled to the bench. On the walls were the crime figures for the area. Rapes were down, pickpocketing and sexual harassment were on the rise.

When I walked into the SHO's room, the subinspector investigating the case was already seated there. "Aayye aayye, Singh sahib, I've called the case officer so that we don't have to keep asking other people for the information you want."

He rang a bell placed at the side of his desk and sent for some more of the syrupy tea I had just finished drinking. "So, Singh sahib, what makes you interested in this? Such things happen all the time."

I told him my editor felt it might be a case of custodial death. He smiled, leaning back on his metal-framed chair. "Aap log to hamesha sensational angle dhundte hain. Bahut seeddha case hai, batao jara Ram Lal ke kiya details hain." ("You people always look for something sensational. It's a straightforward case. Ram Lal, just give him the details.")

Ram Lal didn't waste words. At 3 a.m. the thana had received a call from the councilor's house. When Ram Lal arrived with a constable, Ekka was already lying motionless besides a pile of wood, perhaps already dead. They sent for an ambulance and Ekka was taken to a nearby hospital where he became another entry on the dead-on-arrival list.

Ram Lal was told that an hour earlier the councilor Rakesh Trehan had been woken up by a noise outside his bedroom. He set off the alarm and heard someone running up to the roof. He waited for the servants to arrive before following the intruder. They got there just in time to catch a glimpse of a man running to the edge of the roof. It was only the clatter that followed that made them look behind the house. Ekka, they had told Ram Lal, lay there moaning quietly on a pile of wood, and they sent for the police.

"That's it. It's a simple case. We have checked, the man was a troublemaker, a drunkard. He probably needed money and when he was caught inside the house, he panicked and ran up to the roof," the SHO told me. "I don't know why you're wasting your time." I duly jotted down his words; all the questions occurred to me far too late.

I did obtain the postmortem report from Ekka's sister-in-law and asked the crime reporter to help me make sense of the document. It wasn't all that difficult. On the printed outline of the back and front views of a generic male figure, the specific injuries to Ekka's body had been marked and listed.

The crime reporter was somewhat bemused by my interest in the case. He called up Dr. Mohanty, the physician who had performed the postmortem. The injuries, it turned out, were "not incompatible" with the description of the incident. Mohanty had said, and the crime reporter finally showed some interest in the case as he told me, that perhaps the man may have been beaten by a lathi.

I went back to SHO Puri, who was expecting me. "You seem the stubborn type. You shouldn't take your work so personally, it makes life difficult." I let him have his say before I asked him about the blows from the lathi. Puri didn't even bother to ask me how I knew. "Officially, if you want something from me, I can only say there is nothing to your question, everything is clearly spelled out in the postmortem. But I can tell you something off the record, if you agree."

Today, I know the bastard was uncomfortable at that moment. I should have gone after him, but then you live and learn.

"Things are never the way we write them down in the FIR, certain norms are forced by our legal procedures. We would never get a conviction if we started noting things down exactly as people tell us. Ekka didn't just run up to the roof when he was caught. The councilor got up in the middle of the night—you know how it happens when you drink too much in the evening. He was headed to the bathroom at one end of the corridor when he saw a shadowy figure slipping into his daughter's room. She is a young woman, in college. The councilor switched on the lights and raised the alarm. The servants rushed in from the back. By then, the councilor had already caught hold of Ekka.

"Now, I know what you are thinking. You journalists are not very different from police officers, there is very little about human beings that surprises either of us. She is a rich, spoiled kid, maybe she already knew Ekka, maybe she was the one who called him home. But then again, maybe she didn't. We didn't ask. He is a councilor, a powerful man. Regardless, his rage was understandable. After all, he is a Punjabi. Aren't you one as well?

"Yes, just as I thought, so you should understand. The shame of a man trying to slip into his daughter's bedroom, you would have done the same. Yes, they beat him, beat him badly. Apparently, he managed to slip free as the blows were raining on him and ran up the stairs. They chased him and that is when he jumped off the roof. You already know the rest of the story."

There were several things I should have asked, but as I said, they just didn't occur to me at the time.

He could sense I was out of my depth. "Why don't you check for yourself? Here, let me fix an appointment with the councilor for you." I sat and watched him call the councilor. He broke into Punjabi. "Haanji, haanji, kal shammi aaa jaoga, khul ke gall kar lo, chappan lai nahin hai, samjhada hai, sadde passé da munda hai." ("Yes, yes, he'll come and see you tomorrow evening, talk openly, it will be off the record, he understands, he is a boy from our part of the world.") I didn't need to be told I was being patronized.

I was to meet the councilor at 5 at his showroom. I was back at the house by 3. I didn't have any desire to hang out at the office. The story was beginning to get to me, and I knew I wasn't getting anywhere. On a hunch I decided to stop by the councilor's house on the way to his showroom. Even though I wasn't sure what I'd do at the house, I decided to give it a try.

The councilor's wife answered the doorbell. It took her a while to get there. Gray-haired, dressed in a salwar kameez, she could easily have been a relative of mine from Punjab. She apologized for having kept me waiting. She said she had difficulty walking because of her knees, and the servant was away on an errand. I spoke to her in Punjabi with the deference due to an elder, told her I was a journalist and that I lived not far from her house.

"Yes, I know. When you all moved in, people in the colony were very worried. Five bachelors living on their own, we thought there would be loud parties, people dropping in all the time. It wasn't the kind of thing anyone was used to here. But you boys keep to yourself." I wasn't going to tell her that it was not for lack of trying. She asked me to sit down and hobbled to get me some water.

I found it very difficult to broach the subject. Sitting there, it felt more appropriate to ask how her children were doing, whether her arthritis was troubling her. When I did put the question to her, it seemed a betrayal of the setting, but she seemed to be expecting it.

"Kaka," she began, and I was being addressed as a boy for the second time in two days, but this time it was not meant to be patronizing. "He was a thief. Some of his relatives work here, but you know how these tribals are. He was an alcoholic, everyone says so, and I think he was probably looking for some loose cash or jewelry that he could sell later. The poor man panicked when he heard us and jumped off the roof."

Did she go out and see where he had fallen? I asked.

"Haan, he didn't seem too badly injured to me. I even

made him a cup of tea while we waited for the police to arrive. I think there must have been some internal injuries, but he wasn't complaining of any severe pain."

Was she sure, was she really sure? I repeated slowly in Punjabi.

"Haan kaka, he was sitting in front of me like you are sitting now. God knows what the policemen did to him."

I told her I was going to see her husband and asked the way to the showroom; I shouldn't have. When I got to the showroom, Trehan was waiting for me, already aware of my conversation with his wife. "I didn't realize you lived in Gyan Kunj, we could easily have met there later in the evening."

All I could do was make some vague noises about being unsure of my way. It should have been no big deal, but such interactions are decided by small things. Being in control of the situation is everything; I wasn't.

He was sitting behind his desk in a cabin at the rear of the showroom. Plywood had been used to partition it off from the open floor displaying electronic goods. On one of the walls there was a photograph of him dressed in saffron, staff in hand, on a pilgrimage to a mountain shrine. Snow-clad mountains in the background seemed to suggest it was Vaishno Devi. He must have made the journey a decade earlier—his younger version didn't carry so much flab around the abdomen.

When he spoke there was no warmth in his tone, he was curt, eager to be rid of me. "So ask what you want to ask, I don't see why anyone should be wasting so much time on an open-and-shut case." Even as he spoke, his fingers played nervously on the table; each bore a thick gold ring encrusted with a gemstone.

For the first time I felt a little more sure of myself. "Mr.

Trehan, I don't think there's anything open-and-shut about the case. I've just been to your house and spoken to your wife. I know the SHO wanted this conversation off the record, but I must tell you that everything you say will be on the record."

I had overestimated his nervousness. Today I would have been able to gauge him far better. "I have no desire to say anything off the record. I don't know why you wasted your time speaking to my wife. She wasn't even present, she only repeated what she was told."

"That's not what she said."

"She's been worried ever since that stupid fool died. She thinks the police will come around troubling me and so when a reporter lands up she tries to clear the family of any blame. She slept through much of the incident, and in any case she would have never made it to the back, her arthritis barely allows her to walk. She never even saw the man, and I came and told her he was fine just to keep her from worrying. If you want, you can ask the servant who was there, or the SI and the constable who arrived later."

"But that's not what the SHO told me. He said you'd tell me what really happened."

"That Puri is a fool. I thought you wanted to speak on the record. There you have it—what I have told you, what my servant will confirm, what is in the FIR, what the SI and the constable say they saw, what the postmortem says. What does that leave out, Mr. Singh?"

"Mr. Trehan, you feel you have everything sewn up, but there are things that don't make sense. Isn't it true that Ekka campaigned against you during the elections?"

"Perhaps, but everyone in that jhuggi either worked for or against me during the elections. Does that explain why the others make an honest living and this one steals?"

I sat there noting down everything he was saying. I think I still have the notes stashed away somewhere. Really, though, I was writing things down only because I didn't know what else to do.

I went back to the metro editor. He took me out to the press club later that night. He was far more indulgent of me than he needed to be; at the time I thought much less of him than I should have. I think he sympathized with how I felt about the organization, but he'd also lived long enough to know we all need to get by. It was up to each of us, he told me, to see whether we were eventually left with anything other than money in the pocket.

"Drop the case," he advised, sipping his rum. "You're wasting your time."

Maybe I shouldn't have listened to him, but I did. I've never really forgotten that evening though. So it was no surprise that the details came flooding back when a friend asked me to write about a Delhi I had known. The first words I wrote were the beginnings of this story. Somewhere in the writing I realized I needed to find out where Dr. Mohanty was now working.

Perhaps a sense of failure and the feeling that there was more I could have done spurred me on. Perhaps I wanted to see if it was possible to give a damn after all these years. But then, a lifetime of deciphering the intentions of others had left me no wiser about myself, I just knew it was something I had to do.

I was senior enough now for the young reporter on the beat to treat my words as more than simply a request. It didn't take long—Mohanty, he told me, was the head of the forensics department at the same hospital where he had done that postmortem a decade earlier.

I headed to meet Mohanty the next afternoon, driving through those same streets, past the bridge I used to stroll across. I rarely came to east Delhi any longer. I had fled further and further south in the city, away from this grime. The river, black as ever with sludge, a vast sewer, flowed placidly below. The traffic was far more ferocious. Across the bridge the market was in transition, the old shops I remembered were giving way to even fancier showrooms. As I turned past Radhu Palace, the old structure was barely visible behind the new malls that were being constructed. It was only a matter of time before it would all be torn down for a multiplex. For a moment I even thought of driving into Gyan Kunj, but I was already late for the appointment.

I followed the directions the crime reporter had given me. A final left turn took me to the edge of the vast flood plains of the Yamuna. An old building, looking much like any large office or hospital built by the government anywhere in the country, was in the process of being dwarfed by a new steel-and-glass structure coming up to one side. It would be home to the new Central Institute of Forensic Sciences.

All this I learned from Dr. Mohanty. He still sat in the old building on the top floor. It took me awhile to find the office, walking through interminable lengths of corridors with mosaic-tiled floors. No one seemed to be around, and I had to look into each lab along the corridors, the stench of chloroform and phenyl taking me back to the dissections at the biology lab in school. Finally, a peon directed me to his room.

His secretary asked me to wait in the adjacent library while Dr. Mohanty finished with an appointment. The shelves were lined with books. I glanced at a few of the titles—*Law of Dying Declaration* by S.K. Shanglo, two volumes of Harrison's *Principles of Internal Medicine*, *Embalming* by T. Jayavelu.

My gaze shifted from the shelves to the two posters on the wall in front of me, on either side of a large window overlooking the river. One was titled *Basic Measurements in Hanging: One of the Factors in Deciding the Mode of Death.* The diagrams below had different perspectives of the same drawing that showed a figure hanging from a roof. The measurements that mattered were from hook to knot, knot to toe, hook to ground, loop circumference, toe to ground, and hook to head. For those who could process such information, the other poster dealt with *Types of Manual Strangulation.*

Mohanty was a curiously upbeat character in these surroundings. Bald and bespectacled, he sat in a room crowded by the usual ensemble of mementos and awards. Everything else, however, was dwarfed by a larger-than-life poster of him receiving one such prize. I sat facing him and from the wall to my right, his visage beamed down on him. His mobile rang as soon as I sat.

"No, I don't want a credit card, what would I do with it? A sari for my wife? What sort of chutiya do you think I am? She'll get a sari when I can afford to buy it. You are wasting your time on me, I belong to a generation that believes taking a loan is a sign of failure. Okay, enough, bhanchod, this is my office time, find someone else to trouble." He turned to me. "What can a man do, Singh sahib? These guys never leave you alone. Anyway, tell me what brings you here. Your reporter said it was something personal."

I told him the entire story on the hunch he would react sympathetically to the odd request.

"Not a problem, not a problem, just the kind of case to show you how useful our work here can be. I have records of every postmortem conducted in this hospital for the past thirty years. If you can get me the name and the year, I'll just pull the report out. From what you say, it is a postmortem I conducted. I am sure that looking at the report will bring something back to mind." He sent for his PA, who noted down the name and the date. "It will take them a bit of time, come let me show you around this place."

The crime reporter had warned me about his rose garden— it was always part of the deal when anyone went to meet Mohanty. We walked through the corridor leading to the terrace. It had shelves at eye-level lined with jars of biological curios that Mohanty seemed to delight in. Snakes, the larger ones coiled tight in the jars, fetuses, and severed limbs were followed by a row with deadly poisons on display. It was an eclectic list ranging from ferric sulfate to hydrogen peroxide.

The corridor opened out to an enormous terrace overlooking the floodplains of the river. Along its length ran four rows of roses—yellow, red, white, and orange—neatly arrayed in earthen pots, each labeled with the name of the variety. "I come out here to water them every day. It's therapeutic."

We sat quietly for a while among the roses, overlooking the river that seemed unsoiled from this distance. Then he led me to a wire coop at the far corner of the terrace.

"This is where I rear pigeons. I have collected every conceivable variety from various parts of the country. Of course, I never say this to the doctors, but after they have spent much of their day performing postmortem after postmortem, it's a relief to come out here. They walk past the roses to this corner and then ask the man who looks after the pigeons whether a new brood has hatched, whether an ailing bird is now doing better. After dirtying their hands with death, they come back to life here."

We walked back to his room. The postmortem report was lying on his table. He flipped through it, reviewing it twice. It didn't take him long, then he pushed it aside and looked at me.

"I remember this case rather well. The SHO called in to cash a favor, and there was something I didn't mention in the report."

He paused; the memory must have been vivid for him to recall the case so many years later.

"Ekka died of massive internal bleeding. His lower intestines were torn apart by a blunt object thrust up his anus."

Past where he was sitting, through the window behind him, I could see the city spread out before me. My eyes slowly retraced the path I used to follow, from the new malls coming up at Radhu Palace, the new metro line leading back to the bridge, the glitzy newspaper office that had risen with the circulation. I had tried running away from the tedium on the trail of a man's death. As the years had passed, I had gone further afield, chasing stories with greater skill, some of them taking me far from the streets of this city. But in the end it seemed this is what I had come back to, what I could not escape. What Mohanty had just told me didn't make the case any simpler—either the police or the councilor and his men were capable of such brutality. But at that moment, the facts didn't seem to matter. No one in this city gave a damn, and having made it so far, I was just beginning to realize neither did I.

PART III

WALLED CITY, WORLD CITY

GAUTAM UNDER A TREE

BY HIRSH SAWHNEY

Green Park

It was around 6 p.m. when he left his barsaati. Aurobindo Marg was more hellish than ever because of metro construction.

At the gurdwara he began his walk through Yusuf Sarai. He remembered navigating the neighborhood's maze of backstreets with Lauri when she'd expressed interest in trying bhang. The memory made him wince, I imagine. Most thoughts of her filled him with a mixture of anger and dread.

Between Lahore Jewelers and some sari shops he noticed a new store dedicated exclusively to the sale of Korean plasma televisions. He'd always considered Yusuf Sarai a place where Delhi's real middle class came to shop, the families stacked on Vespas and stuffed into second-hand Maruti 800s. That seemed to be changing, he'd lament to me later.

Crossing the road was a death-defying endeavor. According to his notes, a Blue Line bus and a Honda Accord almost ran him over. Then he spotted the beaming orange sign above the Boogie Down Resto-Bar.

No firearms permitted, unloaded or loaded, read a placard on the first floor of the hastily constructed structure. Standing beside it were some men in cheap black suits, maître d'– bouncers he called them. "May I help you?" the gang's tallest member asked in English.

"I'd like a table," Gautam said in Hindi.

"It's Saturday," replied the tall man in black. "No stags on Saturday." Gautam's worn kurtis and scruffy face often elicited such reactions.

Peering inside the bar, Gautam noticed that in addition to a couple of wives and an Eastern European prostitute, the place was teeming with men. West Delhi teenagers who didn't have the breeding to hit up the five stars; middle managers from domestic corporate houses who bought their suits at Raymond; small-time bureaucrats who extracted enough chai-pani to afford an Esteem or a Ford Ikon.

Had he been somebody else, somebody practical, at this point Gautam would have launched into his dog-eared American English and gotten a table as well as some respect. But practicality wasn't one of his strong points. "And what about all them?" he asked, in Hindi of course.

"VIP customers." English.

"Actually, I have a reservation." The maître d' stared back at him. He'd probably never heard anybody use the word "arakashan" to denote a restaurant booking before. "Under G.S. Lakshman," Gautam continued. Within minutes he was seated at a secluded table sipping a fresh lime soda.

The bar was dark, but lamps he described as "space-age" cast it in "an unsavory shade of orange." Gautam pulled out his notebook and scribbled half-a-dozen pages about the walk he'd just taken. He mentioned the music that was playing, "Hotel California" followed by a set of film songs. Lakshman showed up thirty minutes later looking as gaudy as ever in his silk burgundy kurta and white churidar. I can't hide the fact that I don't care for Lakshman. But we don't necessarily have to like our benefactors.

As the well-fed editor sauntered toward Gautam's table,

waiters bowed and men with hairy ears broke from their conversations to greet him. Lakshman was, after all, a minor celebrity in the Indian capital. The chief lieutenant at a weekly magazine we'll call *Satya—Truth—*he was the one who'd engineered the sting that helped bring down the B Party government, a "fascist, hate-mongering government," as Gautam referred to it.

"Keep sitting, keep sitting," Lakshman said when he got to Gautam's table. "It's great to meet you in person, I'm a big fan of your work."

"Well, it's been almost two years since I've published anything," said Gautam, unyielding to Lakshman's flattery.

"So tell me," Lakshman said, "when did you move to India?"

"I was born here."

"But your accent," Lakshman mused, chuckling his chuckle of self-contentment. "You couldn't have picked that up in a call center."

This question-and-answer period was, of course, extraneous. Lakshman already knew—or so he believed—everything there was to know about the mustached young man sitting before him.

When his mother died, Gautam went to the U.S. on a tourist visa and bought a fake Social Security number. He changed his name to Greg, worked at a Kmart, and became more American than the Americans. After enrolling in a picturesque university, he directed plays and acquired a girlfriend, a blonde from California. But this high life unraveled during Gautam-Greg's senior year. State policemen caught him with enough pharmaceuticals to put down a herd of elephants, and he was indefinitely banned from the country.

"I spent a few years in upstate New York," was all he told

Lakshman. He never told me about his American years either, nor did he write about them in his journals.

"My sister-in-law lives in Toronto, but I prefer it here too," responded Lakshman. "Best of both worlds." His south Delhi Hinglish got under Gautam's skin.

A waiter came, and Lakshman ordered a Johnnie Walker Red Label, some burra kebabs, and mozzarella sticks. Despite Lakshman's insistence that he have something hard, Gautam stuck with lime soda.

"Are you still into making movies, man?" Lakshman asked. He was referring to a documentary Gautam had worked on with the BAFTA-winning American director Lauri Zeller. Gautam didn't like to speak about her, and Lakshman must have known this.

"Lakshmanji," Gautam said, "I'm a teacher now. You told me you had something to say about Khem. That's the only reason I agreed to meet you."

"I was just getting to your friend." Lakshman paused for a gulp of whiskey. "He was a true patriot, wasn't he?"

"I'm no judge of patriotism, but yes, he did good work." Gautam's Hindi was erudite and awkward as usual.

"You know his death was no accident. Gautam, Khem was murdered."

"You think that's news to me?"

"It shouldn't be. But I do have some knowledge that might interest you."

"That would surprise me."

"Gautam, I know who killed him." After making this bold declaration, Lakshman stopped speaking to suck a mutton bone clean. "You're a Hindi poetry aficionado," he resumed. "You've obviously heard of Srirang Kumar, na?"

"Of course." Gautam was particularly fond of one of Kumar's poems, "The Englishman Is Like a Magpie." He'd even written a column on it for *Bibliophile*. "But I don't think you've called me here to discuss poetry."

"Be patient." Lakshman paused again, this time to wash down the meat with some more whiskey. "You must know about Kumar's son," he said, tongue polishing gums and teeth.

Gautam nodded. Who hadn't heard of Ashok Kumar, industrialist, defense contractor, playboy?

"Well, it's the younger Kumar who's responsible for your friend's death." The Canadian Aluminum Corporation, explained Lakshman, had paid Kumar a huge quantity to ensure that Khem would stop getting in its way. "We have evidence: taped conversations, witnesses, bank statements. This might be one of biggest cases of political corruption since Gujarat."

"And?"

"And we want *you* to write the story."

Gautam silently twirled the ends of his mustache and then began shaking his head. "The tribals have been displaced and my friend's already dead," he finally stated. "I fail to see the point of such a story."

"The point?" echoed Lakshman. Then he launched into an oration on the importance of the "fourth estate" in today's climate. Things like, "Now, more than ever, as neo-imperialistic capitalism mingles with our corrupt bureaucracy, it's essential that investigative journalism preserve democracy."

"I'm sorry. I no longer work for the media, especially Indian media," Gautam responded. He'd come to the conclusion that Delhi's spineless editors and their delinquent paychecks weren't worth the trouble.

"Let me finish, yaar. *Satya* has just signed a deal for a tie-up with the *London Tribune*." This article, Lakshman clarified, would not only be a cover story in India, it would also be printed in the *Tribune*'s weekend magazine. "A London publication means London payment. One pound sterling per word!"

The sum Gautam had inherited from the last of his mother's siblings would run out next year. A big paycheck would serve him well. He nevertheless continued on with his protest. "I could never be objective about Khem though."

"Arré, don't you see? Your insider connections make you the best man for the job."

You could consider the day after he met with Lakshman, a Sunday, my third date with Gautam.

Ten days earlier I'd started volunteering at the school where he taught. I told the principal I was an MPhil student doing pedagogical research. Her bureaucratic indifference disappeared when I placed an envelope full of five-hundred-rupee notes on her desk. Despite Gautam's mental turmoil during that period, I managed to get him to notice me.

We'd scheduled to meet outside of Evergreen, where college students were pushing encyclopedias on sweater-clad families who were gorging on chaat and jalebis. Gautam, standing aloof from all this, was petting an overfed stray when I tapped him on the shoulder.

"You look beautiful," he said in Hindi.

I couldn't say the same thing about him. The eyes burdened with purple bags of sleeplessness and ganja, they'd been a constant during our few walks and teas. There was something else though, something new. As I later discovered in his journals, his past twenty-four hours had been particularly tormented ones.

"Green really suits you," he continued. I was wearing a

cheap Sarojni Nagar kameez over a baggy salwar, trying to please him by being the chaste desi girl life had never let me be.

He told me he needed to speak about something important, and even though we were still getting to know each other, this wasn't surprising. There was no one else in his life besides Suraj, and the elite can only relate to their servants so much.

Conversation proved difficult because a loudspeaker was blaring warnings about terrorist threats. Gautam leaned toward me and shouted over the din, "Maybe we could go back to my place?" He tried to feign casualness, but he badly wanted me to come. I hesitated before saying yes though. Too eagerly acceding to his request might not have sat so well with him.

We held hands as we strolled through the market, just another anonymous couple among the Sunday hordes. At the *Asian Age* offices some shoeshine boys called out to Gautam by name but didn't beg him for money. He paused to stare as a tipsy policeman yelled at a sabziwallah for spitting paan on the street. "Kya aap janwar hai, ya inasaan? Are you animal or human?"

Gautam's barsaati was located on top of one of the neighborhood's original houses, built by a Jain in 1961. Besides a fourteenth-century Lodhi tomb where servants played cricket and young journalists smoked charas, this home was the oldest remaining structure on U-block.

A squat ionic column stood near the house's front door, and its latticed stucco exterior had a tasteful but chipping coat of yellow on it. Although the boundary walls of neighboring houses were blooming with chrysanthemums that time of year, the one separating this single-story residence from the street was lined with empty discolored flower pots.

I'd never thought post-Partition Delhi houses particularly

beautiful compared with the architectural marvels of Calcutta, where I grew up. But as Gautam pointed out, these ones were rather handsome, especially next to the soulless builders' flats that were spreading across the city like a virus.

When we were about to climb to the barsaati, a scraggly figure came out of nowhere and started mumbling at us. "Hello, bhaiyya, good evening," the man said, smiling wilily. It was Suraj. "Ah, guest, you have guest tonight," he said in clunky English. A scarf was tied underneath his chin and over the crown of his head. I pulled my dupatta over my face to shield it from his odor, a mixture of sweat, cheap booze, and soot. This was poverty's stench during wintertime, a smell from my adolescence.

He switched back into Hindi. "Achha, sir, kuch . . . ahhh . . . chaye. Okhla se?" He wanted to know if another batch of charas was needed. Gautam became uncomfortable and declined.

His barsaati was in want of some modern amenities that I'd come to take for granted over the past two decades: a Western toilet, for example. But it wasn't lacking what bohemians would call "character," things like old-fashioned split-paneled doors with a sliding rod and hasp, the kind that have become a faux pas in the capital's southern parts.

Gautam went to use the bathroom, and I remained in his living quarters, a sparsely furnished room whose sole decoration was a framed poster of depressed Guru Dutt playing a depressed poet in a depressing film. I stroked the orphaned puppy he'd recently rescued from Deer Park until it got overexcited and pissed on the floor.

A dozen books, both in Hindi and English, were piled atop a rickety aluminum card table. Next to these was a photograph that Gautam had clearly been pondering. It was of his dead friend, who was wearing a khadi kurta on top of some green military trousers. A defender of the tribals but not a tribal himself, this activist looked like your average small-scale landowner from the Hindi-speaking heartland: mustached, paunchy, and balding.

"He's Khem, a dear friend of mine who passed away," said Gautam. He'd returned from the bathroom and was fiddling with his Enbee. The old stereo was his most prized possession.

"Actually," Gautam said with the exaggerated earnestness that was typical of him, "I called you over here to talk about Khem." As an old Hindi record crackled, Gautam told his story.

"It all started six years ago," he explained. He'd just written an article about Orissa, where the state government, then controlled by the B Party, had decided to hand over some bauxite-rich land to the Canadian Aluminum Corporation. But a tribal community resided on the land, and its members formed a movement to protest the B Party's actions. Paramilitary forces, heeding B Party orders, opened fire on movement members during a demonstration.

"Five tribals were killed, two of whom were children," he said morosely.

Lauri Zeller, a new arrival to the subcontinent, read Gautam's article and thought the situation was ripe for a documentary. She persuaded him to return to Orissa with her, and the two spent the next year living with the tribals. "We became very, very close," he explained. He didn't say so, but alone in the tribal community, they became lovers.

Both forged a close relationship with Khem Thakur, one of the movement's main organizers. Gautam believed that Lauri's film should focus on Khem's struggles against corruption and capitalism. Lauri had different ideas though.

She'd started teaching a group of tribal youths how to paint with watercolors. "She decided to make the film about her 'attempt to help these children reflect on poverty and globalization through art,'" he told me, mocking the way foreign newspapers had lauded her work.

By the time Lauri had won her BAFTA for *The Color of Water*, she and Gautam were barely speaking. "I should've seen it sooner," he lamented. "She was an egomaniac—she wanted to exploit India like every other foreigner." He didn't tell me Lauri's side of the story, but I know one of the reasons she broke things off with him: he'd gotten back into pharmaceuticals.

Soon after, Khem died in a mysterious car accident. Gautam tried contacting Lauri for help, but she refused to take his calls. "Actually," he said, his eyes moist now, "she never came back to India after becoming famous." There was more to it than that, I knew, but Gautam wouldn't talk about such things with me or anybody else.

As he recounted his story, I put a hand on his arm. But he turned away from me and began to stroke the puppy, which was chewing on an old chappal by our feet. "It must have been so difficult," I said, mustering up my most sympathetic voice.

He proceeded to tell me about G.S. Lakshman and the *Satya* article, and I listened patiently even though I knew more about the situation than he did. "I have an opportunity to do something for the memory of my friend, to do some good for this corrupt country," he explained. "But I'm not one hundred percent sure I want to."

"What are you afraid of?"

"It's fear, you're right," he said. A breathy laugh of self-loathing escaped through his teeth. "You're very wise. I knew you were the best person to speak with about this." I gave his arm a squeeze. "Anyway," he continued, "I've decided to go through with it."

"Well, you're a very brave man."

He smiled sheepishly. "You smell that?" he asked.

"What?"

"It's smoke from a chowkidar's fire."

"So?"

"Winter has begun."

He turned to look at me with a smile I knew well, one that doesn't care about borders of class or religion. Gautam was hungry for sex.

During the month that followed I continued volunteering at the school. In the afternoon we'd spend hours wrapped in shawls on the terrace, the puppy curled up by our feet. A pair of golden-backed woodpeckers was building a home in the amla tree across the street, and Gautam threw stones at the menacing parrots that were trying to chase them away. At night Suraj would bring up sabzi and rotis for us, and I'd tell stories about my invented childhood in Bihar, so many of them that they began to seem real.

Before sleep there was no actual intercourse but lots of touching. In this department, no matter how hard he tried, Gautam could never be the Indian man he wanted to be. He didn't just stab me with his fingers like some child with a new toy. He used the palm of his hand to rub me between my legs, and I felt things I'd never felt before, not even by myself.

Lakshman told Gautam that he was now representing an important multinational media organization and had to look the part, so Gautam spent a morning in one of Green Park's many salons. He came out looking like a cross between Hritik and George Harrison.

The depression that burdened his eyes began to fade as he flittered around the city investigating Ashok Kumar's connection to Khem's death. He did thorough work and met every type of person imaginable: bureaucrats, ladies who lunched, drivers, and businessmen. Lakshman provided him with a generous allowance to convince people to go on the record.

Within a week Gautam was an expert on Ashok's life story, a story I already knew by heart. Using his father the poet-politician's connections, Ashok became the official supplier of white goods—air conditioners, refrigerators, televisions—to the central government. When the Soviet Union collapsed, Russia turned to India for these products. India put the Reds in touch with Ashok, who supplied them with all the TVs and washing machines they needed for free, bargaining not for cash but influence. Eventually, he became the exclusive broker of oil between Russia and India.

The brat-turned-billionaire soon had more money than he knew what to do with. He had no use for Indian whores anymore. He could fly blondes in and out of Delhi for weekend sessions. He even formed his own security force and intelligence agency. Before long he became a broker not just of oil, but of nuclear submarine deals and the votes of senior MPs. He became a fixer of memorandums of understanding for bauxite mines in Orissa.

"I'm almost done with the research," Gautam told Lakshman on the phone one day. We were sitting on the terrace, and I hummed along to a silly Geeta Dutt song playing on the Enbee. I hadn't heard it in years.

"There are now two witnesses who can connect Ashok directly to Khem's death," he said. He was no longer the disaffected poet I'd met a month earlier. "And there's this accountant who's willing to testify that Kumar received three million USD—cash—from the Canadians. I just need a few more days, and the money trail will lead straight to the B Party. I'm thinking about a short trip to Orissa to round off the article, give it some authentic flavor."

Lakshman firmly cautioned Gautam against this though.

The next morning we were in the middle of pleasing each other when his clunky old Nokia sounded. We were both about to come, and Gautam was irritated by the interruption. So was I.

I picked up the phone from the nightstand, recognized the number at once, and handed it to him. "Hello?" he answered.

Ashok Kumar's voice sounded sinister due to a recent case of laryngitis. He knew exactly what we were up to all the time, and I wondered if jealousy had driven him to call at that particular moment.

Gautam wrote down Kumar's address and then phoned G.S. Lakshman to tell him the news. "This is just what we need," he said. "Some quotes from Kumar will give us more credibility."

Lakshman's response was audible from five feet away. "That chutiya bastard doesn't deserve the right to speak!"

After putting down the phone, Gautam moved to turn on the computer. But I made him come back to bed to finish off what he'd begun.

Around 4 o'clock the same day, he hired an Indica to take him to Sultanpur. It was bitter and gray out, and I stood at the gate waving goodbye like some wife sending her husband off to war.

Gautam's notes from this occasion are particularly vivid. To drown out the chaos of Aurobindo Marg, he put in a CD with the words *Old Hindi Songs for Lauri* scribbled on it. The theme song from his favorite Guru Dutt movie played: "*Yeh dhuniya agar mil bhi jaaye to kya hai?*" ("*Even if you meet with success in this world, what does it really matter anyway?*")

At a traffic light adorned with advertisements for a telecom company there was a knock at the window. A little girl was selling copies of *Satya*. She was barefoot and dirty and held a malnourished infant in her hands. Despite all that was on his mind—or maybe because of all that was on his mind—he gave the girl a ten-rupee note but said she could keep the paper, just like an NRI or some firang.

At Qutab Minar they veered onto MG Road, passing the mangled skeletons of fashion malls, illegal buildings that the Municipal Corporation had torn down to set an example and make the metro's construction a smoother process. "Monuments to progress's war," Gautam called them. After twenty minutes of furniture shops, they turned right at a sign that read *Manhattan Estates* and then drove another kilometer. Two rifle-wielding sentries manned the gate that led to the Kumar farmhouse.

I was all too familiar with the sights that greeted Gautam next: the fleet of antique American cars and the guards armed with semiautomatic weapons and sunglasses; the pool and the pagoda-like temple.

Gautam waited for Kumar in a dimly lit room with hardwood floors and ceilings, a sign of great wealth in a country whose forests have all but been eradicated. One of Husain's Mother Teresa paintings hung on the wall, and a fire crackled in the corner. Its flames flickered so perfectly that Gautam wondered if it was real until a uniformed servant poked at its logs.

"Thank you for coming," said the raspy-voiced man when he entered the room twenty minutes later. Gautam described Ashok as short and handsome. He was wearing a casual suit without a tie and had grown a light black beard during his week-long convalescence. This was the man who'd made me.

During business trips to Calcutta, Ashok always managed to spend a few hours in bed with me. He started to linger longer and longer after our sessions and eventually decided he could use a woman like me in Delhi. I left behind my life of servicing Communist officials and Marwaris in Sonagachi all too willingly and became his pet project, living proof that social mobility actually exists in this country. You must be thinking, *How can a girl from such simple origins evolve into such a creature? That's impossible.*

Well, first of all, I didn't start out life poor; before my seventh birthday I'd worn frocks, taken piano lessons, and learned to sing Rabindrasangeet. Besides, it's not that difficult to hold a wine glass by the stem, use toilet paper, or shout *styupid idyot* at servants. There are many insurmountable challenges in this world, but learning how to mourn the country's rural-urban divide at champagne dinners isn't one of them. All you need is money and the backing of powerful people. Ashok Kumar gave me both.

Seating himself across from Gautam, Kumar started off by trying to charm him. He praised the article Gautam had written about his father the poet. But Gautam wasn't up for chit chat. This was, after all, the monster responsible for the death of his friend.

"Mr. Kumar, you know why I'm here," he said. "I know you're directly connected to the murder of Khem Thakur, and I know about your financial links with the Canadians. Would you like to make a formal response to these allegations?"

"Why would I?"

"Why did you call me here then?"

"Because I'd like to ask you not to write these half-truths about me."

"You can't intimidate me, Mr. Kumar."

Breaking from the conversation, Kumar picked up a phone. He ordered some fresh-squeezed orange juice and cappuccinos. Then he said, "You've learned quite a bit about me, Gautam. Don't you know I never start off a relationship with threats? I first offer incentives."

"Mr. Kumar, I can't be bought."

"Gautam, I've learned a lot about you as well."

"I'm sure you have."

"I know about Lauri," Ashok declared, his eyes surely beady now.

"What does she have to do with any of this?"

"I've found out about your daughter, Gautam. I know Lauri gave birth to a child." These words must have made Gautam sweaty and speechless. He'd never spoken out loud about the daughter he'd never met. "They live in America, which I know is a problem. But I can bring you to your daughter, Gautam."

"How's that?" His question was barely audible, a whisper.

"Just forget about all this nonsense. I'm asking you to forget about Khem Thakur, bauxite mining, and Ashok Kumar."

"And then what?"

"It's very simple. Do that and you'll have a green card."

After his trip to Kumar's palace, Gautam avoided me and started smoking charas with a vengeance again. He stopped sleeping and began taking walks at odd hours, mulling over what would have been an easy decision for most. Children, they say, are the only things that give life meaning. But as he detailed in his journals, choosing to be united with his daughter meant Ashok getting away with it. And Gautam wasn't sure if fatherhood was a responsibility he even wanted. He wasn't sure if he could face Lauri Zeller or forgive her.

We hadn't seen each other for three days when I showed up at his barsaati one evening just before sunset. It had been a particularly biting afternoon, so I'd wrapped myself in a beige shawl. This one I didn't have to acquire for the assignment. My father had gifted it to my mother, and it was the only thing of value she'd managed not to sell. Suraj was pumping water into the tanks and greeted me at the gate. "It's good that you've come," he said. "I'm worried about Gautam bhaiyya."

When I walked into the barsaati, Gautam was taking a hit from his chillum. His eyes were closed and he was relishing this action, as if the pipe were his lover. He'd never smoked in front of me before and looked like a real junkie.

Upon hearing me enter, he opened his eyes but didn't stop sucking until he'd had his fill. Then he said, "I wasn't expecting you," in a soft, airy voice. It was completely devoid of the poise it'd been filled with since we'd gotten close.

"What's going on?" I asked. A small plastic bag with the words *Kunal Medicos* printed on it lay on the card table. Gautam must have picked up some opiates in Yusuf Sarai, where nobody needs a prescription for pills.

"I like your shawl," was all he said back.

He took another hit from his chillum and tried to pass it to me. When I pushed his hand way, he attempted to force the thing to my lips. I'd never seen him like this before.

"Have you gone crazy?" I snapped.

"Just have a hit, try a little," he kept on going.

When I slapped his face, the demons that had been inhabiting his eyes suddenly fled, and a look of panic replaced them.

Then, looking away from me, he drew his hand behind his ear and hurled his pipe at a spot on the wall beside the poster. The chillum smashed into half-a-dozen pieces, and the puppy started whimpering. Gautam began crying too, and he buried his head in my bosom. I held him tightly. It was upon my urging that he slid himself into me that night.

In the morning, we remained naked under the covers despite the cold, and it was then he confessed that Lauri had given birth to his child. He also told me about Kumar's proposition.

Gautam didn't speak about his fear of fatherhood, he just said he was uncomfortable sacrificing the truth for his own selfish ends. "Picking Ashok Kumar over Lakshman and *Satya* is like picking evil over good. It should be that simple."

My response to his dilemma should have come quickly to my lips. But I said nothing. We moved out to the terrace and stared at some local children playing hopscotch and chattering in Hindi on the street below. In front of a neighboring house some laborers were assembling a shamiana for a wedding. "Imagine if that were for us," Gautam said, a faint, wistful smile on his face.

"Nothing could make me happier," I told him.

When he was alone that night, Gautam called Lakshman and told him the article was off. "It's going nowhere, and I'm tired," he said. There was some back and forth, during which Lakshman tried to appeal to his sense of justice and democracy. But Gautam was firm in his resolve to abandon the project.

I was volunteering at the school the next morning when a student stormed through the courtyard and screamed at the principal: "Gautam sir is lying dead in the park, Gautam sir is lying dead in the park!" I ran there as fast as I could.

A crowd was staring from a safe distance: servants walking sweater-clad dogs; prickly old men holding sticks to beat away strays and poor people. I pushed through them and his body came into view. Damaged but not dead, he was sprawled beside an earth-colored Lodhi tomb he often loafed around. An enormous gulmohar tree hung over him. It wasn't Lakshman himself who'd sent the goons with cricket bats to Gautam's flat before dawn. His C Party colleagues had taken care of that.

The sight of his bloodied, maimed face sent a wave of anguish through me.

Two security guards, uniformed UP-wallahs, were attending to his body. A wiry one was dragging Gautam by an arm and his curly locks, and a paunchy one was using a rifle to prod him. The butt of the gun met my leg with a considerable amount of force, and I let out a howl that snapped them out of their sadistic fever.

Once I had their attention, I shouted a series of reprimands in English peppered with words like "idyot." Had Gautam been more alert, it would have unnerved him to hear how naturally such bilious Angrezi spilled from my tongue. But in the nation's capital, the Queen's language is still a deadlier weapon than a Mauser.

After eyeing me up and down, the head guard decided I wasn't a force to reckon with. "Didi," he said, his gaze now inflected with leering. My dress code for this assignment had meant my demotion from "madam" to "sister." "We're going to take him to the police thana. Just listen to me and you'll remain unharmed."

When I dropped the name of some fictitious high-level

official, my mamaji the High Court justice, the guards became uneasy. But what really got them was the sight of the Black-Berry I pulled from my pocket. They couldn't have known what exactly it was or how much it cost, but even they knew it was far more expensive than the toys of the casually rich. I'd kept it concealed from Gautam all these weeks.

The guards helped him up, and I walked out of Deer Park supporting the weight of his semiconscious six-foot frame. After bringing him home, I stayed by his bedside for the next twenty hours. I only left when Ashok called me in for a meeting.

Kumar received me in his mahogany study. He was in a bathrobe and had a stoic look on his face. It was meant to communicate his disappointment in me. "Things have gotten very complicated," was all he said. "I didn't want it to come to this, but it's best to just finish this now. And obviously destroy all his papers." Those were my orders, and they weren't unreasonable ones.

I got up to leave, but Kumar motioned for me to stay. He picked up one of the three phones before him and said, "Bahadur, I'm not to be disturbed for twenty minutes." Then he got up and walked over to the expensive leather chair I was sitting on and untied his robe. There was nothing underneath it, just his hairy body, a gold chain, and the limp organ I was to make hard with my tongue. This was my medicine. I had to win back my place in his good books.

I took the length of him into my mouth. No matter how far I moved away from Sonagachi, this man would never let me forget about the whore I once was.

I returned to Green Park early the next morning, and as I climbed the stairs to the barsaati one final time, the dog began making noise, a series of shrill yelps, the sound of a puppy in distress. When I walked in, the thing pissed on the flats I was wearing, ethnic ones I would've gotten rid of anyway.

Gautam's eyes were closed and his mustache was caked in vomit, but he was still breathing. On the floor was an empty strip of oxycodone, and next to it a brown envelope. Lakshman's people had sent it to him during my brief absence. I thumbed through its contents, five black-and-white photographs.

In one of the pictures I was getting out of a car at the Kumar farmhouse. In another I was wearing a bikini on the beaches of Goa. But strangely, these pictures of me seemed in pristine condition, as if he'd barely glanced at them. Only one had been soiled by tears and fingerprints; it had clearly been too much for him. For me the photo confirmed how tired I'd grown of this life I was supposed to be grateful for.

The photo showed the mother of Gautam's child. She was sitting on a bench having a conversation with my boss. I didn't know it then, but Ashok Kumar and Lauri Zeller had known each other. He'd paid her for knowledge of Khem's movement, and she'd used the money to help finish off her movie. I never confirmed that they'd been intimate, but I wouldn't be surprised.

Staring at the photographs, I contemplated sparing Gautam. Images of us starting a new life together passed through my mind. That's what would have happened in a film. But I knew he'd be more useful dead than alive.

I took out a syringe from my bag and filled it with potassium chloride. Then I jabbed him between the toes. This was the only way I'd ever killed somebody, it was painless and civilized. With all the opiates and benzodiazepines in his system, the coroner would pronounce Gautam dead from an overdose. Nobody would lament the passing of this confused orphan. After shoving Gautam's notebooks and computer into the jute bag he'd used for sabzis, I leashed the puppy and left the barsaati with it.

When I contacted Lakshman, he was surprised to hear from me. It took some arranging, but eventually he was more than happy to print Gautam's exposé on Kumar, which implicated my boss, the B Party, and the Canadian Aluminum Corporation in the murder of Khem Thakur.

Months after the article was published, the C Party won key state elections and handed over Orissa's bauxite mines to more favorable industrialists. The party rewarded Lakshman for his services by securing him a position as an MD in an international media conglomerate.

Three weeks after Gautam's article came out—in London and in Delhi—a Criminal Bureau of Investigation probe was launched. My name came up during the investigation, but I'd long since made it abroad with my Indian pie dog. Ashok Kumar was arrested and caged in Tihar for a few months, where he was allowed to bathe in milk on Sundays. He was of course freed.

In the days immediately after the article's publication, newspapers printed gushing obituaries about its author, referring to Gautam as "one of India's finest young minds." Delhi's intelligentsia lamented his tragic death over kebabs and mojitos for a few months. Then they forgot he'd ever existed.

THE SCAM

BY TABISH KHAIR

Jantar Mantar

A little Turd sits outside the metro exit closest to Jantar Mantar and offers to polish your shoes when you leave the cool, clean interior of the underground for the smog and heat of the pucca-baked roads. You say no, having little time for Turds of that sort and because your boy-servant has already polished your shoes twice this morning, once of his own volition and once because you were not satisfied. So yes, you say no, and *plunk,* the little Turd has deposited a real piece of turd on your shoes. Oh, you do not see him do it, but where else does real turd come from if not from little Turds like him? See, see, saar, says the Turd, speaking Ingliss to you because he can see that you are the type, not phoren but polished. See, see, saar, he says. Ssuu durrty.

The little Turd has made a mistake. Just because you are polished does not mean that you only speak Ingliss. You slap him on the head, twice. It is a language he understands. You thrust your shoe out to him, and say in Hindi-Ingliss-Punjabi: Saaf karo, abhi saaf karo shoes, harami, and you add a few choice gaalis in Punjabi which need not be put down on paper. If you had not added those gaalis, the little Turd might have raised a racket. But he is convinced he has made a mistake. He was fooled by your patina, like those Spanish adventurers were once fooled by the shine of the copper on the Indians in America: What glittered on you was not gold. The little Turd realizes his mistake. He is a quick learner. You have convinced him in two expressive local languages: Punjabi and Slapperi. He wipes your shoe with a rueful pout. Then as you turn to leave, he cannot resist the question. He is still intrigued. He needs to place you. Perhaps he maintains a record of his mistakes. He is a professional, just as much as you or anyone else in Delhi these days. So he asks you with a comic salaam, still in Ingliss, Vaat you do, saab, vaat job-vob, saar?

You have won this battle. You are in an expansive, forgiving mood. You decide to answer him, and mention your profession.

Repoder? Jurnaalis? he says.

Then he shakes his head, as if that word explains his mistake. Jurnaalis, he repeats. Jurnaalis. Repoder.

The street outside Jantar Mantar is a favorite haunt of journalists. Next to the nineteenth-century observatory, there are broad sidewalks, and these broad sidewalks often host impromptu protest groups. Sometimes for months. There is one occupied by victims of the Bhopal gas leak. They have been sitting there, on and off, for at least a few years, down to five or six people now, mostly ignored by journalists. A much larger group, bathed in camera flashes, belongs to the Narmada Bachao Andolan. They are an intermittent fixture on this road, and because their champions include celebrities like Arundhati Roy, they attract media flashlights once in a while.

Actually, they are the reason why that little Turd doing his su-paalis-and-turd-on-shoe scam made such an error of judgment when staff reporter Arvind Sinha of the *Times of India* exited from the metro. Reporter Sinha has long harbored a crush on Arundhati Roy. Hence, he had dressed up with extra care this summer morning and left his Bullet motorcycle behind to avoid the blackening traffic fumes, before doing his round of the Narmada Bachao Andolan protest. Not that it is going to be noticed. The famous Roy is there, but too uninterested in her fame to give interviews, let alone be whisked away for a fawning chat in one of those three-, four-, five-, and probably-more-star hotels around the corner.

So, after jotting down the day's press declaration in his spiral notebook, and pocketing the day's press release, Repoder Sinha heads for one of the four-star restaurants on his own. The Sangharsh Morcha had announced a press meet there, and now that Sinha is here he might as well look in, collect the releases, and, hopefully, guzzle down a cold beer or two. On the way, he notices that a new tent has come up at the corner of Jantar Mantar: It bears the obligatory banner stating, *Justice Delayed Is Justice Denied,* in English. There is no one under the tent—a rickety affair, broad enough to hold four or five people at most—so Repoder Sinha cannot inquire about the nature of the justice that has been delayed or denied, though it is doubtful that he would have stopped to do so anyway.

Past the revolving glass doors of the restaurant, in the air-conditioned, potted interior, Sinha spots the table reserved for the press meet by the Sangharsh Morcha. Not much of the press has met. Apart from Sinha, there are only two other reporters, one of whom is actually the editor of his own newspaper and, it is rumored, subsists on the beer and snacks offered at such meets. Handouts are handed out, appropriate noises are made over soda and lemonade—it appears that the Sangharsh Morcha has a Gandhian aversion to alcohol, which might also explain the low turnout of reporters. Just when Sinha is about to sneak away from the rather drab press meet, the room is visibly brightened by the entry of two women.

Two very different women. Sinha knows one of them: Preeti, who works for one, or probably more, of those internationally visible NGOs. The other is a sturdy blonde wearing a kurta and jeans. Preeti is wearing a kurta and jeans too, but while the blonde looks tired and sweaty, Preeti, like all women of her refined class (at least to Sinha's working-class eyes), never looks ruffled or unkempt. Sinha has seen women like Preeti step out of forty-five-degree heat in July without a bead of sweat on their foreheads, no sign of a damp spot under their armpits. He suspects that their air-conditioned cars offer part of the answer to the riddle of their unruffled coolness, but there are moments when he feels that they are another breed, a superior subspecies that has evolved beyond bodily fluids and signs of discomfort.

Preeti spots Sinha and, ignoring the others, launches into the kind of direct speech that, Sinha suspects, is also part of the evolutionary progress of her subspecies. For God's sake, Arvind, she says, what are you reporter-veporters doing here in this fake palace? There are two dharnas just outside, near Jantar Mantar.

Been there, Preeti, replies Sinha . . .

Not the Narmada one—Preeti is too radical to espouse specific causes—there is another one. From near some Tikri village in Bihar, where there has been a caste atrocity which has not been reported by you guys.

If it has not been reported, it has not happened.

Oh yeah? Ask the woman sitting there and her cute little son. They have experienced it. Father killed, uncles chased away . . .

Just two? A woman and a child?

Both Preeti and her foreign friend nod in affirmation.

A scam then, pronounces Sinha. Look, Preeti, these days

you cannot have a caste atrocity without a couple of politicians turning up to squeeze the last drop of political mileage out of it. If it's just a couple of people, it is a scam. Another way of begging . . .

Oh, you are so cynical, says the foreign woman, in a vaguely European accent.

Not cynical—reporter, staff reporter, contributes Preeti, and introduces the two. The foreign woman is a visiting journalist from Denmark called Tina. But it is spelled with an "e," she explains: Tine.

Why don't you check it out?

Check what out?

Your scam.

Waste of time.

Or afraid to be proved wrong?

I am not wrong.

Check it out then. They are just outside anyway.

What if I am right?

I will buy you a dinner.

Where?

In Chor Bizarre.

Deal?

Deal.

Good. Preeti, you are the witness. Let's go.

The Press Club on Raisina Road, not that far from Jantar Mantar, has sometimes been nicknamed the Depressed Club. Its whitewashed colonial façade has worn thin, its floor stained by tired feet, bleak notices and cuttings on the bulletin boards in the drafty corridor, lawn outside showing only a hint of grass, tables piled with dirty plates, broken chairs, a slight smell of urine from the toilet next to the main entrance.

There, that evening, seated at a corner table, wreathed in miasma, which consists largely but not only of cigarette smoke, we can find Repoder Sinha, Preeti, and Tine. Plates of kebab and beer have been ordered—gin and lime for Preeti—and conversation is going strong. It is still hovering around the scam protest, which—on inspection—had turned out to be that rickety tent with the banner in English: *Justice Delayed Is Justice Denied*.

I told you it was a scam, said Sinha.

How do you know?

I recognized the boy with the woman. He runs a shoe polish scam there. Tosses rubbish on your shoes, so that you have to pay him to polish them up.

So?

So!

So, it proves that he does something for a living. They said they have been here for months, petitioning every person they possibly could. They showed you the petitions and letters that they have actually paid people to write for them.

Another way to beg.

Oh, Preeti, are your journalists always so cynical?

Only the men, Tine. Only the men.

Oh, c'mon, Preeti. Tine doesn't know the place, but you and I know how these things happen.

I am not sure I do, Arvind.

What do you mean?

Look, that woman had a plausible story. Small village in Bihar. Land dispute. Husband killed, murdered one night on the way back from work. Police not interested in clearing the matter. Dismissing it as the kind of thing that happens to people who belong to the so-called denotified tribes. Uncles frightened into moving away. Land forcibly occupied. The woman tries to get justice, finally takes whatever she has and comes to Delhi with all her papers. Sounds plausible to me, given a plucky tribal woman, which is what she seems to be.

She is not a village woman from Bihar, and that boy is too slick. He has grown up here on the streets.

You would be surprised how quickly kids pick up habits and words.

Still, I bet you my bottom dollar—a scam.

Why don't you go to Bihar and check it out? asks Tine suddenly.

Check it out? The woman's village doesn't even have a name. Near Tikri village, she says. Even if I could locate Tikri village . . .

Take them with you, says Preeti. We'll come along. I'll raise the money for it.

I'll have to take leave, Preeti.

Take leave, Arvind.

Take leave, Arvind, will you please? Tine adds, looking soulfully at him with her speckled greenish-blue eyes.

What a waste. Okay, if you ladies insist. Let me see . . .

Time does not fly around Jantar Mantar. That is the magic of such places. The buildings change their billboards; the streets change their beggars, protesters, pedestrians, cars. But all change is for the same. Time simply repeats itself, again and again.

Jantar-mantar, say children: abracadabra. Whoosh! Something happens. Plastic flowers turn into a dove; a rabbit is pulled out of the hat. Jantar-mantar, murmur old women in villages, and they talk in whispers because they are talking of devious doings, black magic, sorcery. Jantar-mantar, say foreign-educated doctors in the cities, and they are referring to the hocus-pocus of quacks, the vaids and hakims who still cater to the rural poor and either heal them or kill them.

But Jantar Mantar in Delhi is a sprawling observatory built in the nineteenth century. It is used to observe nothing. It is useless. Around it rise useful buildings: offices, hotels. Buildings that change and are always the same. About it walk useful people: reporters, politicians, businessmen, doctors, bureaucrats. People who change and are always the same.

So what surprise is there if, a month from the time we last saw him agreeing to go to Bihar, we see Repoder Sinha walking out of the same metro exit where he had encountered the Turd, the boy whom—along with his mother—Sinha and Preeti and Tine had escorted back to Bihar just a few weeks ago? Repoder Sinha has changed and perhaps he is still the same.

In any case, he is looking around. He has been doing this almost every day since all three returned from Bihar: He looks around for the Turd, the little boy, for he knows that the Turd must have returned to Delhi. After all, scams have their fixed scenarios; tricksters their territory.

Repoder Sinha walks slowly, darting quick glances to the left and the right, thinking of that lightning trip to Bihar. He is not sure what happened there, but he will not concede this uncertainty to himself.

The woman and the boy had refused to go back to Bihar; Preeti and Tine had to convince them with assurances of safety and gifts of money. And it had been like that all the way to Gaya, by train, and then to the village of Tikri by taxi: The woman and the boy had wheedled a minor fortune out of the two women. Sinha had expected that; it confirmed his suspicions. But he had not anticipated the certainty with which the woman led them to Tikri and then two kilometres out to a small village and a plot of land which she claimed was the disputed property. That is when it all happened, and Sinha is not very certain even now about what it was.

It was late, the summer evening still steamy, the wind having dropped. Tine was pink, a few beads of sweat had appeared on Preeti's neck. Both were conservatively clad—a reflection of their notions of rural Bihar—in cotton salwar kameezes.

The plot they stood on was rocky; it did not look worth fighting over to Sinha. The woman and her son, the Turd, were pointing out things like the palm trees that demarcated one end of the field, the huts—thatched, hunched—of their village in a far corner, and the small hillock which marked the other end of the field. A fly kept buzzing around Preeti, evading her attempts to fend it away with her anchal, which she wore draped loosely around her shoulders. Tine had discarded her anchal, displaying a rather low-cut kameez that, Sinha felt, was less conservative than most shirts and T-shirts.

As the woman rambled on—the usual lament, how the land was taken away from her, how her husband was murdered, how the police did not listen to her—suddenly, on the hillock, there stood a group of men. They appeared as if by magic—jantar-mantar, Sinha almost thought—burly, impassive men, against the reddening sky, leaning on their staffs. They could have been any group of villagers on their way back from work, attracted by the sight of a taxi and three obviously urban types, one of them a firang.

But that is not what the woman and her son, the Turd, thought. Or pretended. Sinha is not sure. For then there was a cry of fear from the boy and the woman started cursing and weeping. The boy said, Run, ma, run, they said they would kill us if we came back, run. Then both were running—in the opposite direction, toward the palm trees and the brambles and jungle behind the bleak, tall palms. Sinha shouted, but they did not stop. Preeti and Tine had not even had the time to react. When Sinha looked up at the hillock, the men who had been standing there were gone too.

They waited an hour, until it got dark, and the taxi driver insisted on going back, with or without them.

They came back the next day. They spoke to the local police, who denied that there was any land dispute or that any murder had taken place. What woman and son, the thana inspector asked. Sinha's press card turned the police obliging and polite. The inspector took the three outsiders to the nameless village, fetid with garbage next to mud huts with holes in their thatched roofs, and shouted for some old man to come out. Come out, hey you, Dhanarwa! When the man, stubbled, limping, coughing, came out of the low hut, the inspector said to Sinha, Sir, describe the woman and her son to the man. He is the headman here. He knows everyone.

Sinha did as he was asked to do, Preeti adding a word or two of detail.

Description done, the inspector addressed the old man in a gruff tone. So, he said, do you know this woman and the boy?

The old man shook his head silently. A crow cawed and perched on the sagging roof of a hut behind them. With its daggerlike beak, it started to dismember a small rodent held in its talons.

Speak up. Has someone cut your tongue off? Speak up. Not to me, you dolt. Tell sir and the madams here, the inspector barked.

No, huzoor, said the old man.

You do not know the woman? repeated the inspector.

No, huzoor.

Or the boy?

No, huzoor.

The inspector turned to Arvind, Preeti, and Tine, all three now sweating profusely in the hardening sunlight of the late morning. See, sir, he said, see, madam, what did I tell you? 420. The woman was a 420. A chaalu fraud. You should lodge a complaint with us. We will catch them for you.

On the way back the next day, as the train shuddered on the old tracks, Sinha had his doubts. He was familiar with such interrogations by police officers. The way they asked questions often determined the answers. And though he laughed away Tine's offer to buy him dinner in Chor Bizarre on their return to Delhi—I lost the bet, she said—Sinha still could not settle the matter in his mind.

However, Preeti and, especially, Tine had been converted: they spent much of their waking hours on the train trip back to Delhi calculating the money they had paid out to the woman and her boy, the Turd, on the way. By the time the train reached Aligarh, they had agreed on the exact sum of 5,941 rupees.

But doubt nibbled at Sinha. All the way to Delhi. And that is why now, even weeks later, when Preeti and Tine have already turned the experience into slightly different anecdotes for friends, Repoder Arvind Sinha walks past the Jantar Mantar area, on the lookout for that little Turd. Under the tall gleaming buildings he walks, on the broad sidewalks with protest banners, past this useless observatory, always darting glances to the left and right, on he walks in this place that changes and is always the same, looking, looking, looking.

THE WALLS OF DELHI

BY Uday Prakash

Rohini

Translated from Hindi by Jason Grunebaum

I met Ramnivas at Sanjay Chaurasia's paan cart that stood five hundred yards from my flat in Rohini; Ratanlal sold chai right next to Sanjay's. Sanjay had come to Delhi from a village near Pratapgarh, and Ratanlal from Sasaram. They built their shops on wheels so they could make a quick getaway in case someone from the city came nosing around. Cops on motorbike patrol came by all the time, but they got their weekly cut: Ratanlal paid five hundred, Sanjay seven. The two men didn't worry.

All the vendors and hawkers set up camp wherever they could in Rohini's evening market. As night fell, Brajinder joined them, pushing his fancy electric cart, *Kwality Ice Cream* printed in rainbow letters on the plastic panels. So did Rajvati, who sold hard-boiled eggs. Her husband Gulshan was there too, with their two kids. Behind her shop, four brick walls enclosed a little vacant lot. As night wore on, people pulled up in cars asking Gulshan for some whiskey or rum. The government liquor shops were long closed by that hour, so Gulshan would cycle off and return with a pint or a fifth he got from one of his black market connections. Some customers wanted chicken tikka with their hard-boiled eggs, which

Gulshan would fetch from Sardar Satte Singh's food stand up at the next light. Sometimes the customers would give him a little whiskey by way of a tip, or a few rupees. Rajvati didn't make a fuss since it was a hundred times better for him to drink that kind of whiskey, and for free, than to spend his own money on little plastic pouches of local moonshine. You could count on that kind of hooch being mixed with stuff that might make you go blind, or kill you outright.

Tufail Ahmed had come from Nalanda along with his sewing machine, which he plunked down right beside the brick enclosure. He did a little business for a short while. But since Tufail Ahmed didn't have a fixed address, people were wary of leaving their clothes with him. So the only jobs he got were mending schoolchildren's bookbags, or hemming workers' uniforms, or patching up rickshaw drivers' clothes. After a couple of weeks, he stopped showing up. Someone said that he was sick, another said he went back to Nalanda, and still others said he'd been hit by a Blue Line bus. His sewing machine got tossed into the junkyard behind the police station.

That's how it was around here, like an unwritten law. Every day, one of these new arrivals would suddenly disappear, never to be seen again. Most of them didn't have a permanent address where, after they were gone, you could go and inquire. Rajvati, for example, lived two miles from here, near the bypass, with her husband and two kids in sixteenth-century ruins. If you've ever been on the National Highway heading toward Karnal or Amritsar and happened to glance north, you've seen the round building with a dome right beside the industrial drainage: a crumbling, dark-red brick ruin. It's hard to believe that humans could be living there. The famous bus named *Goodwill* that travels from India to Pakistan—from Delhi to Lahore—passes right by that part of the highway.

But people do live there—families, for the most part, and a few others: Rajvati's sister Phulo; Jagraj's wife Somali, who sells peanuts by the gate of the Azadpur veggie market; and Mushtaq, who sells hashish by the Red Fort, and his cousin Saliman, currently Mushtaq's wife. The three women turn tricks. Somali works out of her home in the ruins. She takes care of customers brought to her by the smackheads, Tilak, Bhusan, and Azad, who always hang around. In the evening, Saliman and Phulo go out in rickshaws looking for customers. Sometimes Phulo also works at all-night parties.

Phulo ocassionally sleeps with Azad, even though Rajvati, her sister, and Gulshan, her brother-in-law, both object. Gulshan always says, "Don't lend money or your warm body to anyone living under this roof." Gulshan, Rajvati, and Phulo have the most money of those living under that roof; since Phulo arrived from the village and began to turn tricks, their income has increased so much that they've been scouting land in the neighborhood around Loni Border, where they might build a house someday.

Azad says, "If you move away, don't worry, I'll still manage," but over the last few days he's been shivering and writhing around at night, sick. I had a strong premonition that one day I'd come visit, and Phulo or Tilak or Bhusan or Saliman would say, *What can I tell you, Vinayak? I haven't seen Azad for four days. He left in the morning and never came back. You haven't seen him?*

And Azad wouldn't come back. What about me? Am I any safer than them? I've certainly fallen to a new low, with no work, squeezed on all sides, and now I spend all day long sitting at Sanjay's paan stall, stressed out, useless, numb.

It seems we've gotten off track. I was talking about Sanjay's, the neighborhood paan shop (right near my flat), and then got carried away to sixteenth-century ruins near the bypass. But Ramnivas? I first met him at this little corner paan shop. He'd moved to Delhi twenty years ago from Shahipur, a small village near Allahabad, along with his father, Babulla Pasiya. In the beginning, Babulla washed pots and pans in a roadside dhaba, and was later promoted after learning how to cook with the tandoori oven. Five years ago, he built a makeshift house in Samaypur Badli village, itself a settlement of tin shacks and huts—and just like that, his family became Delhites. Even though the settlement was illegal—city bulldozers could come and demolish everything at any time—he'd procured an official ration card and increasingly had hope they wouldn't get displaced.

Ramnivas Pasiya was twenty-seven—twenty-eight, tops—and lacked any ambition save for a vague desire to see his life circumstances changed. Ramlal Sharma, the local councilman, put in a good word and got him part-time work as a city sanitation worker. His area, Saket, was located in south Delhi. At 8:00 a.m. he'd put his plastic lunch tiffin into his bag, catch a DTC bus toward Daula Kuan, and then transfer to another one that would take him to Saket. Ramnivas would punch in, grab his broom, and head toward the neighborhood he was responsible for. When he got hungry, he'd eat a couple rupee's worth of chole along with the roti he brought from home. His wife Babiya made his food; they'd been married when she was seventeen. Now he was the father of two—a boy and a girl—though he would have had two sons if one hadn't died.

As I've mentioned, I first met Ramnivas by Sanjay's. He had a good reason for frequenting Rohini: He was chasing after a girl named Sushma. She was a part-time servant who did chores for a few neighborhood households, commuting every day from Samaypur Badli, where Ramnivas also lived. He had accompanied her several times, smoking cigarettes or bidis at Sanjay's or drinking chai at Ratanlal's while she worked. Sushma was seventeen or eighteen, a full ten years younger than Ramnivas. He was dark-skinned and lean. Sushma had a thing for him too; you could tell just by watching them walk side by side.

I saw Sushma yesterday, and even today she came to clean a few houses in the neighborhood. Every day, she still comes, just like always.

But Ramnivas?

No one's seen him around for a few months, and no one's likely to see him anywhere for the foreseeable future. Even Sushma doesn't have a clue where he is. If you went looking for him, all you'd find—at most—would be a little damp spot on a square of earth where Ramnivas had once existed; and the only thing this would prove is that on that spot some man once did exist, but no more, and never again.

I'd like to tell you, briefly, about Ramnivas—a simple account of his inexistence.

Two years ago, on Tuesday, May 25, at 7:30 a.m., Ramnivas, as usual, was getting ready to go to work in Saket, forty-two kilometers from where he lives. Sushma was already waiting for him by the time Ramnivas got to the bus stop. She was wearing her red polka-dotted salwar, had applied some special face cream, and was looking lovely.

The previous Saturday, she had accompanied Ramnivas for the first time to a movie at the Alpana. During intermission, they'd gone outside and snacked on some chaat-papri. In the theater and afterwards on the bus going home, Ramnivas inched closer and closer to Sushma, while Sushma repeatedly deflected his advances. After they'd gotten off the bus and were walking home, Ramnivas announced this before parting: If she wasn't at the bus stop waiting for him next Tuesday, it meant she wasn't interested, and they were through.

Now it was Tuesday. His heart sank as he left the house, thinking as he often did that Sushma was having serious doubts. When he saw her at the bus stop waiting for him, Ramnivas was so overjoyed that he declared they should ride in an autorickshaw instead of taking the bus. He insisted and insisted, but Sushma wasn't persuaded. "Why throw away money? Let's just take the bus like we always do." Ramnivas had fixed on the idea of sitting very close to her in the little backseat of the rickshaw and maybe even copping a feel—and was therefore dismayed at her refusal. But Sushma's coming to the bus stop was a yes signal to Ramnivas, and the man was now beside himself. He sensed that his life was about to turn a corner, and soon he would be free from the shackles of home.

He was always picking fights with his wife Babiya. Even though Ramnivas's paycheck wasn't enough for Babiya to cover household expenses, he'd let loose. "It's like your hands have holes in them! Look at Gopal! Four kids, parents, grandparents, and God knows who else to support, makes less than I do, and still gets by! And you? Night and day, bitch and moan." She'd remain silent but glare at him with flames that licked at the inside of his head all day long.

That Tuesday, as they parted ways—Ramnivas to Saket, Sushma getting off the bus in Rohini—he told her he'd leave work early for Rohini and be at Sanjay's by 2:00, where she should be waiting; then they'd return to Samaypur Badli together. Sushma said that she didn't like waiting for him at Sanjay's (Santosh, the scooter mechanic, was always trying to flirt with her; and Sanjay, too, was always cracking dirty jokes), but in the end, she agreed.

And then, for the very first time, Sushma, very slowly and very deliberately, instructed Ramnivas to absolutely bring her some of those chili pakoras, the ones he'd been going on and on about that they sell by the Anupam Cinema. When Sushma made her request, Ramnivas could swear he heard a note of intimacy in her voice, even a hint of possessiveness, and it made him feel very good indeed. He said casually, "I'll see what I can do," but had a very hard time concealing the fact that he was jumping for joy.

Ramnivas went on his way, happy, singing that song from *Kuch Kuch Hota Hai*. After punching in, he told his boss, Chopri sahib, that he needed to leave work early to go home because his wife had to be taken to the hospital. Even though Chopri sahib usually gave employees a hard time about leaving early, for some reason he readily agreed.

That day, Ramnivas was sweeping the floor of a fitness club in a building that housed various businesses. Cleaning the gym wasn't technically his responsibility since it wasn't a government building, but Chopri sahib had instructed him to work on it, explaining to Ramnivas that rich people and their kids went there every day to lose weight.

The gym had every exercise machine imaginable. The prosperous residents of Saket and their families spent hours on them. A beauty salon and massage parlor occupied the first floor. Middle-aged men of means would go for a massage and, occasionally, take some of the massage girls back to their cars and drive away. Ramnivas had seen policemen and politicians frequent the place.

Govind's chai stall was right outside, and he told Ramnivas that a girl named Sunila earned five thousand for accompanying gentlemen outside the massage parlor. "Who knows what these fucking big shots do with themselves in there," Govind said. "I've seen them throw these wild after-hours parties, boys and girls right from this neighborhood." Indeed, while cleaning the bathrooms, Ramnivas sometimes stumbled on the kind of nasty stuff that suggested that someone had had a good time, and it wasn't so fun to clean up.

What a life these high-rollers have, Ramnivas thought to himself. They eat so much they can't lose weight. And look at me! One kid dies from eating fish caught from the sewer, and the other is just hanging on thanks to the medicine. Then he remembered Sushma. His envy faded away and he set his mind to his work.

As he was sweeping the floor of the gym, the rope at the handle of the whisk broom that fastened the bristles together began to unravel. He was almost done, working on the cramped corridor between the bathroom and storeroom where hardly anyone went. But now he couldn't finish his work properly. Annoyed, Ramnivas banged the butt of the broom against the wall to try and right the bristles. *What was that?* Sensing something strange, he again banged it against the wall. This time he was sure. Instead of the hard thud of a thick wall, he heard something like an echo. It was hollow, a fast layer of plaster had been applied to it. But what could be behind it? Ramnivas wondered. A table and chairs and a couple of burlap sacks stood between him and the wall. Ramnivas moved them to make space. Then he hammered the butt of the broom into the wall, hard.

It was just as he suspected: A few cracks began to show in the plaster, which soon crumbled away, exposing the inside. Ramnivas peeked in through the hole he'd opened, and his breath stopped short. He went numb. Holy cow! The wall was filled with cash, stacks and stacks of hundreds and five-hundreds.

He drew his face flush with the hole and took a good look. The hollow was pretty big, a long tunnel carved out on the inside of the wall. Nothing but stacks of cash as far as he could see, all the way on either side until the light failed and the money was lost in the dark. Ramnivas's heart raced. He kept glancing around to see if anyone was there.

There was no one, only him. Before him stood the wall in the big gym, at A-11/DX 33, Saket, against which he'd banged his broom and opened up a hidden cache of bills.

"Dirty money . . . dirty money . . . dirty, dirty, dirty!" came the words, like a voice whispering into his ear. His hair stood on end.

Ramnivas didn't move for a few minutes, trying to figure out what to do. Finally, he grabbed his bag from the table in the corner and, peering around to make sure there wasn't anyone watching, took two stacks of five-hundred-rupee bills and stuffed them in his bag. Then he grabbed one of the burlap sacks and placed it in front of the wall to cover up the hole along with the table and chairs. He hoped no one would suspect anything in this forgotten corner of the gym.

It was only 11:30, and Ramnivas still had the better part of his cleaning rounds to finish. Instead, he went right to the office, hung up his broom, and said that he had received a phone call alerting him that his wife had taken a turn for the worse. He needed to go home right away.

Each stack of cash contained ten thousand rupees, meaning that Ramnivas had twenty thousand. He'd never seen this much cash in his life and was so scared that he rolled up his little bag and shoved it down his pants for the bus trip. If any of his fellow passengers had taken a good look at him, they would have instantly realized this was a man in a state of high anxiety.

Ramnivas took a rickshaw from the bus stop to Sanjay's. He found Sushma joking around with the scooter mechanic, Santosh. This upset Ramnivas, but what really unnerved him was when Sushma said, "Enjoying a rickshaw ride today? Did you knock over a bank or something?" But then she added, "You said you were coming at 2:00, and it's not even 1:00. How did you get out so early?"

Ramnivas laughed; maybe it was seeing Sushma. He relaxed, his worries slipping away.

"I ran as fast as I could!" Ramnivas said, looking at Sushma and chuckling. She too began to laugh. "Can I buy you guys a cup of chai?" Ramnivas then asked, turning to Sanjay and Santosh.

"What's the special occasion? Did you get overtime?" Santosh replied, taken aback.

Sushma was also startled, since Ramnivas was known for being such a penny pincher. She never liked the way he'd come around Sanjay's and try every trick in the book to convince someone to buy him a cup of chai. This day, however, Ramnivas didn't just include Sanjay and Santosh in the round of chai, but also Devi Deen and Madan. And not just plain old chai, but the deluxe stuff—strong, with cardamom.

Sushma protested—why throw money down the drain like that?—but Ramnivas didn't listen. He hired an autorickshaw for the rest of the day and took Sushma on a whirlwind tour of the city. He fed her chaat-papri, splurged on bottles of Pepsi, bought her a handbag in Karol Bagh, and a five-hundred-rupee salwar outfit with matching chunni from Kolhapur Road in Kamala Nagar. Sushma felt indescribable

happiness each time she touched, or even looked at, Ramnivas. The sad and worried little Ramnivas of yesterday (on many
occasions Sushma had thought, *Enough is enough*) had suddenly
blossomed into an uncannily happy, Technicolor lover. Though
his hair was unkempt, his stubble getting scraggly, and his bidi
breath hard to take, whenever Ramnivas kissed Sushma in the
little backseat of the rickshaw, for some unexplainable reason,
she felt as if she were rolling around on a bed of flowers.

There's no way Sushma could have known what accounted
for Ramnivas's surprising turnaround. She knew this much:
She'd done well by showing up at the bus stand that Tuesday
morning, after having spent the whole night thinking, *Do I
show up? Do I not show up?* It turned out she'd made the right
decision. *There is someone out there in the world who loves me!*
Sushma thought, overflowing with joy. Even after Ramnivas
had gotten her pregnant and then paid for her abortion at the
Mittal Clinic in Naharpur, she'd remember the whirlwind trip
that day two years before in the autorickshaw.

The roots of happiness lie hidden in money. From there,
a tree of pleasure can grow, and flourish, and bear the fruit
of joy. Maybe the best qualities of men, too, lie locked inside
a bundle of cash—this is how Ramnivas began to think. He
was a new man: Everything had changed. Life at home had
also improved substantially. First, his wife Babiya seemed content all the time, and now cooked the most delicious food.
They could afford to eat meat at least twice a week and eggs
every day. The kids asked for ice cream, and the kids got ice
cream. If a guest came knocking, Babiya would bring out the
good stuff: Haldiram's namkeen snacks and Britannia biscuits.
Ramnivas bought a sofa, a TV, a VCR, a double bed, a fridge,
and a foreign-made CD player from Palika Baazar, and announced that it was only a matter of time before he bought a

computer for the kids. He said everyone knew that there was no getting ahead without one. He planned to get them computer courses and then send them both to the States, where they'd make six-figure salaries.

Ramnivas's relatives, who'd always steered clear of him, suddenly started showing up at his place with whole families in tow. His stock within his own caste community was on the rise, and he was often approached for advice about matrimonial alliances between families. He got all sorts of letters and wedding invitations. If he felt like it, he'd go. If he didn't, he wouldn't. But when he did—what a welcome he got!

Meanwhile, Ramnivas had begun drinking every day, and his liaisons with Sushma also became a daily occurrence. By then, Babiya knew all about the affair but had decided to keep her mouth shut. She knew enough about the kind of man Ramnivas was to feel confident he'd never leave her or the kids.

Sometimes Ramnivas wouldn't come home until well after midnight. Sometimes he'd disappear for a few days— sometimes with Sushma, who now owned several salwar outfits, complete with matching sandals and jewelry sets. She used to go toe-to-toe with Ramnivas no matter how small the squabble, but now, fearing he might get angry, Sushma silently put up with more and more. On several occasions her mother cautioned, "How long will this last? You have to stand up for yourself and tell him that what's yours is yours. And *he* is yours, honey. People are beginning to talk." But Sushma would reply, "I'm no homewrecker, Amma. He has kids, don't forget. Let it go for as long as it goes." And she was sure it would go on for the rest of their lives.

If people asked Ramnivas where he'd gotten so much money, he'd say he'd invested in a half-million-rupee pyramid scheme in Saket, or that he was playing the numbers and kept hitting. Or that he'd won the lottery. Or—and this he reserved for only a few—that he'd met a great holy man near the mosque who whispered a very special mantra in his ear that caused future stock-share figures to flash before his eyes. In turn, Ramnivas whispered the same mantra into the ears of several people, all of whom failed to see the numbers flash before their eyes.

Whenever Ramnivas felt like it, he'd go and fill up his bag with a few stacks of cash from the wall in Saket. It was amazing that no one had stopped him or arrested him, and no one had moved the stacks of rupees around. Spending the money as he pleased for so long with no one stopping him had turned Ramnivas into a carefree man, and so his daring grew. And yet he was still beset with worry that one day the rightful owner of the money might show up and take it away. So with foresight, he bought a ten-acre plot of land in Loni Border and put it in his wife's name. He took three-hundred thousand and deposited it into various savings accounts in several banks—all under different names.

Things began to crumble about eight months ago.

Ramnivas made big plans to take Sushma on a trip to Jaipur and Agra, where, of course, they'd have their photo taken in front of the Taj Mahal.

They found a taxi driver the moment they stepped out of the train station. Ramnivas instructed him to take them to a hotel. "What's your price range?" the taxi driver asked, sizing him up.

Ramnivas could tell that the driver thought he was an average joe, or worse, some schmuck. "It doesn't matter so long as the hotel's top-notch," Ramnivas said firmly. "Don't take me to some cut-rate flophouse."

The driver appeared to be around forty-five; he had a cunning look on his face and dark eyes as alert as a bird of prey. He smiled, asking sardonically, "Well, there's a nice three-star hotel right nearby. Whaddya think?" The man must have been expecting Ramnivas to lose his cool at the mere mention of a three-star hotel, but Ramnivas was unfazed.

"Three-star, five-star, six-star—it's all the same to me. Just step on it. I really need a hot shower and a big double plate of butter chicken."

The driver gave him a long look, which he followed with a piercing, hawklike glance at Sushma. Pleased with himself, and mixing in mockery, he added, "Yes sir! On our way! And do you think I'm gonna let you settle for a plain old hot shower? I'll see to it you have a whole big full tub of hot water! And butter chicken? You'll get triple butter chicken!"

Ramnivas laughed at this and said, "That's more like it! Now step on it."

The taxi driver then asked, "So where are you from, sir?"

"Me? I'm a Delhite. What, did you think I was from U.P. or M.P. or Pee Pee or someplace like that?" Ramnivas quipped, smiling at Sushma as if he'd just won the war. "I come to Agra every couple of weeks with the company car," he added, hoping that this shrewd driver wouldn't ask him about his big job. What would he say? Grade four sanitation worker? Broom pusher? Fortunately, the driver didn't follow up.

When they got to the hotel, the driver told him, "Go and see if they have any rooms. If not, we'll try someplace else."

Ramnivas left Sushma and went inside. When he got to the reception desk and heard the rate, he wondered if they should find a cheaper place to stay. But he soon signed on the dotted line for an air-conditioned room with a deluxe double bed for fifteen hundred a night. The man at the reception desk sent a bellboy to fetch the luggage.

When Sushma arrived upstairs, she looked a little worried. "Gosh!" she exclaimed. "What kind of a place is this, anyway? Everything's so shiny and polished, like glass. I feel like I shouldn't touch anything. What if it gets dirty? There's something about all this stuff that gives me a weird feeling."

"Just enjoy yourself. We've still got plenty socked away, so why fret?" Then, lovingly, he added, "Come here and give me a big smooch. And crack open that bottle in my bag while you're at it."

The knock on the door came at half past 10 that night. It had already been a long day of sightseeing at the Taj.

Ramnivas wondered who it could be so late. He opened the door to find two policemen. One was an inspector, and the other, the inspector's sidekick.

"You've got a girl in there?" the inspector asked in a scolding voice.

"Yes," Ramnivas replied. The inspector and his sidekick came in. The name *V.N. Bharadwaj* was engraved on a little brass tag pinned to his uniform. The way he was looking at Sushma! A fury began to build in Ramnivas, but he was too scared to say anything. Sushma was wearing her pink nightie, and you could see right through to the black bra he'd bought for her. And beneath that was her fine, fair skin.

"Something tells me she's not your wife," the inspector declared. "So where'd you pick her up?" The man's square face housed cunning little eyes that kept blinking. His hair had been turned jet-black with unspeakable quantities of dye.

"She lives next door. She's my sister-in-law," Ramnivas said; he was a terrible liar.

"So, you've been having a little party!" the inspector continued, glancing at the fifth of Diplomat on the table. Then he gave Sushma the hard once-over. "She ran away. You helped her. You brought her here. My guess is she's underage." He turned to Sushma. "How old are you?"

She was scared. "Seventeen," she said.

"I'm taking you down to the station—both of you. We'll find out from the medical reports exactly how much fun you've been having." He pulled up a chair and sat down. "So where'd the money come from? A three-star hotel? AC? My guess is this isn't your usual style. Did you steal it? Or knock someone off?"

Ramnivas had a good buzz going, and he should have been able to pluck up his courage; but Sushma telling the truth about her age had unwittingly thrown him to the wolves. He felt as if he was walking right into their trap. He thought quickly, and a smile took shape on his face. "C'mon, inspector, just give the word. Another bottle?"

"That I can order from the hotel. As for you two—I'm taking you to the station. Get dressed. Is she coming like *this*? With her see-through everything?"

"What's the rush? The station goes wherever you go, inspector. The inspector's here, so we can work things out right now," Ramnivas suggested with a little laugh.

He was surprised at himself. Where had this been hiding? He took a quick look at the sidekick, who was standing by the bed, to see if he could get him to go along. It looked like a yes, Ramnivas thought: The sidekick was busy staring at Sushma, but seemed to give a little nod when his eyes met Ramnivas's. "Aw, they're just kids, Bharadwaj sahib," he said. "They come to see the Taj. Let 'em have their little party. You and me can have some fun with her too. Whaddya say, pal?"

Ramnivas didn't like what the sidekick was hinting at. "Wait just a minute," he said. "Look, Bharadwaj sahib, as far as some food and drink go, just say the word and I'll have it sent up in no time. But you've got to believe me that she's really my sister-in-law. I swear!"

The inspector began to laugh. "Uh-huh. You need an AC hotel room in order to polish off a fifth of the good stuff with your underage sister-in-law? And then let me guess: The two of you were singing hymns and clapping your hands? But now that you mention it, go get a bottle of Royal Challenge and order a plate of chicken. Actually, don't move." The inspector sat down on the bed. He pressed the intercom button at the head of it that got him to the reception desk, placed the order, and then stretched out on the mattress. He loosened his belt buckle and regarded Sushma, who was sitting at the foot of the bed looking as if she wanted to crawl under a rock. "And you—go sit in the chair in the corner and face the wall. Don't make me crazy. I lose it a little when I drink, and then the two of you'll go crying to your mothers about big bad Bharadwaj. I just can't help it, like when I see those pretty Western girls that come here on vacation." He had a big laugh.

They killed the bottle in just over an hour. First, Ramnivas finished off his own fifth, and then he joined the police in a few more shots from theirs—by the end, he was completely drunk. The inspector and his sidekick left the hotel room sometime after midnight. They settled on five hundred to let the matter slide; later, the sidekick shook him down for an extra hundred. By the time they'd gone, Ramnivas was utterly spent, so drunk he was queasy and started getting the spins. Sushma helped him into the bathroom and poured cold water over his head, but Ramnivas lay down right there on the bathroom floor and began to retch. Out came all the butter chicken, the naan, and the pulao. After the vomiting subsided he clung to Sushma, but everything was a blur, so he went straight to bed.

In the morning, Sushma told Ramnivas that after he'd gotten drunk he told the police about some cash hidden behind a wall somewhere in Saket. Ramnivas instantly sobered up. He'd been so careful about keeping his secret! He hadn't even hinted about it to Sushma or his wife. In the end, a little booze had turned the sweet smell of success into a putrid pile of shit.

He made a few excuses to Sushma about something coming up back home and canceled their trip to Jaipur, then decided to take the next train back to Delhi.

Just as he'd feared, a police Gypsy idled in front of his house, waiting for him the next morning. "The assistant superintendent wants to talk to you," a policeman said. Ramnivas got into the Gypsy.

This was some eight months ago—I think it was a Tuesday, and there was a light cloud cover. It seemed it might start to drizzle at any time. That day, I saw a very nervous Ramnivas at Sanjay's; he was waiting for Sushma.

I ordered two cups of deluxe chai from Ratan Lal, and got my first inkling of how desperate Ramnivas was when I saw him down the piping-hot tea in one gulp, burning his mouth and everything else.

It was early afternoon, and Ramnivas, eyes full of pleading, looked at me and said, "I've gotten into a big mess. Way in over my head. Help me find a way out—please! I won't forget it for the rest of my life."

I asked him to tell me all about it, and he did; and now I've told you everything he told me. When he finished—just as I was about to see if I could find some way to help—Sushma showed up.

"Meet me here tomorrow morning. I've got to go," Ramnivas said, and the two of them jumped in a rickshaw. I watched them ride away until I couldn't see them any longer. That was the last time I saw Ramnivas.

He hasn't come back to this little corner of the street. He'll never come back. If you ask anyone about him, no one will say a word.

And if you keep going from this corner to the sixteenth-century ruins at the bypass, and ask Saliman, Somali, Bhusan, Tilak, or Rizvan about Ramnivas, you'll get the same blank stare. Ask Rajvati and her husband Gulshan, who sell hard-boiled eggs at night—they'll all give you the brush-off.

Even the fair and graceful Sushma, who comes every day from Samaypur Badli to clean people's homes, will walk right past you at a brisk pace without so much as a word. That's how bad it is. Nowadays, she's been seen with Santosh munching on chat and papri in front of the Sheela Cinema.

And if you happen to travel to that little settlement by the sewage runoff and manage to ask for the address of the tiny hut that Ramnivas had converted into a real house, and, once there, ask his wife Babiya or his sickly son Rohan or his daughter Urmila, *Where is Ramnivas?* you'll face a stare as blank and cold as stone. They'll say, *He's out of town.* If you ask when he'll be back, Babiya will reply, "How should I know?"

No one in all of Delhi has any idea about Ramnivas—that much is clear. He simply doesn't exist anywhere—no trace is left. But I'm about to give you the final facts about him.

If you read any of the Hindi or English newspapers that come out in Delhi—say, *Indian News Express, Times of Metro India,* or *Shatabdi Sanchar Times*—and open the June 27, 2001 edition to page three, you'll see a tiny photograph on the right side of the page. Below the photo, the headline of the capsule news item read, *Robbers Killed in Encounter*, and below that, the subheader: *Police Recover Big Money from Car.*

The three-line capsule was written by the local crime reporter, according to whom, the night before, near Buddha Jayanti Park, the police tried to stop a Suzuki Esteem that bore no license plate and was traveling on Ridge Road from Dhaula Kuan. Instead of stopping, the people inside the car opened fire. The police returned fire. Two of the criminals were killed on the spot, while three others fled. One of the dead was Kuldip, a.k.a. Kulla, a notorious criminal from Jalandhar. The other body could not be identified. Police Assistant Superintendent Sabarwal said that 2.3 million rupees were recovered from the trunk of the car, most of which were counterfeit five-hundred-rupee bills. He stressed the importance of information provided by the Agra police in netting the loot.

If you were to examine the photo printed above this news item, you'd notice that the car is parked right in front of Buddha Jayanti Park. The dead man lying faceup in the street next to its back door, mouth open, pants coming undone and shirt unbuttoned, chest riddled with bullet holes, is none other than Ramnivas—the "criminal" who, to this day, remains unidentified.

Now, listen to what happened that day, a few hours before the encounter.

According to Govind, who sells chai in front of A-11/ DX33, Saket, that night at 10, a police Gypsy came with three plainclothes cops. They went into the gym, kicked everyone out, and then themselves left. An hour later, as Govind was closing his stall, the Esteem pulled up. It didn't have any license plates, and a Sikh, not too tall, not too short, got out.

Ramnivas stepped out of the backseat right after him. They went inside and stayed for about an hour and a half. They kept carrying stuff from the building and loading it into the trunk of the vehicle. An undercover Ambassador car pulled up right around the corner, and followed the Esteem when it began to pull away.

Govind said Ramnivas looked incredibly stressed, his eyes glazed over like a corpse's. He'd tried to say something to Ramnivas, but the Esteem was gone in a flash—the Sikh was driving.

According to what Ramnivas told me about the space behind the wall in the gym at Saket, it must have been pretty large. Conservatively, I figured it had to have been an area of about twelve by four feet. Ramnivas said the space was crammed full of hundred- and five-hundred-rupee bills. Based on that, I did the math. What I came up was that there was easily anywhere from a hundred to a hundred-and-fifty million rupees in there.

Do you remember the case where the Central Bureau raided a cabinet minister's house, along with a few of his other properties? The investigation was launched by the government that had just come into power, and the cabinet minister under investigation had been part of the previous government. The minister was charged with taking something like a billion rupees in kickbacks from a foreign company that supplied high-tech equipment. The man did a little time, and was later released. He then joined the very same government that had earlier begun the investigation. It's clear that Ramnivas, guided by auspicious astrological alignments, or just dumb luck, had discovered a problem with his broom; and in order to solve it, he began banging the butt against the wall. He figured out the wall was hollow, got his hands inside, and was suddenly face-to-face with money hidden from the eyes of the Central Bureau and the tax man. It was unaccounted money, untraceable money—dirty money.

You already know that only a few lakhs of rupees were recovered from the trunk after Kuldip, a.k.a. Kulla, and Ramnivas were killed on Ridge Road that night—and a large part of that cash was counterfeit too. This, when we know that there was some one hundred-and-fifty million rupees taken out of that wall. What happened?

Kulla, a career criminal, had so many cases pending in court that the police could use him as they pleased. He worked as an informant, reporting to the police station each and every day. He spied for them, pimped for them, and provided false testimony as needed. But they say that a few days before that fatal episode, he got into a fight with the station superintendent, who accused Kulla of playing both sides and being on the take from another party. *He's become more trouble than he's worth. Let's make the problem disappear.* So the police killed two birds with one stone, disposing of Kulla in a manufactured encounter and getting their hands on the cash. A police captain plotted the whole thing with a couple of trusted underlings: low risk, high payoff. The cops split the spoils among themselves, and they didn't forget their friends in Agra. And the officer behind the plot received a medal and promotion for his good deed that day.

It doesn't matter how many weeks or months or years I've got left in this sorry life before I also disappear—but I, too, would like to enter into a world of my dreams, just as Ramnivas did.

So that's why every night at midnight, when all of Delhi is asleep, I put on some black clothes, sneak out of the house, and spend the rest of the night scraping out the walls of Delhi.

Treasures beyond anyone's wildest dreams are hidden in the countless hollows in Delhi's countless walls. I'm sure it's there. My only regret is that I've wasted the last decades of my life before starting out with my pick and trowel.

So if you read this story, go and buy a little pickax and get yourself to Delhi right away. It's not far at all, and it's the only way left to make it big. The other ways you read about in the papers and see on TV are rumors and lies, nothing more.

CULL

BY MANJULA PADMANABHAN

Bhalswa

The slender black police transport sprang into the sky above headquarters, then shuddered to a halt in mid-air. Dome, mission-commander of the two-man team inside the vehicle, frowned as he punched the com-link on his helmet. A vacant hiss greeted him.

"Transmission failure?" he wondered out loud. "I'm raising clean air."

Mission coordinates from the dispatchers were normally fed simultaneously into the commander's helmet and to the transport vehicle's self-guiding system.

But today, silence.

Dome stabbed at the com-link button repeatedly.

Blank.

"Oh, come on, come on," muttered Hem, copilot. "We're losing time . . ."

In Dome's three years of airborne service he had never yet been dispatched without directions. Finally—a couple of squawks in his earphone and—

"*What?*" Dome swung around to face Hem. "Can you believe this? They're asking for a *visual* search!"

Hem groaned, though he took the precaution of covering his mouthpiece with his hand. Profanity, even to the extent of rude noises, was strictly forbidden amongst uniformed officers. "We'll never find the sucker."

"Apparently the call came over some sort of outdated radio device—" Dome listened to the dispatcher's voice squeaking in his ears, trying to make sense of what he heard "—reception garbled . . . just the name: Golden Acres." He glanced toward Hem. "Ever heard of it?"

The copilot shook his head, scowling. "Nah," he grunted.

Directly beneath them was the gigantic administrative complex known as the Hub. It served as the absolute nerve center of Dilli Continuum, glittering capital city of the economic behemoth of Greater India that sprawled across the whole of South Asia. The six-lane avenue called Rajpath that had once stretched from the presidential palace in the west to the national stadium in the east had been replaced by a long straight block of buildings four stories high. It was crossed by a matching block at its midpoint. From the air, the combined blocks of the Hub looked like a colossal plus-sign.

Nothing now remained of the old white-walled bungalows of the past, the hexagonal roundabouts, the graceful tree-lined avenues. The presidential palace along with all historical monuments, including ancient forts and tombs, had been dismantled and rebuilt in vast underground museums.

The Hub bristled with dish antennae and the long whiplike lances of directional audio-scopes. Flat green lawns provided a boundary between the structure and its parking vaults. A battalion of employees moved in and out of the place in four daily shifts, ensuring that it remained awake and operational twenty-four hours a day, year in, year out. The strictly linear grid of streets that contained and defined the city originated from this central location.

"It'll take *forever*," snarled Hem. "Do we even know what to look for?" Pilots were encouraged to compete for the fastest response times. Weekly and monthly bonuses were awarded on the basis of nanosecond differences in their scores.

"An area of desolation is what we need to find," said Dome, repeating what he'd heard over his earphones. Now he pulled down his helmet visor, reading information off its glow-screen. "No solid structures. No roads. No landmarks . . . Wait . . . incoming images . . . hmmm. Dense smoke haze. Can't see much through *that*. Okay, they're saying to head north and east—the caller will send up a flare five minutes from now."

Precious minutes spilled from Hem's time-cache as the transport hummed high above the taut regularity of the city's streets below. In every direction beneath them the rigid graph that originated at the Hub had wholly replaced the tangled web of the old city's narrow streets. Avenues met at precise right angles and at every intersection artificial cherry trees in permanent full bloom had taken the place of dusty neems and soaring silk cottons of the past. Surface vehicles were regulated by magnetic strips embedded in the road surface. From the air the neat rows of residential buildings looked like identical wooden blocks, color-coded by locality.

"It's some kind of dump," said Dome, listening to the dispatcher. "The world's largest—two thousand acres—occupied by squatters . . ."

It was difficult to make sense of the information. How come he'd never heard of it? How could such a vast area have gone unregulated and unreported to the extent that its coordinates weren't available to dispatchers? What was the meaning of such obscurity?

Four minutes passed before the transport was hovering above a cloud of pollution that blanketed the area like a thick gray lid. The machinelike regularity of the city's streets had ended abruptly at what looked like a wall or a moat, zigzagging at sharp angles. Beyond it was the fog.

"It's been used as a dump since the mid–twentieth century," said Dome. "Used to be on the northern-most boundary of the city . . . along some kind of ancient highway—G.T. Road, they used to call it, stands for Grand Trunk—and a bog or a lake called Bhalswa . . ."

While the modern Continuum had developed southwards, the northern dump had become a lawless, cancerous wasteland. Its residents were declared illegal squatters but were too numerous to be moved out by force. Rather than risk the disapproval of their international business partners, the government had chosen the alternative of maintaining the dump as a ZZ: a Zero Zone. They suppressed all information going in or coming out of the area while leaving the inhabitants severely isloated. In an operational sense, the sector did not exist.

"That's the flare," said Hem, pointing toward a flash of pink light that fountained up above the murk.

"Yes," said Dome, "set me down there."

He, like Hem, wore full-body protective armor. It was designed to protect the wearer against all foreseeable threats, mechanical or chemical. Hem positioned the transport above the locator flare as the mission commander descended from the transport on a steel cable attached to his suit.

The air had the consistency of thin gruel, stirred by the gale from the transport's whirring rotor. Dome wondered, as the murk enfolded him, if his helmet's air filter would be overwhelmed. It was equipped to process and neutralize gas attacks but not such dense concentrations of airborne particulate. He was trained to suppress all emotions and reactions, yet his nerves were twitching and a bead of sweat trickled down his forehead. He hated to acknowledge these signs of weakness, minor though they were.

Then his feet touched down and he went into a defensive crouch, automatically scanning and processing information.

On the ground, a taser.

Beside it, a body.

The taser's handgrip glowed cherry-red in the heat scanner Dome wore as a monocle clipped to his visor, over his left eye. The red glow meant that the weapon had been handled very recently. Yet its muzzle appeared blue and cold in the heat scanner: Whatever the cause of death, it hadn't come from this small weapon.

Visibility was low. Air unbreathable. Operational area flat, open, a circular clearing forty feet in diameter and—

Ah.

There was someone else present. A man.

Dome straightened up, his movements slow and deliberate. Civilians were known to be nervous in the presence of the tall crisis-response officers in their gleaming body suits.

From the man's string-vest, loose khaki shorts, and bare feet, Dome guessed that he was a resident of the Acres. Dress codes elsewhere in the city were as strict and formal as the building regulations, with low tolerance for bare skin. The man was short, wide, and wiry, his black hair close-cropped and his eyes set deep beneath a jutting brow. He was clearly unarmed and did not appear to be offering any threat.

He stared expressionlessly at Dome for a few seconds before shifting his gaze downwards, toward the body.

The space the two men were standing in was bounded by compacted mesas of garbage that rose steeply, perhaps three stories high. Every visible surface was the same mottled silvery-gray freckled with cerulean blue: thirty years' worth of plastic bags, fused and solidified. Blue was the only color that did not fade. From the open area, pathways radiated between the mounds in five directions. Languid streamers of lime-green vapor seeped continuously from the ground, gradually merging into the mauve haze overhead.

The body looked flat and curiously two-dimensional, like something out of a police training demo, a corpse-icon painted onto the floor. It lay at 2 o'clock to the north pathway, its right arm angled over its head, left leg bent outward. The whole body was a uniform cola-brown in color, glittering slightly.

The shifting vapors made it difficult for Dome to see details. For instance, there appeared to be no obvious variations to suggest clothing, skin, or hair. Dome frowned and turned off the heat scanner to look again, but could not make sense of what he saw. From his belt he now unclipped the slender telescoping lance known in police circles as a "whisker." Its tip was sensitive enough to provide chemical analyses of anything it was poked into. He pointed it toward the inert body, not yet touching it.

Dome tightened the focusing ring on his monocle. With the heat scanner turned off, he now saw that the figure was covered in a layer of some substance from head to foot. Still not making sense of what lay before him, the police agent extended the tip of his whisker toward the corpse's right calf and tapped it.

Immediately, the glittering mantle that covered the body parted and drew back, as if alive.

It *was* alive.

Dome's arm jerked back reflexively, the whisker twanging upwards.

The other man's lips stretched wide, exposing his crooked teeth in a sly grin.

"Roaches," he smirked. Clearly, he was amused to witness the agent's discomfort. "The insects found him before anyone else." He spoke in a mixture of dialects built upon a base of Hindi and Punjabi, instead of the mandatory Hinglish of urban dwellers across the nation.

Dome clenched his teeth and swallowed hard as a wave of nausea caught him unawares. A glimpse of raw red flesh had winked on and off for the instant that the blanket of insect bodies had parted. Not only was vomiting into a face mask physically dangerous to its wearer, but to show weakness in the presence of a mere civilian could result in the loss of one month's pay: Police agents had to maintain their dignity under all circumstances.

"And it's been here how long?" he asked finally, when he had control over his voice again. "The body, I mean."

"Early morning," said the other man. "Or anyway, that's when it was noticed."

Dome nodded, just as his body armor registered a movement behind him—

He had no time to react.

Two, maybe three bodies hurled themselves at him, pinning him down. There were a couple of sharp grunts from the attackers as the suit attempted to repel them with shocks. But they wouldn't be shaken off. Then, as quickly as it had started, the assault was over and Dome was soaring up and away, suspended from his umbilical cable, returning to the transport overhead.

He struggled briefly against the blackout that inevitably attended the conflict of pressures his body was subjected to as it rose. Then the void overtook him and he knew no more.

Three hours had passed since Dome and Hem had returned to the station. A detailed debriefing had been ordered.

"It was planned," Dome insisted. "It must have been. I didn't see any of the others—never got a chance. And the witness gave no indication whatsoever."

He had already described the corpse. Obviously, it had just been a pretext to get him in place. In retrospect, the presence of only one resident in that open space, the relative silence in that teeming, congested colony, the staged presentation of the body—all of these had been transparent indications that a trap had been set up.

But for what?

Dome claimed that his attackers had made no effort to cut the cable that connected him to his transport. They had merely pinned him down for a few moments and then withdrawn. "They weren't really trying. I can't be sure but my impression was that they *let* me go—they fell away as soon as the copter began pulling up." He shook his head. "It doesn't make sense."

He'd returned to consciousness once Hem had reined him into the cockpit and secured him in his seat. Meanwhile, back at the station, a full alert had been sounded. Dome was rushed into quarantine and given a thorough physical examination during which he was anesthetized. Then he was coated in a thin layer of antibiotics and brought to a secure room for the debriefing, sealed into a clear plastic recovery bubble with its own air supply. He was told it was for his own protection.

Two bureau chiefs were present now, along with a dozen officers of Dome's rank. Hem, however, was absent. There were two other men in the room, both civilians. They wore the pale linen suits of high-ranking government officials. The fact that they were not introduced made it clear that they belonged to one of the ultra-secret services. The kind that the media were not authorized to make direct reference to without fear of losing their licenses.

One of these men spoke now.

He was the taller of the two, sleek with the confidence that comes with absolute power. His skin was brownish-purple and cratered with old acne scars from youth. Anyone else would have had the unsightly texture surgically smoothed away, but this man had chosen to keep it, along with the iron-gray of his hair. He was a realist. A pragmatist who had no use for outward frills and no obligation to maintain an attractive exterior. He wore wrap-around shades, impenetrably black, over his eyes.

"Are you aware," said this man, his head turned toward Dome, "that there have been precedents?" His voice was soft, without weight, and his lips barely moved. He may well have been a physical mouthpiece for someone else, someone speaking through him via a remote mic. "This is not the first episode of its kind."

"Oh?" That was Police Chief Mana. A tall woman built like a tank on two legs, hair pulled back in a wispy ponytail. She spoke in a rasping bark. "We are aware of only two previous incidents—*accidents* is what we called them."

"Officially, yes, they were accidents," said the linen suit, turning his head toward the chief. Dome saw that his throat moved as he spoke. Apparently the voice was his own. "But I am authorized to tell you now that they were controlled experiments. And not the only ones. There were others. None were successful—if by success we mean that our operative survived with his skin intact. In another sense, they were wholly successful. They confirmed our suspicions that the sector known as Golden Acres has ceased to be a mere eyesore and embarrassment to the capital city of our glorious nation, the premier world power of our time, and has become, instead, a threat."

There was a silence.

The meeting had been convened in a room with scenic windows.

Dome was seated a little apart from the others, in his recovery bubble, close to the window. From the corner of his eye he could see the picture-perfect vista of the city, its avenues stretching away to infinity, its rigidly linear buildings, its silently speeding vehicles. For security reasons, the Hub was taller than any structures in its vicinity.

He'd been working here ever since he earned his body armor at the age of twenty-two. He was lean and handsome, his black hair cut short, a neatly trimmed mustache over his top lip, his nose straight, his eyes clear. He was four years away from being eligible for marriage, but the Police Bureau had already cleared his application for a spouse and all the benefits that came with one: two-bedroom apartment, private transportation, paid holidays. The woman, a fellow officer suitable to his rank and physical dimensions, would be chosen for him by his seniors. As was normal with all salaried personnel in the country, it was the employer's prerogative to choose mates for their dependents. Until then, young adults lived with their parents, under conditions of strict celibacy that included medication to suppress unseemly desires.

Premier world power. The words strolled luxuriously through Dome's head, like an emperor touring his estates. Dome felt the familiar rich thrill lapping through his consciousness. It was grand, it was heady, to belong to a nation of such consequence. *World power! Yes, that's what we are!* he thought. *A glory to behold, the envy of all other nations!*

The reference to "controlled experiments" barely penetrated the light haze that enveloped his senses.

Instead, he allowed himself to be mesmerized by the view

from the window. Blinding white clouds drifted lazily against the dizzy blue vault. He could see the darting profiles of police transports as they sped across the city's skies. He wondered how soon it would be before he would be released to duty once more. He wondered if the faint flush of heat he felt at his temples was a reaction to the antibiotics coursing through his system. There was a faint nausea too and the first stirrings of a headache. He registered these impressions with surprise but no actual alarm.

The silence in the room deepened in some way.

With a guilty start, Dome returned his attention to the others around him. He had the oddest impression that his distraction had been noticed, even though no one was looking directly at him. In fact, they seemed to be avoiding his gaze in some subtle way, as if peering around him rather than at him. He told himself he was imagining things.

The man in the linen suit continued now, in his weightless voice, as if he had not paused to ensure that Dome was listening. "Clearly, it is a threat that we can no longer tolerate. Five years have passed since we cut their water and power supply. The area continues to be used as a dumping ground for every kind of waste—toxic, nontoxic, wet, dry, what have you. They have no sanitation facilities, no access to any medical supplies, no health-related technology. No supplies in the form of fresh food, no manufactured goods. Their air is unbreathable. They live ten to a cubicle, each cubicle the size of an aircraft toilet." He paused for maximum effect. "Yet they *thrive*." On the final word, his voice swung down like an axe, exposing the heart of his passion.

That repulsive vitality!

The man's nostrils expanded, and he exposed his teeth in disgust. "The time is long overdue," he whispered, "for that zone of filth and human degradation to be extinguished. Snuffed out. Erased." He turned his head slowly, taking in his audience one at a time, yet excluding Dome. If his voice had been soft before, now it was little more than a purr. "We all know the realities: We cannot use military force without attracting the attention of the world's moral matrons. But the residents of the Acres have steadfastly refused to submit of their own accord. In such a situation, I think you will all agree, we have few choices . . ." He paused once more. "Yes? May I assume agreement?"

Dome's forehead puckered in confusion. He glanced around the room and saw, to his surprise, that heads were nodding. Whatever the linen suit was talking about, the other members of the audience seemed to be in on the secret. Now the hairs on the back of his neck stiffened. His heart began to thump within his chest. What were the others nodding over? He could not remember hearing of any resolution. Had something been discussed in his absence? Had some crucial decision been made?

No one was meeting his eye.

The unnamed man's head was swiveling around now, toward Dome. "Yes," he said. "Yes, young man. You have every reason to look bewildered. That is because you do not realize that what began as a routine operation has ended very differently. Even as you sit there, believing that you are the same young officer who leapt into his transport to respond to a distress call this morning, the truth is, you have been damaged beyond repair by the encounter. What may have appeared to be a long and fruitful life ahead of you has today, in the space of a few brief minutes, been reduced to a week, maybe two."

Dome stammered, "Sir—I—what . . . ?"

"It is the latest strategy of the denizens of Golden Acres.

They use various pretexts to lure government agents to their environment, then jab them with microfine needles filled with infected blood and send them back. No doubt they have found ways of harvesting the hospital wastes that are dumped on their land. No doubt they find painkillers and hypodermic syringes along with all the rest. It is swiftly done, perhaps using a mild anesthetic, so that the victim is not even aware of what has happened to him. But we have seen the results and, I assure you, what I say is true. While you were unconscious during your physical exam, I was able to reveal to your colleagues the site of the puncture wound, deep within the crease of your right armpit. The infection will be fatal and incurable, a cocktail of TB, hepatitis, and SARS, plus a speeding agent which causes the germs to go to work at twice their natural speed."

He paused, like a college lecturer who knows when to give his students time to absorb a nodal point in their instruction.

"I have informed your colleagues that only one course of action is available to you, and of course we will offer you a couple of hours to adjust your mind to these new realities. It boils down to this: We will send you back in there, loaded with contagions that *we* have prepared for just this purpose. Whereas the technology of the squatter community has not progressed beyond the primitive skin-puncture delivery systems of the mosquito, ours spreads through a modified rhinovirus via skin contact and then to the mucus membranes. Death follows in forty-eight hours as the lungs clog up with fluids. When the contagion spreads amongst the residents, they'll have no option but to come streaming out of there like rats from a burning warehouse. We'll have specially prepared containment hangars ready for them. Their bodies will be disposed of safely, with no risk of further contamination. It should take about a fortnight. From the very start, we shall announce the outbreak of an epidemic of catastrophic proportions and declare to the world that for the sake of the entire human species we will have no option but to raze and sterilize the entire area . . ."

Bureau Chief Mana raised her hand. "Excuse me, sir, but how will you defend this action in the eyes of the international community? Whatever justification you offer, however catastrophic the disease, human beings cannot be destroyed like poultry at the time of the avian flu epidemic! This action *will* be defined as a planned genocide, with severe economic sanctions to follow—"

"We shall refer to it as *culling*," said the man, cutting in swiftly, before Mana could build up steam. "You are familiar with the term, no doubt? It belongs to the era of big game hunting, when licenses were issued for thinning out herds of animals whose populations were rising too steeply in game sanctuaries. But we shall redefine the word to mean, *Removing a percentage of the human population so that the species as a whole might survive*. It is a useful word. We hope to make it very popular."

He turned back to Dome.

"You realize, I am sure, that you will be a martyr to our nation's greater glory. Not that your role can ever be acknowledged: This entire operation, including your trip this morning to the Acres, has already been erased from the record. Even as we speak your copilot is having the memory of his flight flushed from his brain. You cannot have any contact with your parents before you vanish from their lives forever, apparently in a tragic encounter with enemy agents. However, your service record tells me that you are a model citizen, for which reason I do not doubt that in your final moments, you will find tremendous satisfaction in the knowledge that your name will be honored and that your family will benefit to the tune of . . ." He mentioned a very handsome sum.

The interior of Dome's head had filled with a loud buzzing sound, but aside from that he felt very little. The initial shock he had experienced upon hearing the news had dissipated. He felt detached, as if he were listening to a recitation about someone else's life, a stranger on the evening news, the synopsis of a tri-vid.

The man continued: "Of course, in case this option does not appeal to you, there is one other we can offer. You can choose to be extinguished immediately and painlessly." He paused once more. "After which your body will replace the one you saw this morning." He smiled mirthlessly.

When Dome woke again, he found that he had been sealed within a heavy sack. He was lying on his side. Naked. He could see nothing at all. He wondered whether he'd gone blind. He felt utterly limp; disinclined to engage with the hectic activity he could sense taking place around him, outside the bag.

He was being pulled this way and that, then hands were reaching around the bag, patting it down in order to determine his position within it. Many voices were speaking all at once, some giving instructions, some passing comments, some complaining. The complainers were louder, perhaps because they were not actively engaged in pulling.

"Leave it—*leave it!* Whatever's in there, it can only be more trouble for us—"

"No. We take all the rest of their garbage. This is just another part of it—"

"How do we know it's a living being? Maybe it's just one of their new machines—"

"Maybe it's a monster, come to eat all of us alive . . ."

In amongst all the hubbub and the tugging, some hands located Dome's head and began to reposition him so that he was in a roughly seated position, on the ground.

"Knife—knife—who has a knife? We'll have to cut the bag open."

Children took up the cry, calling in piping voices, "Knife—knife—someone bring a knife . . ."

Inside the bag, Dome was experiencing the unfamiliar sensation of being drenched in sweat. He could not remember the last time he had ever felt so unbearably hot. And the air! Even through the sack he could taste its rasping texture. Thick. Sulfurous. Gritty.

He used his hands to push the heavy material, a mixture of leather and plastic, away from his face. "Here!" he called. His throat felt as if it had been scrubbed with sandpaper, producing only a shadowy whisper of sound. "I have a knife!"

His whisker had been left to him, looped around his wrist. Releasing the slender, razor-sharp tip of the instrument, he sliced through the skin of his confining sack and wiggled his head through the resulting slit. Then he collapsed on his side, gasping painfully. The light from half-a-dozen hissing gas lanterns blinded him.

Arms and hands reached out to hold him up once more. Tumblers of water were pushed toward his mouth. All around him were the faces of strangers, thrust toward him, their skin glistening with sweat, their eyes agog with a combination of concern and curiosity. He could smell their breath, their sweat, their unwashed clothes.

"Don't—" gasped Dome, his voice hoarse, "Don't get close to me. Mustn't . . . mustn't touch me . . . Stay back!"

But they misunderstood him.

"See! He's afraid of us—*us!* What a chickenheart—what a dickhead . . ."

The language they used was similar to what the man beside the morning's corpse had spoken, an amalgamation of many tongues. Dome could understand some words better than others. There were even a few Hinglish phrases woven in amongst the medley.

Raucous gusts of laughter rippled through the gathered crowd as they ridiculed him for his fears, and pitied him too. Here he was, abandoned to their care, a naked stranger and— trying to push them away! The glasses of water were shoved ever more insistently toward his mouth. Hands were reaching to pull away the bag in which he had come, to free him completely from its grip, even as another cry went out for cloth, a plastic sheet, anything to cover the stranger's nakedness.

A fit of violent coughing convulsed him. His joints felt spongy with weakness.

"Please!" he rasped. "It's not safe—not safe for *you.*"

But his voice lacked power and no one could hear him. Even as his senses swam, bodies were pushing all around him, holding him up, shifting him to a different location. There was nothing he could do. The deadly virus was already slithering into new hosts, fresh from his skin. Bitter tears joined the sweat pouring down his cheeks. The linen suit's cruel scheme was working like precision electronics.

Some hours later, the young ex-agent had been reestablished in the hut of a man who introduced himself as Shankh. He seemed to be the same person who had been standing beside the morning's corpse, but the difference in his behavior made it hard to be sure. He was no longer reserved and self-effacing, but welcoming and friendly.

Inside the hut were Shankh's wife and two other women who may have been cowives or sisters, it was hard to tell. Dome was lying on gunnysacks spread out on the floor, which was clean and dry. The dwelling was perhaps six feet square and a little less than that in height. The only source of illumination was a gas lantern. The women were crouched in the far corner, talking between themselves, while Shankh was turned toward Dome. There were at least three infants inside the hut and a couple of chickens, pecking here and there on the floor. Blocking the entrance were the head and forequarters of a huge portly animal that had settled itself down right there.

"What is that creature?" Dome asked.

Shankh replied, smiling at the ignorance of the visitor, "A pig. Have you never seen one? We know that you eat them from the pictures on the tins of food products that you city people throw away."

A pile of old newspapers sealed within plastic bags formed a bolster for Dome to lean against. He was wearing borrowed clothes, a string vest and a thin cotton lungi. Still practically naked by his standards, yet he didn't have the energy to care. His head was spinning with fever and his speech was reduced to a bare trickle of sound.

"Never mind pigs. Listen to me, Shankh," he whispered. "Please . . . there's something terrible I must tell you . . . even though it's too late."

Shankh's smile didn't waver as he listened.

When Dome was finished—it did not take long—the other man said, "Bas? That's all you've brought for us—one more disease?" He threw his head back and laughed. "Never mind! We'll accept it graciously; after all, you know what they say about beggars . . ."

Dome's heart contracted with sadness. "You don't understand. This is something worse than anything that has yet existed—it's been *designed* to destroy you—"

"But we refuse to be afraid," interrupted Shankh. "And you know why?" He waggled his finger in the air. "Because whatever's thrown at us, we grab it, recycle it, and return it with interest. So they have cooked up a new disease in their medical factories? Good. Wonderful. We will circulate it through the living factories of all our hundred thousand bodies, and some of us will die, and some of us will live, and those who survive will repackage that same disease and send it back out to your friends in the city, so that they can enjoy it too." He laughed once more and patted Dome's hand. "So stop worrying! Cheer up. Let's eat."

The women brought food on tin plates. Later someone brought a herbal infusion that would help Dome with his breathing. Later still, in the darkness of that steamy night, a young woman joined him on his gunny bed and showed him a definition of hospitality that he had never known before.

The remaining two days of Dome's life were spent peacefully and comfortably, given the circumstances. With the desperate thirst of one who is about to leave this world forever, he wanted to understand how the residents of Golden Acres had survived, what gave them the incentive to keep fighting.

According to Shankh, it was simply a question of perspective. "From the bottom of the pit, all roads lead *up*," he explained, smiling. "So in one sense, this is an extremely positive place to be. Rich people throw away things at such a rate that for us, living in the dump, we only have to wait long enough before whatever we want comes sailing out of the sky—for free! Cars, food, books, furniture, machinery, medicine, bottles, toys—you wouldn't believe how much gets thrown away. And very often in its original packing. So we're not complain-

288 // Delhi Noir

ing. We take what we need, repackage the rest, and send it back out."

A week after Dome died, a new product began to appear on the shelves of fashionable stores in the city. Small black tins of pickled beetroot, straight from Russia, according to rumors. The labels looked like burnished gold and each tin was secured within its own individual membrane of cling film. A flattened medallion of red sealing wax provided a guarantee that the contents were authentic and had not been tampered with in transit.

It proved to be very popular and the entire stock sold out even before the first case of a terrifying new strain of flu was reported in the Continuum.

Among the first hundred people to fall ill was the man in the linen suit.

He, more than anyone else, should have known exactly how soon he would succumb to the mysterious fever that had already felled dozens of victims. He had no family and all his staff had deserted him the moment he began to manifest the telltale symptoms. As he lay in his silk pajamas, alone in bed, writhing with joint pains and gasping for breath, his attention was caught by something on his bedside table. It was a little black tin that he'd bought at great expense a few days earlier.

"Tasty stuff," he wheezed to himself, as he fished for the last few morsels with a silver pickle fork. "Might as well finish it." With streaming eyes, he squinted at the gilded label, embossed in running script with the product's name: *D'Ohm's Pickled Beetroot.*

"D'Ohm's . . ." he said aloud. "Doesn't sound very Russian!"

It reminded him of something.

Some*one.*

If only he could remember who! He sensed a gigantic truth swirling in the ether, just out of reach of his understanding.

But a spasm of coughing shook him just then.

A day later, he was dead.

GLOSSARY

The following glossary provides simple explanations of certain Indian terms used in *Delhi Noir*. These words come from Hindi, Punjabi, Urdu, English, and Bengali.

aarti: Hindu ritual that usually occurs at the end of religious ceremonies.
abhi aaya: I'll be right there.
achaar: pickled vegetables or fruits.
adda: station; den for thieves.
almirah: closet.
amla: *Phyllanthus emblica*; the Indian gooseberry tree.
anchal: end of a scarf, sari, or other garment.
Angrezi: English language.
aunty: term of respect used for older female family friends, neighbors.
ayah: nanny.
baba: old wise man; also used colloquially to express frustration or irritation.
babu: midlevel civil servant.
bahoot: very.
bahu: daughter-in-law.
baingan bharta: curried eggplant.
bakra: goat.
bakwas: bullshit.
bania: trader, shopkeeper.
banyan: undershirt.

barfi: sweetmeat made from milk, sugar, and other ingredients.

barsaati: single-room top-floor flat of a post-Partition north Indian home.

bas: stop, enough.

basti: settlement; often used to describe marginalized urban areas.

beta: son; child.

bhabi: sister-in-law.

bhaisahab: respectful way to address a brother or older male.

bhaiyya, bhayya: brother.

bhanchod, bhenchod: sisterfucker.

bhang: leaf or flower of the cannabis plant consumed in the Indian subcontinent; often used in drinks or food items.

bhavra: bee.

Bhumihar: caste found in states like Bihar and Uttar Pradesh that consider themselves Brahmans.

bibiji: mother; madam; term of respect for older women.

bidi: Indian cigarette rolled in tobacco leaves.

biji: mother; term of respect for older women.

bindi: decorative or religious dot women wear on their foreheads, in previous times to denote marital status.

brake lagao: put on the brakes.

bua: aunt; father's sister.

chaalu: shrewd, cunning.

chaat: savory snack often made with tamarind yogurt.

chacha: father's younger brother; colloquially, used to denote fondness or respect for nonfamilial relations.

chai: tea.

chai-pani: literally, the tea and water served to guests; figuratively, a small bribe paid to the lower echelons of the bureaucracy.

chaiwala: person who serves tea.

chal: come on; let's go.

chamchagiri: sycophancy; ass-kissing.

chapatti: round whole-wheat flatbread cooked on a stovetop.

chappal: open sandals.

charas: hashish.

choder: fucker.

chodo: let go, drop it.

chokra: young boy.

chole batura: fried round bread made of wheat, flour, and potato accompanied with spicy chickpeas.

chotey: young one (affectionate).

choukhat: threshold.

chowkidar: watchman.

chunni: long scarf women wear with a *salwar kameez*.

churidar: long, tight pajamas worn with *kurta* or *kameez*.

chut: cunt.

chutiya: moron, loser, fucker.

da: suffix that shows respect for men.

daal: curried lentils.

dargah: mausoleum.

desi: countryman; colloquially, from India or the subcontinent.

dhaba: inexpensive roadside restaurant frequented by workers, truck drivers, and travelers.

dhanda: trade, work.

dharamshala: cheap hotel for pilgrims.

dharna: sit-in, protest.

dhobi: person who washes and irons clothes.

didi: sister.

Dilli: Delhi.

Dilli-wallah: someone from Delhi.

dupatta: long scarf that women wear with a *salwar kameez*.

falooda: noodle served over *kulfi*.

fauji: soldier.

firang, firangi: foreigner (somewhat derogatory); from *Feringhee*, Persian for Frank.

gaali: abusive terms.

gaand: ass.

gali: lane, alley.

ganji: undershirt.

ghada: rounded earthen vessel for storing and cooling liquids.

ghazal: poetic form consisting of rhyming couplets and a refrain.

ghee: clarified butter.

gora: white person.

gulmohar: *Delonix regia*; royal poinciana trees; when in bloom, they have bright red or orange flowers.

gurdwara: Sikh house of worship.

gutka: intoxicant made from tobacco, betel nut, and other spices.

hafta: one week; refers to weekly protection money paid to police or gangsters.

hakim: traditional doctor.

harami: bastard.

haveli: old mansion or residence.

huzoor: sir.

Jai mata di: Hail to the mother goddess.

jalebi: fried sweet dipped in sugar syrup.

Jat: north Indian caste.

jawan: soldier.

jhuggi: thatched hut.

ji: suffix that indicates respect.

jooti: shoe.

kaabadi: physical-contact sport.

kaana: blind in one eye.

kadai: deep wok.

kaftan: one-piece dress.

kameez: shirt.

katta: single-shot country-made handgun that's illegal, inexpensive, and crudely made.

kewra: *Pandanus odoratissimus*; a fragrant flower whose essence is used to flavor food.

khadi: homespun cotton popularized during the independence movement.

khamba: colloquially, a 750 ml/1 liter bottle, usually of Indian-made foreign liquour; literally, a column or pillar.

khus: type of grass used to cool buildings.

kikar: *Acacia nilotica*; a thorny small tree with yellow flowers.

kirpan: dagger carried by Sikhs.

kulfi: ice cream made from boiled milk.

kurta: loose shirt.

kurti: contemporary, casual, and shorter version of a *kurta*.

lakh: one hundred thousand.

lathi: wooden baton carried by a policeman.

loocha-lafanga: lecherous male.

Lucknow: capital of Uttar Pradesh, once a seat of Awadh (Muslim) power.

lungi: garment which consists of a single piece of cloth wrapped around the waist and legs.

madarchod: motherfucker.

mai: female domestic worker.

mai-baap: mother-father; colloquial, benefactor.

mandir: temple.

marg: street.

masala dosa: south Indian dish consisting of a thin rice-flour pancakes wrapped around potatoes.

Mataji: Mother (respectful).

matthi: salty fried snack made of flour.

mixie: blender.

muhalla: neighborhood.

mundu: cotton garment worn around the waist; akin to a *lungi*.

namaste: Hindu greeting of respect; literally, I bow to you.

namkeen: salty snacks.

neem: *Azadirachta indica*, a fast-growing tree in the mahogany family.

Narmada Bachao Andolan: An NGO that opposes the Sardar Sarovar Dam being built on the Narmada River.

nimboo: lime.

niwas: residence.

NRI: nonresident Indian.

nullah: large open drain; stream.

paan: betel nut.

paise: monetary denomination less than a rupee.

pakora: snack fried in chickpea flour batter.

pallu: end of a sari.

PCO: public call office; a place to make local phone calls.

prasadam: edible Hindu blessing.

pudiya: twisted pieces of paper that are used to store small things.

pucca, pukka: full, complete; certain.

qawwali: form of Sufi devotional music.

randi: prostitute.

rangbaz: colorful character.

rehvaasi: resident.

roti: bread; food.

rudraksha: berries from a *Elaeocarpus ganitrus* tree used to make special prayer beads.

SHO: station house officer.

saab, sahab, saheb, sahib: a superior; during colonial times, a
white man; South Asian term of respect meaning sir, mas-
ter, or lord.

saaf karo: clean it up.

saali: wife's sister.

saas: mother-in-law.

sabzi: vegetable.

sabziwallah: vegetable seller.

salaam: Muslim greeting.

salwar: baggy pants.

sandow: sleeveless undershirt popularized by the early-twentieth-
century strongman Eugen Sandow.

Sardar: man who practices Sikhism.

Sardarni: woman who practices Sikhism.

sari: female clothing garment consisting of five yards of
fabric.

satya: truth.

shaitan: devil; colloquially, naughty.

shamiana: large, often luxurious tent for a celebration.

shikar: hunt.

shradh: in Hinduism, the name of the ceremonies performed
by relatives of the dead.

sidey: sidekick.

surahi: round earthen pitcher with a long neck.

tandoor: drum-shaped clay oven.

thakur: landowner.

thana: police station.

theek hai: it's okay.

thulla: traffic policeman; fat slob.

tiffin: container in which a meal can be packed.

vaid: practitioner of ayurvedic medicine.

veshya: prostitute; whore.

wala, wallah: suffix indicating an association with some type of activity.

yaar: friend; dude; man.

ABOUT THE CONTRIBUTORS

OMAIR AHMAD is the author of a novel, *Encounters,* a novella, *The Storyteller's Tale,* and a collection of short stories, *Unbelonging.* He studied at Delhi's Jawaharlal Nehru University and has worked as a journalist and policy analyst.

HARTOSH SINGH BAL trained as an engineer and a mathematician before turning to journalism. He is coauthor of *A Certain Ambiguity: A Mathematical Novel* and is currently working on a travelogue set along the Narmada River.

NALINAKSHA BHATTACHARYA has published three novels and some short fiction in India and the U.K. A civil servant by profession, he has lived for more than twenty years in R.K. Puram, where his story "Hissing Cobras" is set.

SIDDHARTH CHOWDHURY is the author of *Diksha at St. Martin's* and *Patna Roughcut.* He studied English Literature at Zakir Husain and Hindu Colleges in Delhi University (1993–98). In 2007, he held the Charles Wallace Fellowship in Creative Writing at University of Stirling in Scotland. He currently lives in Delhi and works in the publishing industry. "Hostel" is taken from his forthcoming novel, *Dayscholar.*

RADHIKA JHA, born in Delhi in 1970, is the author of *Smell* and *The Elephant and the Maruti.* She has received the Prix Guerlain and writes and performs Odissi dancing. She has also worked for the Rajiv Gandhi Foundation, where she started up the Interact Project to educate children of the victims of terrorism in different parts of India. She now lives in Tokyo with her husband and two children.

RUCHIR JOSHI, a writer and filmmaker, lived in Delhi from 1997 to 2007. Joshi's first novel, *The Last Jet-Engine Laugh,* was published in Britain, India, Australia, and France to critical acclaim. His films include the award-winning documentaries *Eleven Miles, Memories of Milk City,* and *Tales from Planet Kolkata.* Joshi is now taking a break from Delhi and spending his time between Calcutta and London.

L. Franchi

TABISH KHAIR was born and educated in Bihar, the Indian state that provides Delhi with much of its "migrant labor." He has worked as a staff reporter for the *Times of India* in Delhi, and he continues to visit the city regularly. A poet, novelist, and critic, Khair's latest book is the novel *Filming: A Love Story.*

Lars Kruse

PALASH KRISHNA MEHROTRA was educated at St. Stephen's College, Delhi and Balliol College, Oxford. He has two forthcoming books—*Eunuch Park,* a story collection, and *The Penguin Book of Schooldays,* an anthology—and is currently working on a nonfiction book on India called *The Butterfly Generation.* He writes a column for the Delhi tabloid *Mail Today.*

Rose George

MEERA NAIR grew up in five different states in India before coming to America in 1997. She is the author of *Video: Stories,* which won the Asian American Literary Award in 2003. Her work has been featured in the *New York Times* and NPR. She is currently finishing a new novel. Her earliest memory of Delhi is of a predawn bus ride. A fellow traveler, shaken awake, let loose a string of Punjabi profanities. He was about five.

Joe Tabbaca

MANJULA PADMANABHAN, born in 1953, is a writer and artist who lives part-time in Delhi. Her books include *Hot Death, Cold Soup, Kleptomania, Getting There, This Is Suki!* and *Hidden Fires. Harvest,* her fifth play, won first prize in the 1997 Onassis Award for Theatre in Greece. She has illustrated twenty-four books for children including two of her own works, the novels *Mouse Attack* and *Mouse Invaders.*

UDAY PRAKASH writes poetry, fiction, and journalism and is also a filmmaker and translator. He has published four collections of poetry, eight collections of short stories, and three books of essays. His latest work to be translated into English is a novella entitled *The Girl with the Golden Parasol.* He began living in Delhi in 1975 and stayed there until 2005, when he moved to nearby Ghaziabad.

Anjali Wason

HIRSH SAWHNEY has written for the *Times Literary Supplement,* the *Guardian, Time Out New York,* and *Outlook Traveller.* His parents migrated from Delhi to New York in the 1960s, and he moved to the Indian capital's Green Park area in 2005. He splits his time between Delhi and Brooklyn and is working on his first novel.

KOMPAKKAMMA

IRWIN ALLAN SEALY is the author of the novels *The Trotter-Nama, Hero, The Everest Hotel, The Brainfever Bird,* and *Red,* and a travel book, *From Yukon to Yucatan.* He is at work on a narrative poem set in Fatehpur Sikri, a conversation with the Mughal Emperor Akbar. Sealy is a graduate of Delhi University and lives in the foothills of the Himalayas.

MOHAN SIKKA currently lives in Brooklyn, New York. His story "Uncle Musto Take a Mistress" was published in *One Story* and won an O. Henry Award. He spent part of his childhood and teenage years in Delhi, where he lived in various railway colonies, including the one adjoining Paharganj depicted in his story "Railway Aunty." Sikka is completing a story collection and planning a novel.

Also available from the Akashic Books Noir Series

PARIS NOIR
edited by Aurélien Masson
300 pages, trade paperback original, $15.95

All original stories from Paris' finest authors, all translated from French.

Brand-new stories by: Didier Daeninckx, Jean-Bernard Pouy, Marc Villard, Chantal Pelletier, Patrick Pécherot, DOA, Hervé Prudon, Dominique Mainard, Salim Bachi, Jérôme Leroy, and others.

"Rarely has the City of Light seemed grittier than in this hard-boiled short story anthology, part of Akashic's Noir Series . . . The twelve freshly penned pulp fictions by some of France's most prominent practitioners play out in a kind of darker, parallel universe to the tourist mecca; visitors cross these pages at their peril . . ."
—*Publishers Weekly*

TRINIDAD NOIR
edited by Lisa Allen-Agostini & Jeanne Mason
340 pages, trade paperback original, $15.95

Brand-new stories by: Robert Antoni, Elizabeth Nunez, Lawrence Scott, Oonya Kempadoo, Ramabai Espinet, Shani Mootoo, Kevin Baldeosingh, elisha efua bartels, Tiphanie Yanique, Willi Chen, and others.

"For sheer volume, few—anywhere—can beat [V.S.] Naipaul's prodigious output. But on style, the writers in the Trinidadian canon can meet him eye to eye . . . Trinidad is no one-trick pony, literarily speaking."
—Coeditor Lisa Allen-Agostini in the *New York Times*

HAVANA NOIR
edited by Achy Obejas
360 pages, trade paperback original, $15.95

Brand-new stories by: Leonardo Padura, Pablo Medina, Carolina García-Aguilera, Ena Lucía Portela, Miguel Mejides, Arnaldo Correa, Alex Abella, Moisés Asís, Lea Aschkenas, and others.

"A remarkable collection . . . Throughout these eighteen stories, current and former residents of Havana—some well-known, some previously undiscovered—deliver gritty tales of depravation, depravity, heroic perseverance, revolution, and longing in a city mythical and widely misunderstood."
—*Miami Herald*